MW00437752

FULL BLOWN

Rage

By Ken Gross from Tom Doherty Associates

A Fine Line
Full Blown Rage
Hell Bent
A High Pressure System
Rough Justice

FULL BLOWN
Rage

KEN GROSS

A TOM DOHERTY ASSOCIATES BOOK

NEW YORK

This is a work of fiction. All the characters and events portrayed in this book are fictitious, and any resemblance to real people or events is purely coincidental.

FULL BLOWN RAGE

Copyright © 1995 by Ken Gross

All rights reserved, including the right to reproduce this book, or portions thereof, in any form.

This book is printed on acid-free paper.

A Forge Book
Published by Tom Doherty Associates, Inc.
175 Fifth Avenue
New York, N.Y. 10010

ISBN 0-312-85757-8

Printed in the United States of America

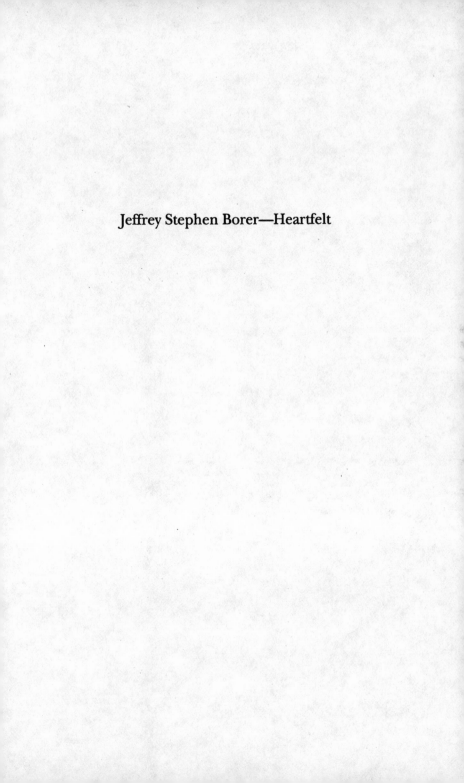

Jeffrey Stephen Borer—Heartfelt

FULL BLOWN
Rage

prologue

EARLY JUNE

"A glass of white wine," she said, and the nondescript young man in the wilted tan suit nodded and promised that he would be right back. Laurie Drake watched him turn and twist through the blaring, sweltering summertime crowd in the clammy brownstone on Manhattan's West Ninety-first Street. She experienced a sudden emotional loop of rising and sinking expectations. Well, she thought, trying to regain her balance and put the best face on matters, it was true that he was a little clumsy and he didn't make her heart leap, but on the other hand—and this was no small consideration for a lonely and plain woman of late youth—at least he would be back with the wine. She could count on that.

At that moment in her life, that was worth more than all of the chisled features and princely charms of all the desirable but unreliable men who vanished behind the first excuse. On the other hand, this particular young man must have his own hedged bets. Because Laurie Drake was acutely aware that she, too, would be there when he came stumbling back, no doubt spilling the wine as he made his way through the slowly circling crowd.

It was comforting that there would be no surprises with this man. He was a perfect example of a type. Reliable. He would return and he would be wearing an apologetic grin and he would be moist with eagerness. The only real surprise was the awakening of an old ember of enthusiasm. She even allowed herself to imagine companionship—she didn't expect much more—before she came to her senses and told herself to expect nothing but a compromised glass of wine.

A lifetime of social defeat had left its marks on Laurie Drake. She had been aware of her exact physical limitations since the fifth grade when a teacher had to select her dancing partner. There were some women who could compensate in other ways. But Laurie had no female cunning in that department. She had no radiant or fascinating or exotic fallback. Her tactic in public was blunt and defiant. She wore no makeup, presenting herself in a plain, unambiguous wrapper.

To make matters worse, Laurie tended to freeze in light conversations. Small talk and wit in the service of courtship were beyond her competence. She considered banter as evasive and misleading as powders and rouge.

There was an interesting by-product of Laurie Drake's outlook on the world: a heightened sensitivity. She became expert at detecting every shade of cruelty and deceit. At parties she sat quietly in corners, a spectator, watching the ebb and flow of traffic. Her watchfulness was harsh. The predatory men and boys in their greedy sweeps of the available females would lock eyes with her for an instant—displaying an unexpected flash of bared teeth—then rush off searching for defenseless victims.

Of course she was conscious that she was only asked to attend parties in order to flesh out a room, or to lessen the glamorous competition, or out of simple pity. Still, she came, as if she had to be squeezed like a lemon out of every last lingering sour droplet of hope.

As she sat on the couch waiting for the wine, she overheard one cool and trendy woman speculate to another about why a man who had recently arrived was so slow in removing his hat. Why, the first woman wondered, did the man stand in such obvious discomfort, sweat pouring down from under the hat like rain? The equally stylish and scornful friend took one quick look at the man and replied with a world-weary certainty, "Bald."

Laurie Drake wanted her to be wrong. Just once, just this one single time, let the smug woman be wrong about the man in the wet baseball cap! Then the man lifted the hat like a surgeon removing stitches and Laurie saw a shower of light sparkling off the bare scalp. The cynical, smug woman was right after all!

"What do you do?" asked her clumsy young man in the wilted tan suit, handing her the unspilled wine.

She hadn't noticed him coming back and for a second she couldn't manage a reply. She shook her head and took the glass. It was red wine, she noted.

"I teach," she said finally, offering him her stiff-arm gaze.

"Really?" He nodded, took a sip of his own wine. "They only had red," he explained. "Where do you teach?"

"At City College," she continued. "I teach history at City College." His head was bobbing out of confusion and fear, she thought. He was, she decided, a shoe salesman. A bad shoe salesman. Maybe a bank teller. He had, she noticed now as she studied him more closely, looking for defects, the way she did when she was examining a term paper, the expression of one of her lost students, hopelessly unable to follow the lesson. An "F," she concluded.

"Modern, American, ancient, European?" he asked brightly.

Again, he surprised her. "All," she said.

"Too young to be tenured," he said.

She was too flattered and impressed to contradict him. "Uptown campus?" he asked.

"What do you do?" she asked.

He turned and looked around the room and for the first time she felt a vague but definite uneasiness. "Engineer," he said, and she knew that he was lying. Kids faking answers to pop quizzes hit the same false note. The lie sent the first quiver up her spine.

"Laurie Drake," she said, holding out her hand.

"Ed Barnes," he said, and her instincts told her that this was another lie.

His grip was powerful, surprising for a man with drooping shoulders and small stature. The nails were even and clean. They didn't match, somehow, the bland young man who wore them. He lied and he had manicured hands and he had sudden poise. It gave her another shiver of emotion.

"History was one of my best subjects," he said.

"Really? Not mine."

He paused, slow to respond to the polished old attention-getter. He was either stupid or careful. She decided on careful.

"So how come you teach history on the college level?" he asked finally.

The woman on the couch next to Laurie, bored by the conventional turn of the conversation, got up with a theatrical sigh of disappointment—they were spoiling her entertainment—and moved to a more animated part of the room. The plain man who called himself Edward Barnes took her place. They might have been alone for all the attention they paid to the festivities. Suddenly the music stopped. Lights dimmed and an excited undertone heralded the arrival of a great cake. It was the centerpiece of the party and a surge of fresh energy swept through the room. The occasion had taken on the flesh of excitement with the outbreak of song and wide, self-conscious grins.

"People do the thing at which they are second best," she said, ignoring the singing of "Happy Birthday" and the applause. He leaned close to hear better, to signal the exclusivity of their conversation.

"That's a new one," he said. "I always thought you were supposed to give life your best shot."

She shook her head, modestly conscious of the tight little-girl cuteness of the gesture. She rolled her eyes and gathered her thoughts, then explained. "It's something I read. Mailer, I think. Maybe not. It's a very elegant idea. You shouldn't do the thing you do best because you love it too much. The passion makes you unreasonable. You expect too much and extinguish the flame. See what I mean?"

He nodded tentatively. "We are talking about work. A career?" he asked.

"Career. Work. Love. Anything. You can't function when it means too much. If you do the second-best thing—the thing that matters a little less—you can do it well."

"So you should marry the man you don't care all that much about?"

She blushed. "If you're smart."

"Cold-blooded idea," he said.

She shrugged. "I teach history. I function."

"Norman Mailer taught you that?"

She waved a hand in the air. "You can also blame my mother."

"I'm too busy blaming mine."

She laughed. She was amused, titillated, eager, operating at her best pitch of enthusiasm. "I think Mailer wrote it, but he stole it from my mother."

"Your mother and Norman Mailer. I like that."

She leaned closer. A confidence. "It was a collaborative stroke of genius. Mother said that I was very good at math and science and didn't need to take extra courses.

I'd study them anyway. However, since I didn't much care for history—couldn't tell one Punic War from another . . ."

"Homer, right?"

"Hannibal," she corrected.

He nodded. "Athens versus Rome?"

"Rome versus Carthage."

"Good that I stuck with thermal dynamics."

She stared at him for a moment. Somehow, and she could not say how, she knew that he was aware of the differences. He knew that it was Hannibal and Carthage. She could not say how she knew, but she was certain. "You should take one of my history classes. I'd let you sit in."

He looked around, a change of subject. In the dining room the cake was being carved up.

"Do you know the birthday girl?" he asked.

He changed subjects with flustering speed. To distract and divert. She had no objection. It was a carnival ride and she had decided to stay on. "I think it's a birthday boy," she said, gesturing at the group gathered around the dining room table. He had just wandered in, she speculated, or been someone's spare friend. Harmless enough. "Daniel," she said, indicating the group near the table. "The one wearing the blue paper hat."

"Friend?"

She gazed over wistfully, weighing such a possibility. "Colleague," she said. "He's an instructor in my department."

He nodded, then leaned over and whispered, "Wanna split?"

Momentarily she looked alarmed. "Split? Where?"

He held out his palms. "Anywhere. I like to walk."

She was not dressed for walking. Her shoes were tight. But she didn't want to let this thing go. It had all the indications of an adventure. God knows she had few enough of those.

"Lead on," she said, gathering her purse, pocketing her eyeglasses, and carefully leaving her untouched wineglass on a table slippery with spilled beverages.

She felt excited—an electric jolt, not knowing whether to take his hand or to stay at a distance. The tension of the distance, together with the open question about whether or not they would eventually touch, was dizzying. She walked in a state of utter confusion.

They experienced a preview of August as they walked. The streets were steamy with leftover oven warmth from the day. Dog droppings and torn newspapers and rotting fruit lay under the extra gravity of summer. Little pools of foul water from open hydrants attracted swarms of insects. Homeless men in layers of rags pulled supermarket carts swollen with bedouins' burdens against the traffic. The tenements were empty of their occupants, who sat like melted wax on the stoops, the men with basketball bellies, drinking beer, and the haggard women fanning themselves with paper bags, astonishingly young under the stress of brute poverty and male oppression. Sticky children burned off ice cream running back and forth on the street, like convicts marking off the space of their prison cells.

"Gee, doesn't the night air feel terrible," said Laurie, aware of the unfriendly eyes watching their progress across ninetieth Street.

"Not like home," agreed the man who called himself Edward.

"Where's that?"

"The Village," he said. Another lie. She was accumulating his lies. She was certain that she would recognize a truth.

They stopped at a diner on Broadway and had iced tea

and he rummaged through her life, taking the usual history of marital status, everyday habits. He told her nothing but lies, which told her a story of sorts.

She decided to take him home. She had no reason to do it—she had every excuse not to—but it had been a long time since she'd brought a man into her home and she was peculiarly stricken with loneliness on that summer evening. There was also this other factor, something energizing and wildly romantic in his brazen pack of lies. She pushed aside the warning voice and led him to her bed.

It was a bad mistake.

one

MID-JUNE

Nothing fit. Maggie Van Zandt felt bloated, swollen—dangerously unsettled. It could go either way: she could hang on and act normal or get crazy. She prowled the fitting rooms and clothing departments of Saks Fifth Avenue like a panther. She pulled on a pair of summer slacks and popped a button. A row of speed bumps appeared down the front when she closed a silk blouse. Even her shoe size deserted her. Not that she had gained weight or even had a problem in that realm. She knew what the damn problem was. She was caught in some humid lunar female riptide. Hormonal fluids were flooding her body. Sooner or later she knew that she would dry out and get back into her regular size and her cranky but manageable moods. But that didn't help, not at the moment, not when her skin felt as tight as a wet suit.

"Maybe we should try this?" suggested the saleswoman in the "junior" dress department, holding up the next higher size. The saleswoman was one of those brittle professionals, starved into her own size four, and she addressed Maggie with the detached mildness of a keeper.

What was more infuriating, she didn't listen. Maggie had just told the woman—twice—that she was a size six, had been a six for her entire adult life and left clear the implication that she was not prepared to consider any other size.

"Look, this is not a denial thing. And I'm really not having trouble with reality." Maggie spoke slowly, putting forth her best sarcastic interpretation of the truth. When faced with obtuse functionaries, Maggie had no idea how to behave. "I am a size six," she insisted. "Really. No matter what you think, no matter what the label says." The saleswoman didn't blink. Maggie couldn't stop. "Are we having a communications event here?" Still, the saleswoman didn't crack. Her only reply was a condescending smile. Maggie answered the saleswoman in kind. She glared ominously, then did something impetuous, which was not unusual, given her tendency to shock. She opened her purse, as if searching for proof of her size-sixness. She made sure to open the purse flat so that the saleswoman would see the gun. The flash of the revolver broke the discipline of the saleswoman's face. She paled and retreated, mumbling something about coming right back.

Maybe, thought Maggie, watching the woman's pace quickly increase, just maybe she had gone a tad too far. No, no. She shook off the self-reproach; she was definitely in the right. She had been badly provoked by a size-four retail bulldozer. It was not her fault that the saleswoman's eyes grew like dinner plates at the sight of the gun. Still, prudence nudged her into her own brisk escape gait toward the down escalator.

Halfway to the third floor, she spotted her friend Cissy going the other way. It didn't matter that they had come shopping together and expected to bump into each other; they both lit up at the encounter, as well as at the actual silliness of the sight when their paths crossed, like bandoliers, on the up and down escalators. They exchanged signals. Maggie smirked and rolled her eyes, then looked down. It meant that Cissy should board the next down escalator. Cissy grinned and held up two large shopping bags, which meant that her trip to ladies' suits and accessories had gone without a hitch. Everything fit Cissy. She was always a perfect size, even when she was in the grip of a gender undertow.

Maggie accepted this inequitable truth about her friend without vindictive afterthoughts. Some people were gifted when it came to finding clothes that fit, cheap apartments, and sweet cantaloupes. Maggie would have resented someone else—anyone else—but not Cissy. Not that she could explain the singular amnesty she awarded her friend. She knew only that there was a bond of instant sympathy between them. It ran deeper than logic, and was undisturbed by the peculiar incitement aroused by opposites. Cissy was always well groomed; Maggie was a slob. Cissy dined with men of aristocratic polish; Maggie dated civil servants. Cissy always had a handkerchief; Maggie mopped her nose with toilet paper.

None of it mattered. Maggie and Cissy had fallen into a lifelong friendship the moment they'd met at a party years earlier, talking together suddenly, as if they were picking up the thread of a conversation left off in another life. Maybe it was the simple shock of an authentic transcendental event. They were standing in a group—very intellectual, very high minded, very correct—who were discussing the elevation of Elie Wiesel to Nobel laureate.

"Has anyone noticed that he doesn't smile?" interjected Maggie suddenly, without thought.

There was an awkward silence. Faces turned, as if looking for guidance. "Well, I've never seen him smile," pressed Maggie, who felt pushed to defend herself.

Eyes widened, but voices were strangled.

Then Cissy broke the enchantment with an explanation. "Maybe, having been through what he's been through, his face is frozen into an expression of permanent sorrow. A public mood of perpetual mourning." She shrugged and continued. "If I had been through what he's been through, I'm not certain I could ever smile again." Then she smiled generously at Maggie. It was a great-hearted gesture, the smile. "Of course, it doesn't explain Mr. Elie's wandering hair," Cissy added, taking a bite out of the brittle moment.

The thing Maggie appreciated most was that Cissy didn't offer her interpretation with any kind of superior or harsh condescension. It was simply an explanation. And a sensible one. Then Cissy did something else that was considerate: she pulled Maggie away from the pack, sparing her from those who had not recovered from the shock of her high blasphemy.

"Oh, I'm such an asshole," said Maggie, looking back and seeing the astonished aftermath of her remark.

"Well, you're not a Jew," said Cissy simply. "It's like not being Black and disparaging Jesse Jackson. You can't do that; you have to earn it. We Jews are obliged to respect Wiesel's show." She smiled. "The man was in a concentration camp and that gives him a very high credit line when it comes to sainthood. Personally, I've always been a little bothered by the hush. It's like you're in a tomb when he enters a room." She smiled again. "It's not his fault. I can even live with the fact that he employed a public relations firm to get the prize. The point is, he writes well and he does speak for six million dead. That's a pretty heavy load and he's entitled to some extra slack." Then she held out her hand in friendship and smiled again. "I'm Cissy Stone."

"And I'm a jerk. I should stick to attacking Alan Alda."

Cissy laughed. "Personally, Bill Moyers is my pet peeve," she whispered.

And so they were already fast friends. Later—when they found that it was something more than a passing shadow of sympathy and affection, and spent more time together—Cissy introduced Maggie to museums and tricky dinner parties and high culture. With all the contacts and in all the settings, she never gave Maggie away.

They were conspirators. Cissy, with her Ivy League glaze, made adjustments for the fact that Maggie had had an uneven education, having dropped out of City College after her second year, and Maggie grasped that Cissy, in spite of her training and background and lofty contacts, scraped by on a hard-earned income. Maggie admired all the effort Cissy put out in order to keep up the façade of a graceful life.

For the past six months, Cissy had been unemployed and was on the last lap of her secret unemployment insurance. The shopping expedition at Saks was to perk up her wardrobe in order to impress the style-engrossed editors at *The New York Times,* where she had high expectations of a new job as a fashion editor on the magazine.

"Nervous?" asked Maggie.

They were in the eighth-floor cafeteria, perched on the hard metal grillwork chairs, waiting for the waiter, who stood chatting nonchalantly with a waitress.

"No," replied Cissy, looking around casually. "Not nervous."

It was too early for lunch—just after noon—and they were both more tired than hungry. The overpriced cafeteria, even with the clash of expensive perfumes and heavy colognes, along with the dense contempt of the waiter and waitress, was a relief. Maggie looked around, following Cissy's eyes. It was, she thought, a room full of well-behaved, grown-up grade-schoolers. Everyone with their arms in the air, as if they were bursting with proof that they had done the homework assignment, while the waiter and waitress exhibited the blunt force of indifference.

"Why should I be nervous?" asked Cissy, her arm obediently in the air as if she, too, had the right answer and wanted her share of attention. She didn't look at Maggie. "The job's in the bag. All I have to do is pass the physical."

"Liar," said Maggie, and Cissy kept up her show of indifference, swiveling her head around the room, as if it was her duty to inspect every outfit and every table combination.

Then she stopped, turned, and broke into a laugh while plunking her elbows on the table. She bent over and confided in that voice that was both throaty and operatic, "Scared shitless."

Maggie nodded, shook her head, then made her own reassuring sounds. "Don't be stupid. The job's in the bag. All you have to do is pass the physical."

Cissy laughed deeper and Maggie smiled. She liked that laugh—so intense, so unguarded. Mostly, Cissy kept it bolted down—until she was sure it was safe to let it out.

Maggie sensed something behind her and saw Cissy's expression change. She started to turn to see what it was, but before she could shift her weight she saw the rough texture and whiffed the familiar scent of cops. There was a policeman on each side of her, each guarding an arm. They put me in the box, she thought, recognizing the tactical competence of controlling her ability to resist.

"That's her!" cried a voice.

It was the size-four voice. It had gone from dull to shrill, but there was the unmistakable ring of Maggie's enemy hiding behind the cops.

"Excuse me, ma'am, could you step outside with us for a moment?" said the officer on Maggie's right. He was tall and young and athletic. It was only a matter of seconds, but Maggie was calculating quickly. She had a flair for clear thinking in a crisis. She knew that the one on her right, the larger officer, was on the verge of snapping her arm in two. She could see him measuring the distance and plotting his moves. The other officer was dark and silent. Even more dangerous, she thought. He would be the one to break training and start shooting.

"It's okay," she said, and although she knew better—after all, she was a veteran!—she made a phantom move toward her purse.

Before she could utter another sound, the second cop grabbed her in a choke hold and the first flung her purse out of her reach. That was nice, she thought, even as she gasped for air and began to grow dizzy. She respected the first cop's presence of mind in getting the suspicious purse out of her reach.

Then both cops wrestled her to the floor and in the background, Maggie could hear the screech of bystanders. They were heading for the exits. It was a small satisfaction to see the waiter and waitress also running for cover.

It was Cissy who saved her. She could hear her friend in the fuzzy distance of her consciousness.

"She's a policewoman!" shouted Cissy.

No, no, Maggie wanted to correct her. I'm on the job. We don't say policewoman!

She saw dimly, as the dark one kept her pinned, the tall cop going through her purse, taking charge of the gun quickly, then examining her wallet and gold detective-lieutenant's shield.

"Sorry, Lieutenant," he said, handing back her gun and purse while Cissy held out a glass of water. The dark officer said nothing, just hung back sullenly, as if he suspected that this was one more lawbreaker stunt.

Maggie sipped the water, took in some air, and then kicked the table. "Damn!" she said looking at the long tear in the blouse, ripped during the fracas. She saw the size four cowering in the corner. She looked paralyzed.

"I'm going to need something to wear," she hissed.

"Size six," quivered the broken saleswoman's voice.

two

Eric Miller awoke in a shivering sweat, bewildered at finding himself in his own apartment. Technically and legally it was his apartment. Emotionally he had no home. He sublet the apartment in a gently threadbare section of Manhattan known as Kip's Bay, but in spite of the fact that he'd lived there for five months, it always felt as if he was waking up in a strange motel room. For the first moment of every day of his life, he was disoriented and trembling with a vague but palpable fear.

The furnishings belonged to someone else; they still bore the owner's lasting imprint. It took work for Eric to focus closely and arrange all the connections.

Not that he would have changed anything. The apartment was within his price range and it was centrally located on East Thirty-seventh Street. The city lay spread out in all directions from that Midtown hub. Finding the apartment had been a stroke of luck.

During the previous winter, the apartment's owner had gotten into an ambiguous but risky quarrel with a neighborhood panhandler. (On his way to pick up his morning newspaper, the apartment owner had given the man a quarter. On his way back home, the beggar held out his cup again, not recognizing his benefactor. The owner grumbled about the beggar's ingratitude, and the beggar launched a vicious stream of threats that froze the apartment owner's heart.) After that, like many of the aging residents in that nook of the East Side, the owner abruptly moved away. He had grown weary of the mean, downward drift of public manners.

In his haste, the owner had left behind every stick and bolt of furniture. The realtor had made it a selling point, and Eric didn't argue. The heavy drapes and Victorian couch and sagging easy chair suggested a different, distant world. He had inherited thick, old walnut dressers and desks, and weighty armoires. On the surfaces of the wooden pieces Eric found the shadows of the framed photographs that had stood there for long decades. He felt cheated of their companionship.

Until this morning, Eric had taken comfort in the cranky nostalgia of his neighbors, who never tired of complaining about the decline of life on their portion of the island of Manhattan. On this particular morning, however, he felt a deeper, more intense unhappiness. Now he had solid grounds for his despondency.

He lifted his head and felt the weight of the impending doom that had kept him awake and pitching all over the bed until an hour before the alarm went off at seven. He lay there until it was time, then picked up the phone and hit the buttons with a deliberate, pointed hostility. "I'll be late," he told Harry Graham, his supervisor.

"Fine," said Graham. To Eric, the voice of the supervisor had a flat, empty sound. He heard no trace of interest or sympathy.

"I have an errand—I may even take the whole day," Eric said, trying to provoke a challenge.

"Fine," said the supervisor, unprovokable.

Eric put the receiver back in the cradle gently; it was either that or smash it to pieces.

Peering through the blinds, Eric saw the cars and trucks maneuvering slowly in and out of the Midtown Tunnel; the traffic looked like reluctant cattle being pushed to slaughter. Everything agreed with his collapsing spirit. His throat tickled and his head ached; his fingers felt numb as he forced himself to go through the usual morning routine of bathing and breakfast. The shower scalded his face before he realized that he had not touched the "Cold" knob, the coffee tasted like lighter fluid.

He stood naked before the full-length mirror examining his reflection, as if he could see the fatal transformation. He looked hard, but there was only the familiar reflection staring back at himself. No lesions. Not yet. He was a medium-sized man who had just turned thirty, but he recognized that he had crossed some imperceptible line and was no longer young. It caught in his throat when he realized for the first time, in a definite, conclusive way, that he would never be old.

Not that it surprised him. He had grown accustomed to disappointment. If he had a gift, it was for open-ended resignation. He had no other special talent. His looks were unremarkable. In fact, his features were relentlessly average in a gray, inoffensive way. His hair was dull and dirty brown and cut conventionally. His forehead was flat and unmarked by age or anguish, and his nose ran a certain, regular distance down his face. But even his co-workers would have trouble picturing him, much less describing him. The only truly distinctive thing about Eric Miller was his rage. It was bottomless.

Most of the time he had it under control. But there were flashes like lightning when he wandered the streets searching for release—some way to vent his unfathomable fury. He didn't look for fights, and in fact seemed mild. But he ran riot in his own subtle way. He would crash a party, find some poor, lonely prey and make up a name, like Edward Barnes (he had no home, and so it made little difference if he had no name), make up a new career, a new background, then do whatever emotional damage he could manage before leaving the victim in confused suspense. The wound of a phantom entanglement was as deep as any inflicted by a straight razor, but it bothered Eric that he couldn't see the eruption of blood or hear the cries of pain. He could only imagine the harm he inflicted as he made his way to work every day, looking like any other normal citizen.

"I'm afraid the news is not good," the doctor had said the previous evening in a voice that had not quite mastered the art of pity. The doctor was too young and too pink with his own good health to be taken seriously. Eric just sat there, sinking in the chair.

Finally, in a voice that trembled, Eric suggested, "It's only a cold," as if the excuses and explanations he made for himself had not occurred to the young, robust doctor.

The doctor shook his head. It irritated Eric that the doctor's great shock of hair waved like wheat when he moved his head. It was a cute mannerism, and he was certain that the doctor was aware of it, used it. It didn't seem fitting for brushing off hope.

"What are the chances," began Eric, choking slightly, "of a mistake?"

The doctor didn't answer right away. He frowned, as if unprepared for such a simple inquiry. Eventually, he spoke. "We'll do another test," he said. A trace of charity had found its way into his voice. It was the sad note of resignation in Eric's question that had broken through the sugary crust of optimism that forms over people gifted with looks and luck. The doctor softened. "Of course, another test," he said.

Eric felt a great, resentful bile of hate in the pit of his stomach.

It didn't take long before he realized that the second test would only confirm the first, and on the morning after his doctor's visit, having stood under an unrefreshing shower and swallowed an acrid breakfast—after the sharp, impersonal exchange with the supervisor—Eric left the apartment he didn't own. He couldn't get away fast enough. He locked the three bolts of the door knowing that there was nothing inside to steal. Locks and bolts were just a brute habit of suspicion and mistrust, his own unpleasant comment upon the human race. Then he came out into the early summer heat and began to walk. He had no particular destination, but he enjoyed walking through Manhattan. He was a sailor, watching the sea from the high deck of a great passing liner, appreciating the thrill of being close to the ocean, but always, inevitably, untouched by it.

He hiked at a businesslike pace through his own alien neighborhood, avoiding eye contact with merchants and residents, who had already written him off as one more cold-blooded trespasser. Eric actively dodged personal contact, but soaked up the inflection and texture of the area. The early structures in Kip's Bay were nineteenth-century brownstones with bulging bay windows, trophies built by complacent burghers as a sign of rank. Later came the low-slung, high-striving apartment houses with chipped cornices and blind cherubs that seldom rose above ten stories, meant to shelter a solid mercantile legion. There was, Eric had to admit, a sensible, human scale to those first plantings.

But during the building- and investment-crazed previous decade of the 1980s, the banks and realtors had

thrown up a scattering of modern glass and iron towers—
forty-story skyscrapers that looked like middle-finger insults among the discreet brownstones—intended to ac-
commodate the paper sharks and junk-bond merchants of
Wall Street. Like the illusory boom of the takeovers and
buyouts, the gaudy new apartment goliaths seemed, for all
the cost and effort, tinny and alarmingly insubstantial.
Eric took some satisfaction in the vacancy signs that never
went away.

He crossed Park Avenue and headed west. The uniformed doormen in the big buildings with fancy awnings
nodded at him out of custom, ignoring his lack of interest.
It was enough that he was a familiar face, a regular, and
they saluted his resident rank with a dip of their heads.

He swam against the tide of office workers, who were
heading up Madison Avenue to the white-collar spawning
grounds of Midtown. There were derelicts on Fifth Avenue, asleep in the doorways of vacant stores; in spite of the
rising temperature of a hot June morning, in their soiled
layers of blankets and clothes, they were bundled against
the cold winds of contracting and grudging charity blowing from one end of the city to the other.

Better off, he thought bitterly. The homeless, hacking
parasite with a coal miner's hide has a better chance of
survival, he thought miserably, than I do. By Sixth Avenue,
on fire with self-pity, Eric was firing curses like arrows
under his breath at everyone he passed: the brittle professional women in their careless chic; the Armani men in
their iron masks, holding on to their leather briefcases as
if they contained nuclear codes. Even the bicycle whippets
slaloming through traffic in their tight spandex shorts and
racing helmets were not spared. "I hope you wind up
crushed under an eighteen-wheeler," he said out loud. A
young, pretty woman heard him, turned her head in momentary shock, then remembered that this was New York

City and swung back to face in the opposite direction and quickened her pace.

Eric laughed.

"We can start on the AZT right away," the doctor had said.

"If the second test confirms the first," Eric had interrupted.

The doctor had grown solemn. "Of course," he had said in a tone that held out little hope. "The cold symptoms are not severe and you seem to be in pretty good shape. . . ."

Eric sat on the lip of the chair, listening through the whistling in his head. "I work out," he lied.

"The treatments are usually pretty successful," he said. "For a while. We have to keep close tabs on the T cells and watch out for any infections. . . ."

The doctor was, Eric realized, plotting the final days of his life from a script already written in stone.

The Star Billiard Academy was located on Fourteenth Street, one flight up. The entrance was on Eighth Avenue and Eric had to stare down a sullen junkie who blocked his way. The junkie moved slowly enough to preserve his dignity while gradually giving way. Eric had his hand on a Swiss army knife that he kept open in his pocket. It wouldn't have taken much for him to use it.

The stairs were covered by wet carpeting, and the banister shivered when he touched it. The kid who ran the pool parlor had a cigarette dangling from his mouth. "We're not open yet," he said belligerently. The half-smoked cigarette bobbed with each word. The sign above his head said that the billiard parlor opened at nine. The clock read 9:20.

"I'll take table eight," said Eric. The kid behind the

counter, his rolled-up sleeves revealing a tattoo of an anchor on one arm and an eagle on the other, measured his opponent, then decided it wasn't worth a brawl. He reached down under the counter and came up with a tray of balls and some blue chalk.

Eric racked the balls, broke the pack, and missed every shot. He was not a bad pool player, but he couldn't concentrate. Not on this morning. He kept looking out the window at the drug transactions and the gypsy Rollerbladers and the wild-eyed punks and the sightless cops and the steady stream of ordinary civilians who swerved in and out between the outlaw packs, gazing past the immediate demented chaos to some imagined far-off vista of sanity.

He was one of them now, Eric thought. One more condemned desperado.

"You wanna shoot some eight ball?"

The kid who ran the parlor was no youngster. Now, as he stood in the light near the window, Eric saw that he was in some delayed stage of middle age. Forty something, simulating a mutinous peak of adolescence, thought Eric. The vest and the tattoos and the slope of long hair were designed to prolong something long gone. The lean and unshaved face was creased and scarred from too many bad calculations. A heavy gold ring hung from the right earlobe. The eyes were pockets of suspicion. The stringy arms held a pool cue with intricate designs—his own, not one of the public cues spread around the room. The smile was a twisted and taunting insult.

"Rack 'em," said Eric.

The "kid" nodded and went to work. He slammed the balls into the rack, tightened them up, cleared the table of lint. Then he turned and faced Eric. "Ten a game?"

Eric shrugged. "Make it twenty."

He lost the first game, then the second. After the third the kid held out his hand for the money.

"Lemme look at your cue," said Eric, handing him three twenties.

"Why?" asked the kid.

"Maybe you cork it," said Eric. "Rack 'em again."

The kid handed him the cue, the prospect of a bigger hustle blinding him to the danger. Eric took the cue, examined the handle and the pretty design, then slid both hands down to the narrow tip. He held it like a baseball bat. The kid wasn't watching; he was busy putting the balls in the rack, trying to guess how many twenties he could glom before the sucker ran off. Maybe he should lose a few to whet the sucker's appetite. That was what he was thinking when the first blow landed. It hit square on the back of his head and sent him crashing into the wooden frame of the pool table, where he lost four of his front teeth.

"Aaarrgh!" came pouring out of the kid's mouth, along with a spray of spit and vomit and blood. His skull was splintered and blood was seeping out of his ears and nose. He lost consciousness.

"Fag!" hissed Eric, cocking the pool cue and whacking the kid in the back, breaking two ribs. "Filthy fucking fag!" He kicked the kid, rolling him over, and carefully broke both kneecaps with the stout pool cue. He aimed and landed the blows deliberately, a marksman, each explosion accompanied by a venomous cry that had been bottled up since he had learned the cause of his endless cold.

"Fag! Fag! Fag!"

Finally, he was done. He broke the kid's pool cue in one last act of punishment.

He left the kid on the floor, bleeding and unconscious but still alive. The aging kid had finally achieved permanent youthful status. He would spend the rest of his life in a gurgling, infantlike coma.

Eric felt a moment of exhilaration, then complete deflation. He ran out of the building, stepped over the dazed junkie, and headed north, back to his apartment. He wasn't afraid of being caught—he was surprised at how immune he felt. And as he ran through the streets of Lower Manhattan he told himself that he had done nothing wrong, he was merely dispensing justice. After all, homosexuals had fatally assaulted him. He did not deserve to die. He was an innocent bystander!

But clubbing the kid did not answer the deep rage Eric felt at the mortal wrong that had been done to him. True, there was some physical satisfaction, some transient release in the act of breaking a man's skull. But it was primitive and messy and, in the end, not enough. It did not educate anyone, except some repulsive pool-hall lizard. No, he was definitely not satisfied with what he had done. He had to find another way to instruct the world about the real danger of AIDS.

He slowed to a walk and began to plan his new line of attack. It would have to be more shrewd. And more deadly.

three

LATE JUNE

The bag was leaking badly. Maggie held the brown paper sack containing her breakfast at arm's length, clutching the top in her left hand like the neck of a dead chicken. In the other hand was her trusty tote bag—a dense swamp awash with crumpled reports, extinct newspapers, fading receipts, mysterious notes, stale breath mints, loose dental floss, snowflakes of torn paper on which were written long-forgotten six-digit telephone numbers, two eyeglass cases, and one floating pair of cracked glasses. At the bottom of all that commotion was a toxic mass of chewed-up dross that had lost all possibility of identification. It was not the tote bag of someone in firm control.

As she entered the station house of the Seventeenth Police Precinct on East Fifty-first Street, Maggie was aware of all eyes turning in her direction with the usual uncharitable blend of amusement and disdain. None of the men and few of the women were certain that a young, female detective-lieutenant should be in command of a crack homicide squad. Their confidence was not boosted by the clear trail of dripping coffee she left from the rolling sidewalk cart outside to her second-floor office. The coffee fell like incriminating footprints as Maggie advanced through the security screen and the reception area, past the high magistrate's desk and the disapproving scrutiny of the duty sergeant's ruefully wagging head, then climbed the rickety stairs to the cold warren of doors marking off the various sections and divisions of the Manhattan North Police Command. By the time she kicked open her office door, dumped all of her other gear on her desk, and placed the sopping bag on the curdled blotter, the cup inside the container was bone dry. The only coffee left had soaked into the now-spongy bagel.

A large, peaceful-looking man with the knowing and sympathetic eyes of a basset hound brought her a fresh serving in a chipped mug with the police department emblem baked into the side. He performed this task with the quiet dignity of someone who recognizes and forgives harmless idiosyncrasies. Maggie preferred the stronger brew from the cart outside, but she accepted the weaker precinct version from her loyal deputy with a barely audible, growling thank-you. She needed the caffeine.

With a sigh, she turned to the material waiting for her professional attention. There was a pile of telephone messages, as well the thick brown overnight report folder of daily homicidal mayhem in her "Active" basket.

"What've we got?" she asked through the first mouthful of hot liquid as she quickly skimmed the telephone messages, all of which contained some element of reproach from a superior or else some racking obligation to call someone back. She hated returning phone calls, especially when they required groveling or equivocation. The calls could wait. In any case, it normally took a few heartbeats, together with a scalding slap of coffee, to transform Maggie from a muddled, half-awake civilian into an efficient, masterful sleuth. It took a little longer before she was willing to suffer annoying phone calls.

"Just the usual mishegoss," said her deputy, a loyal old

police dog named Sad Sam Rosen. She nodded, listening not so much for the words, but for a telltale pitch signaling alarm. A sarcastically soothing tone from Sam meant that there was no emergency; it meant that she had time to adjust to her weighty position as head of the Manhattan North Detective Command. It meant she didn't have to speak to anyone for a while.

Maggie Van Zandt had picked Detective Sergeant Rosen as her deputy for a variety of reasons, but mostly for the great comfort of his concrete presence. Sam was steadfast and capable and loyal. A hulking, scrupulous, and meticulous man, he had spent twenty-four years on the job building up a great fund of solid street wisdom. He had also picked up a completely misleading reputation for thick-witted sluggishness. It was based on a complex legacy of bigotry within the department, and reinforced by his own bullheaded restraint. The fact that he was Jewish as well as Black reinforced high negative leanings in the narrow and suspicious fold of the police department. Sam regarded the low opinion of his peers as one more passive form of abuse.

But Maggie quickly saw through all the defenses and camouflage. Sad Sam was a pistol and had a real sneaky sense of humor. She knew that in spite of his lumbering size and sleepy manner, he could outrun and outslug the youngest, meanest, and brawniest villain. Apart from his physical competence, Maggie appreciated the fact that Sam's apparent reserve was born of a deeply sensitive nature. Like the best of his breed of cop, Sad Sam did not trust words. They were too imprecise; he did not recognize in the narrative the grim and complicated world of the street.

Two decades earlier, when he was brand new on the force, a newspaper had published an account of a robbery in which he had been the first uniformed officer on the scene. He was disgusted by the garbled depiction of the event. It didn't match the butchery and anguish of what he had witnessed. Sam Rosen didn't see a "victim," as depicted in the newspaper. "Victim" sounded clean, almost peaceful. Also slightly pitiful and maybe gutless. In the arid newspaper story, the blood-drenched, sightless "victim" was laundered into a statistic. But Sam remembered a guy with half his head blown away and his brains stuck to the shelves of his own liquor store. That was his "victim."

And calling the villain a "suspect"—well, that one really struck a nerve. This "perp" had been conferred with a purely technical innocence by the press for reasons that were swinishly self-serving and timid. Libel-law and politically correct reasons. Sam had captured an armed thug. He brought him down after a grueling uphill chase. Now the same snarling, unrepentant murderer with a rap sheet that ran the full text of the criminal code was kissed with the presumed-innocent category of "suspect." Not as far as Sam was concerned.

He understood the underlying motivation, he was aware of the cautious excuses, but he could not reconcile the two versions. Victims and suspects were not stick characters who could be disinfected or dismissed by cagey newspaper accounts. The individuals were, themselves, haunting and vivid, not to mention often savagely dangerous. And so after that first warped experience, he employed a cryptic, noncommital silence. It was preferable to the glib, stammering, and garbled categories of newspapers and locker rooms. He didn't mind at all that his silence was misconstrued as a kind of dull evasion. He welcomed the misreading. It became, in fact, a layer of protection against the raw, voluptuous scrambling of reality.

Maggie had recognized instantly that this was a man who, when he did report, was thoroughly accurate. He was a perfect counterpoint for her wild, speculative impulses. She needed his spare and faithful lucidity.

"A drive-by on East One-eighteenth Street," he said in his flat, emotionless voice. He was reading from his copy of the overnight detective reports that Maggie could not yet bear to face. "Drug thing. No perps yet."

She nodded in numb recognition that they lived in a world of routine drive-by outrages. They both knew and accepted the sad truth that the perps would inevitably show up again at the site of a future social insult. If there was any consolation, it was in the certainty that sooner or later the drive-by killers would be caught. Drive-by shootings were never a once-in-a-lifetime thrill.

"Dead baby in a garbage can on One-sixty-eighth Street," he continued. "Mother's fourteen. Says it was born dead and she couldn't afford a funeral. Bruises say something else."

She listened with the anesthetized earplug of professional detachment. By the time she had become a detective, Maggie had learned to shut out the unproductive outrage. She performed a kind of defensive triage to save her sanity. The full range of human malice—murder, rape, torture, child abuse, serial slaughter—was too great for any mind to bear and remain in balance. If she absorbed it all, every gruesome detail, she would end up running wild and tearing out her hair. She could only listen selectively and pick out those tragedies about which she could do something. The rest, she told herself coldly, was just the six o'clock news.

Maggie took a bite of the bagel, squirting coffee on her clean blouse. She looked down sorrowfully, just above her left breast pocket, as if the stain was a birthmark over which she had no power.

"School shoot-out. Two dead."

"Drugs?" she asked. She didn't look up from the blouse.

"No," replied Sam with a sigh of resignation. "This was over a girl."

"A girl?" She looked up from the stain. "I hope she was worth it."

"She was the shooter," Sam said.

Maggie blinked.

"She was getting in touch with her anger." Sam shrugged. "The two guys had a duke-out over the girl, then decided that she wasn't worth it. They made friends. Laughed about it." Sam smiled weakly. "The girl was offended. She thought she was worth it. So she smoked them both in the cafeteria." He was reading from the report. He raised his eyebrows in a kind of salute. "A born banger. Only took one shot for each. Right in the heart."

Maggie raised her head, then nodded. "Well, they were asking for it. Somebody tells me I'm not worth it . . . !" Then something occurred to her. "She had the gun on her? In school?"

"Borrowed it. From a girlfriend."

Maggie gave a melancholy shake of her head. "I used to borrow lipstick when I went to high school. . . ."

"Junior high," corrected Sam.

For an instant, Maggie stopped, caught by surprise. A milestone. Something had happened. She had grown accustomed to high school felons. Big-time crime in high school had become almost routine, which was why there were cops and metal detectors in bad schools. But now the killings had leached down to junior high school. Kids twelve, thirteen. She felt a chill, as if a shadow had inched closer to a new dark age.

Sam went back to the reports. "Murder-suicide in a swank apartment on East Fifty-fifth Street. Lawyer with heart problems couldn't face taking care of a wife with terminal cancer."

"I take it that the local shoes are working the outstandings," she said, brushing the coffee stain into a wider blotch.

Sad Sam nodded.

She opened the case folders and read the raw DD 5 report of the precinct detective on the murder-suicide. Manny Stern, a criminal lawyer with some skill. She had seen him in court. Good on his feet. Wore tailored suits, fancy hankies in his breast pocket, and expensive jewelry. She remembered the scent of cologne when she thought of Manny Stern. The story of a suicide and homicide didn't smell right—not like fresh pine, not with a man who flashed diamond cuff links. She looked at the photographs of the apartment, then looked back again at the typed report. Sam slumped into a chair and waited for her to finish. It took a few moments.

"These people were well-to-do," she said.

"Well, they weren't civil servants," replied Sam. "I'd say they were comfortable."

"Collected expensive paintings and sculpture."

"Could be. Who said?"

"The sister-in-law," said Maggie, indicating a spot in the detective's dense report.

"So?"

She looked up, put the lens that fell out back into the socket of her eyeglasses, then explained. "Monet, Picasso, Braque—that's a lot of dough," she said. Then she thought about it some more. "Put somebody on this one, Sam. Somebody with a brain."

"You know something, or is this just a hunch?" he asked.

She looked up and smiled. "Sam, make the assignment. I got a reason." She was studying the pictures. She examined one in particular. "Look at this," she said, poking him gently. She held up a wide-lens shot of the murder scene. Everything looked in place to Sam.

"You don't see it?"

He shook his head.

"Look at the wall, up here." She pointed to a corner of the photograph, near a fireplace. There was an outline clearly visible—a place where a large painting had hung. Now a cheap print hung like a postage stamp in the shadow on the wall. "There's something suspicious about a rich lawyer sticking an undersized print in a space where an expensive painting used to hang."

"The sister-in-law says she thinks that he sold the paintings and whatnot to pay expenses. Man couldn't work. Had a bum ticker. Sold his paintings." He held out his arms as if that was a reasonable explanation.

Maggie shook her head. "He wouldn't leave that mark. Not in a million-dollar co-op. He'd've put another painting up there. Something that fit." She shook her head more emphatically, punctuating the opinion. "Let's check it out. See if the paintings are registered, insured. If somebody peddled them."

The more she thought about it, the more she felt a tickle of misgiving. The story was flawed. Manny Stern, a lawyer with diamond cuff links and a baroque style, would not sell his paintings quickly; he'd have several bank accounts and lots of insurance.

Sam looked down at his own copy of the DD 5. Smiled. "I'll get Neeley to take a run at it."

"Neeley?"

He laughed. "He's a fiend about art," replied Sam without looking up. "Year ago he took me to our storage vault on a lunch break just to show me a hot Matisse somebody recovered."

"Really? Was it great?"

"The hot Matisse? Rather have a hot corned beef sandwich."

* * *

They were at lunch at the nearby deli on Lexington Avenue; the corned beef reference had given them both an irresistible cholesterol craving.

"The squad detective—who caught it?" she asked with her mouth full of french fries and pickle.

"Bukowski," he replied, almost choking as he swallowed an unchewed portion of his sandwich.

"Do I know him?"

"If you don't, you're not missing much. He made gold because his father and grandfather were cops. Lots of rabbis in the family. Not much else to recommend him. Busts down doors and busts in heads. Thinks that's where the term *bust* comes from. A family tradition. He comes from a long line of lousy cops."

She laughed. She was always pleased with his candor. "Good that we get our own guy on the case," she said.

They buried themselves in the corned beef for a while, washing it down with soft drinks. Maggie was glad that she didn't have to shop for clothing today.

"What kind of cop would you say that I was?" she asked.

He took a moment to answer. "Not a ball-buster," he said finally. It was a high compliment.

"That's good," she said.

He studied the meat in his sandwich—a piece of stage business to give him time to consider the question. "You move," he said. "Like that Manny Stern business this morning—you really haul ass when you want to move."

"Yeah, well, I get that from my father."

"Was he a cop?"

She shook her head. "A contractor," she said, mashing the food in her mouth, throwing back a slug of cherry soda. Then she paused. "But he was fearless, you know? I went along on some jobs when I was a kid and I was impressed." She collected the parts of the story to get it right.

"The man had no fear." She laughed. "I remember a job. There was some work with a patio and the owner of the house had another problem with a wall. Wanted it moved or opened. Who knows? This was somewhere—I don't know—maybe Queens. Oh, I remember: The guy said that he wanted a door there—to get to the kitchen or the toilet. But the guy says, too bad, it can't be done because the wall is filled with wires and pipes. Can't be disturbed. Ruin the infrastructure. Well, can't be disturbed. You couldn't say a thing like that to my father. The old man liked to disturb walls. He takes a sledge hammer and starts whacking down the plaster while this guy stands there holding his head, his mouth flapping and his eyes popping. He can't even speak. My father really went to work. Beams, wires, pipes— tore through everything. He did not give a shit. He says anything that he breaks, he can fix. Pipes, wiring—it's all man-made. He can rewire the electricity, reconnect the pipes, shore up the beams. And he did."

Maggie shook her head, smiling. "The man was fear- less. Really. Fearless. He would go through anything. A bulldozer. It made me a little aggressive." She took a bite of a pickle. "You know, life's a lot like that wall full of wires and pipes and beams. You can't be shy about making a door for yourself. You gotta go through a wall, just go. You gotta break down some walls in the PD, go get an ax. My father taught me that." She attacked the food.

He laughed. "Meshugge," he said.

Her beeper went off when she was blissfully wiping the last smear of ketchup from her plate. It was the chief of detectives, and he said that he had to see her. He was in his car on his way across town and would be in her office wait- ing. "Be there!" he snarled.

Maggie didn't take it personally. That was his way. He was the same miserable, bad-tempered foe who had ar- gued against her appointment to head the homicide squad. His reasons, he said at the time, were self-evident. He could have meant Maggie's sloppy administrative skills or her defiant nature. But he hadn't. He'd meant gender, pure and simple. He had only given in under hard and direct pressure from a police commissioner who wanted to appease the female lobby.

"Trouble?" asked Sad Sam.

"Trouble is our business," she said in arch dramatic tones, picking up the check.

"I thought it was avoiding trouble," mumbled Sam, leaving the tip.

four

TUESDAY, JUNE 29

"Professor Drake's office."

"Is she in?"

"She's busy right now. Can I take a message?"

"When will she be free?"

"Well, she's got an appointment and then an interview
and then another meeting. You wanna leave a message?"

The girl's voice sounded young. Nevertheless, Eric
Miller thought that she was a master at grown-up evasion,
which was the most important requisite for the job of answering a busy college professor's phone. A gifted student,
no doubt, sweating out her summer working on the translucent telephone line.

"I'll call back," he said.

As he replaced the receiver, Eric noticed that he was
clutching a handkerchief. He didn't remember reaching
for it. But he remembered precisely the moment when
he'd started to carry one regularly. He awoke one morning—after the screening and tests had been repeated
twice, confirmed and reconfirmed seropositive—and experienced a vast and terrifying uncertainty. Not just a

pause for a reconfiguration of his life or a philosophical misgiving, but something more elemental: dread. It was a moment when he grasped, finally, that he was going to die.

There was nothing he could do about it. His body belonged to the virus. And the ground shaking under his feet was not his own doing. In the end, he convinced himself that he was just a bystander at whatever sinister and tragic drama was being enacted inside himself. And so he plunged ahead, doing just what he was doing—fully, totally, savagely committed to the lethal mission he had chosen. Of course, in order to carry out his scheme, he couldn't start on the medical protocol. No disabling or unmasking drugs. No surrender to the inevitable. Not yet.

There were no symptoms. He inspected the surfaces of his skin daily, looking for the telltale lesions of the fateful carcinoma. And, of course, he waited for the cough. When it came, it would not be just a simple respiratory static reflex. It would be a cough that would never end. Like some finely calibrated Richter scale, he listened for the first distant rumble of his own extinction, all the while clenching a handkerchief as if it would shield him against the shock.

Eric had no illusions that he would be saved by a miracle cure out of the research labs. That would come—if ever—too late. He'd be stricken fatally long before that. He imagined in detail the long, lingering death, swallowing the poison AZT three times a day, suffering the nausea and havoc to his body, without any proof that it did any good at all. The exact medical trajectory was inescapable: first there would be episodes of opportunistic infections, followed by periods of remission. None of it would be decent or painless. None of it would be without its own heaping measure of humiliation. He'd be in and out of the hospital, monitoring his diminishing T-cell count like a miser, all the while growing progressively gaunt and grasping at wild, useless homemade cures. He would eat carrot extract and ingest Mexican compounds, and still get sick.

It was, of course, utterly inescapable. Eventually, there would come one last chapter when he would just get worse. Period. If he accepted that dreary fate, his only aim would be to retain enough strength and enough sense to end his life peacefully, in some twilight of overmedication.

That was the concluding nasty secret about AIDS, and he knew it instinctively, even before someone from the Gay Men's Health Crisis told him in whispers that a lot of the afflicted went out with a quick combination of lethal pharmaceuticals. Already he had begun to hoard sedatives. If he didn't have another prospect in mind, he would have already elected that mortifying swan song.

What ate at him was the discreet and pervasive scorn. Counselors obviously didn't believe him when he declared himself heterosexual and drug-free; they would suggest with mulish regularity that he come to terms with whatever risk factor put him in this pickle in the first place. Unprotected sex. Drugs. Whatever. Like priests pushing for confessions, they paraded their disbelief openly. Of course the suspicious mind-set was not unfamiliar. When he was on the sidelines, taking blood from people he regarded as wicked sinners, he, himself, had doubted everyone, too. All the blood technicians would roll their eyes at yet another spurious disclaimer from yet another poor bastard in some advanced stage of denial. Mostly, the technicians were right. Mostly, the avowed innocents turned out to be abusers of something or closet somethings.

But Eric was not ready to be dismissed with that kind of contempt. He didn't want to hear the doctors speak to him in harsh, unsympathetic practical terms, erasing whatever Hail Mary hope he'd found for temporary refuge. He wanted the respect he felt his due.

It stung, because he regarded himself as an unsung hero of the war on AIDS. He had been on the front lines when other lab technicians quit rather than draw the toxic blood. Changing occupations hadn't even occurred to him when he'd heard stories about doctors and nurses becoming accidentally infected. It hadn't really been courage; it had been a lapse of imagination. He just never thought that he would catch it.

And he wouldn't have been infected, except for a tiny slip. Not that he was careless. In fact, he considered himself a casualty of excessive caution. He had been wearing two pairs of the latex gloves that April morning when he took the fatal blood sample. But the extra gloves made him clumsy. He always treated the needles and blood as if they were plutonium, but while extracting a needle from the arm of an apparent drug addict with track marks up and down his arms, he experienced a sudden spasm in his taut nervous system. The point of the instrument went through both gloves. If he could, he would have sliced off the finger right then and there.

He didn't say anything, just rushed into the bathroom, leaving the addict looking bewildered. In the bathroom he ripped off the gloves and squeezed the puncture wound with all his strength to force out the blood, like clearing out the venom from a snake bite. Then he punched an extra hole in his thumb to encourage more bleeding. He bled as much as he could, but he knew it wasn't enough. He scrubbed his hand over and over. It wasn't enough. Whatever had taken place in that flicker of a second was already over and done.

Two days later, when he saw the drug addict's HIV seropositive blood report, his knees sank and he left the lab early. It was then that he made the first appointment, under the invented name of Edward Barnes, with an out-of-the-way internist. It was, of course, too early for the tests to show up positive. It took weeks for the antibodies to incubate. He waited to take second and third tests, but it was an ordeal that tested his sanity. It was during that period that he crashed a party in a brownstone on the Upper

West Side of Manhattan and slept with the unsophisticated college professor.

He thought, Why not? Husbands infected wives. Wives infected lovers. Everyone got even with somebody. The world spun on a vicious cycle of spite. So why not put a superior college professor with no known risk factors in fear of her life? Why not educate her? Of course, this was before he was certain, before he had gone over the edge and decided on the calculated path of punishment.

When the incubation period was over and the test came back positive, Eric was not surprised. There was even a small measure of relief in confirming the worst. Now he had no farther to fall. But, as the counselor said, this false tranquillity was followed by a rising anger. In Eric's case, because he believed himself blameless—even martyred— the resentment rose to a great bile of hatred. Eric felt robbed even of the pity he didn't want. He had to act on this anger or explode. The question became, How?

He wanted to educate the self-righteous bystanders who clucked with remote sympathy. They wrote big, deductible checks, yet ever so slightly averted their heads lest they inhale the floating contaminated spray when they spoke to an AIDS victim.

It was after witnessing a few such encounters from behind the one-way mirror of his secret infection that Eric decided to educate the world in his own subtle fashion.

Everyone witnessed the slow, skeletal extinction of young artists and athletes; they watched it in the newspapers and in dewy documentaries and in angry plays. But public sympathy was centered on homosexuals, intravenous drug abusers, or hemophiliacs. No one gave a thought to the rare straight, unaddicted victim in low-risk categories. Like himself. This was where he intended to draw attention. He had to make the earth tremble for everyone. He had to show something new, not just the known misery.

Chief of Detectives Larry Scott stole one more glance at his reflection in the window of Maggie's office. It was a twitch, this checking up on himself. He was simply unable to digest the brutal fact that he was aging. The boyish face—a face that he had carried unmarked past his thirties—had begun to pleat and crinkle and droop into the pulpy bookends of matching jowls. When he ran a comb across his head it plucked out hair like wisps of floating dandelion seeds. He arranged the remaining strands across his scalp and tacked into the wind when he walked so as not to disturb the carefully organized and sprayed fan of modesty. But in every car and shop window he was confronted by the terrible shadow of his father and his father's father walking in his footsteps.

The latest humiliation was something that should have been inconsequential; it had occurred right outside on the street. A man had called him sir. Hadn't recognized the chief or known his rank. Just a quick, reflexive remark after they'd accidentally bumped into each other, but it had bite. The offhand simplicity was crushing. "Pardon me, sir!" The respect was for the seniority of age.

At that instant Scott was forced to admit to himself that he was no longer the fabulously bright, youthful executive crashing his way through all the police department promotional ceilings in his rocket to the top. He was, alas, just another moderately high-ranking police officer of nascent middle age who had already reached the far limits of his ability. Soon he would begin the countdown to a pension. He yearned for a whisper of the old compliments about his remarkable youth and his immeasurable future. But as he turned and caught his reflection one more time, he realized that he was forty-one and no one found that fact at all surprising.

It was at that ripe and aching moment that Maggie came barreling into her office, catching him looking at himself. Once again, he found himself flustered and annoyed at her sudden and knowing intrusion. She had a gift for making him uncomfortable, as if she could read his secrets.

"Chief," she said in a borrowed baritone, wearing that cryptic grin that made him squirm.

For a moment he forgot himself and started to chew her out—it was his first impulse whenever she moved into his crosshairs. But then he remembered why he was there. His hand began to flutter, and he slapped on a cheerless grin to signal his harmless intent. Still, he couldn't help being critical. She looked sloppy. No makeup. Broken fingernails. And she wore an outfit more fitting for a chase than a photograph. He wanted his senior officers looking crisp, not dangerous.

It didn't make Maggie any less appealing to Chief Scott. On the contrary, her untidy look caught in his throat. He felt drawn and surprisingly protective toward her. Her lush vulnerability was at drastic odds with her prickly personality; the combination was intoxicating. Chief Scott was batty about Maggie Van Zandt. The insubordinate manner acted like a dizzying scent. He would never dare admit it. Or do anything about it. Not with a woman spilling over with complaints and difficulties like Maggie. Not with the civic thought-police ready to pounce at the first hint of male-to-female interest.

There was a time when a chief could, with some probability of success, make clear insinuations to which a female officer with ambition would eagerly respond, as the price of doing business. Nothing complicated. Nothing messy. Nothing that would leave a damaging aftertaste. A few afternoons in some clean and discreet hotel room. Such things were done—he had done them—even in the age of female emancipation. But with Maggie Van Zandt, he knew that he would be spinning the cylinder of a loaded revolver. He would not dare even make an off-color joke in her presence; she'd have him busted for sexual harassment, he was positive. The odd thing was, he was certain beyond any doubt that she was not a mindless, bluenose feminist radical. He guessed that she had a healthy and active libido under all that grit. But she'd turn him in, nonetheless. Some distorted notion of entertainment. She'd enjoy seeing him twist in the wind. He couldn't take a chance with her.

It made Chief Scott's teeth sore to think about her temper and pride and operatic crusades. These were possibly the traits that heightened her charm. Maybe the worst part of it was that she seemed so amused by him, as if she were the mother allowing him to play chief.

"You better sit down," he said, removing the smile.

Maggie smelled authentic trouble.

Outside the office, Sergeant Rosen was reading a fresh case. A young publishing assistant with a nice apartment on the intellectually superior Upper West Side of Manhattan had had her throat cut. This one should bounce, he thought. He looked up in time to catch the eye of his boss, Maggie, who then rolled her eyes to signal her own distress. He stuck his head in the office and asked in his dour manner, "Mind if I sit in?"

"Better wait," said Maggie quickly, shaking her head.

Scott, who was not gifted with tact, welcomed emotional reinforcements. "No! No! Come in here," he said, waving Sad Sam into the office.

Maggie turned to Sad Sam and said in a loud whisper, "Bad news."

They were interrupted by a uniformed policewoman who brought in a tray of coffee. Again Scott welcomed the delay. Anything to postpone what he had come to do. The uniformed officer deposited the tray, smiled at the chief, then left. Sad Sam and Maggie and Scott picked up the heavy wooden chairs and arranged themselves in cozy proximity. They fussed with sugar and cream and stirring.

"Bad news, Maggie," confirmed Chief Scott without looking up from his cup.

She thought, Demotion. He was finally going to get his revenge with a drastic solution to their feud. She couldn't imagine what had provoked it. It wouldn't take much. The incident at Saks? No. Scott didn't give a shit about that. Well, he did, but there wasn't much to it. It was too vague, and no complaints or charges had been filed. A little misunderstanding that made a nice item of gossip. Proof of Maggie's wild, cowgirl nature. Had to be something stupid, like not filing reports on time or screwing up her budget or messing up the statistical virtual reality by which he lived. The man was devoted to body counts. It was the root of the hard friction between them. They had gone toe-to-toe over the difference in their theory of how to run a homicide command. Chief Scott was committed to the traditional idea that the only reliable way to measure success was to match a conviction with a dead body. One murder, one prisoner. You get a drive-by, send out a flying squad, and round up a gang. Somebody's guilty of something. And it plays on the tube.

Maggie disagreed. She was convinced that there was a more subtle role for a highly trained homicide detective. It was no trick to round up known gang-bangers. Just run the blue broom down any ghetto street. But that was a job for uniformed cops who operated like an army in big sweeps. No big brainpower required for that.

She argued that the trained and disciplined homicide specialist should take a more sanguine, circumspect view of death. The shrewd detective should put sudden death in a social context, see coincidence as a red flag. He or she should attach motive and meaning to little things and, above all, look beneath the surface. A heart attack could be the aftermath of a stickup. An accident had consequences. Look for the motivating factors of money, lust, or revenge. Uncovering a cheating spouse or a disgruntled worker required effort, legwork, and sneaky, back-alley tricks. In the really interesting cases—the carefully plotted murders—nothing was the way it seemed. Everything was all staged. The homicide specialist had to have an intuitive sense of what small thing stood out, seemed misplaced, hit a false note and cried murder.

What Scott called squandering man-hours Maggie considered preventive medicine, deterrence. Cracking a solitary murder case with a squad of intelligent cops was not a waste of time, even if it was true, as Scott insisted, that the same number of police officers could, during the same period of time, round up ten homicidal gang enforcers. No, Maggie insisted, the single murder had to be solved. It was nothing less than a grand, cautionary statement made on behalf of society that every life was precious, that every killer would be hunted to the ground. It was a vast accusatory finger warning would-be master criminals that brains and effort would be spent prodigiously—disproportionately—to bring in a single killer.

On the other hand, she was aware that the city was entering another election season and the circus of photo ops and sound bites was at hand. The mayor, a good-hearted but essentially soft man, would need the boost of police pit-bulls to convince an already skeptical electorate that he had the mettle for another term. The public had no stomach for parlor mysteries—not when they couldn't walk the streets or bike in the parks unmolested. They wanted action.

Chief Scott was one of the architects of blunt, street-tough politics. A couple of beefy cops with some surly malefactor hung out between them was the real coin of political currency in a close election. Solving some ten-year-old family-fortune mystery poisoning didn't reassure the citizens about their safety. Above all, what the political managers and spin doctors didn't want was the image of some dippy, thirty-four-year-old female detective lieutenant with mustard stains on her blouse clinging to the mayor when he promised to bring in the killers by the scruff of the neck.

This was what Maggie told herself—the underlying reason for the demotion or transfer—as Scott worked up enough courage to speak. She was in a mild panic because the truth was that she didn't want to lose the job. There was something deeply fulfilling, as well as conclusively righteous, about tracking down a killer. There were very few areas in life in which there was such unequivocal certainty. There was none of the squeamish ambivalence she felt when locking up some pathetic drug addict. There were no moral misgivings about hounding someone who only wanted to feed a family. Murder was clear-cut. Simple.

"If it's the charts . . ." she began.

She owed Chief Scott an updated pie chart for his presentation to the high police chiefs who met weekly to critique each other. Scott was a demon for pie charts and graphs, which, like Ross Perot's, bypassed flabby rhetoric and demonstrated vividly the marching, climbing bars of progress.

Scott shook his head. It was not the charts. He held out an envelope, his eyes still fixed on the floor. He can't even face me, she thought. Little worm! She looked at the envelope, realized that it was private, not official. It had been sealed and opened, dusted for prints. She felt the residue. On the face of the envelope was her name: *Maggie Van Zandt*. Inside was familiar stationery. Cissy's.

A rare, icy crawl of fear climbed up her back. A swarm of confusing possibilities blocked her usual lucid behavior. Maggie was one of those born soldiers who did not panic under gunfire. Ordinarily, the noise and smoke and whistle of combat did not affect her ability to think coherently. During a shoot-out in East Harlem, Sad Sam had watched her walk upright and unafraid past cringing commanders to the communications van, shaming and inspiring the other officers on the scene. She would have made a great general, he thought.

But at the moment Maggie was far from an inspiring warrior. What was going on? she wondered. Was this some sort of trial? Some test of her poise? She was aware of Sad Sam's evident concern and the uncertainty and anxiety on the face of Chief Scott. It was not a test. She didn't speak, but suddenly she knew that she held something volatile in her hand.

Carefully, she looked at her name. Chief Scott got up, the scraping of his chair disturbing her concentration, walked to the window, and stared out at Fifty-first Street. Sad Sam moved in closer, her faithful sentry.

She opened the folded paper and wanted to weep before she even knew why. The room was as quiet as midnight. She hadn't breathed since Chief Scott handed her the paper. She read the writing and sobbed, "Oh, dear God!"

The paper fell from her hand. Automatically Sad Sam reached down and retrieved it. He handed it back to Maggie, but had time to read the single sentence.

I will miss you.

"She, uh, took an overdose," said Chief Scott haltingly.

five

Maggie was startled to find herself standing up; she didn't remember getting out of the chair. She circled the desk quickly, as if she had banged her toe and was walking off the pain. Her fists were clenched white and her eyes rolled around in her head like loose marbles.

She wanted to cry, but she didn't dare start. She showed only a ferocious front to the chief and Sad Sam. But no matter how hard she tried to fasten in on it, the idea of Cissy Stone committing suicide would not sit still.

Cissy couldn't be dead, not according to Maggie's reliable touchstone logic. She'd spoken to her yesterday. Less than twenty-four hours ago. It was impossible. Cissy's words—she remembered the sound of her words, but she couldn't remember exactly what she'd said. Something about lunch. Cissy had sounded perky and lighthearted and forward-looking. Cissy-like. Nothing suicidal. No trace of terminal plans. How could she be dead by her own hand if she had mentioned lunch?

"They found her this morning," said Chief Scott softly.

Maggie shot him a warning glance that said, Don't push me, not now! He was too dull to read it correctly.

"The cleaning girl," he continued, as if she needed detailed proof that he wasn't lying.

"Chief," said Sad Sam in a silky voice, trying to shut him up gently.

"What?" cried the chief in a voice that was too loud. This was no business of a sergeant.

Sad Sam just shook his head and turned away. He couldn't bear to look at Maggie.

"We were supposed to have lunch," declared Maggie. It was an intense statement. It suggested a logical flaw in the suicide account; she and Cissy had a lunch date. That proved a completely different intention. She'd found a hole in the story and she wanted to widen it.

It was a natural, normal reaction to unbearable news. Maggie was no different from any other shocked survivor. She was splashing around in the choppy waters of denial.

Sam brought her a fresh cup of coffee. She hadn't heard the door open or close, but there he was, holding the coffee mug, so he must have gone out to get it. Her throat was dry and she tried to swallow a mouthful. She almost strangled; it was like trying to gulp down a rock.

"I know you were friends," said Scott.

"An overdose of what?" she asked, regaining her composure. She sat down. She had taken on a frosty mask of professionalism.

Chief Scott shrugged. "A cocktail," he said. "All kinds of drugs. She had a large supply."

"What, exactly?" she insisted, bending over a notepad, forcing him to recognize an official burden to be accurate—he was committing himself to a written record.

Chief Scott was unprepared for the role reversal. She was the commanding presence now. This must be how the suspects felt under her probing hammer. Chief Scott wavered as she bore in on him. She laid deductive traps, fixed her attention on obscure discrepancies. His impulse—like those unlucky suspects who came under her grilling—was to unravel and gush out quick answers. It was a game, and she was better at it than he, firing back his mistakes and inconsistencies with bewildering speed. This was why she had become the head of the homicide command, he thought.

"Well, actually, all we have now are empty bottles," he answered docilely. "There was Diazepam, which is a generic tranquilizer. Librax. Valium. Some other stuff. We have to wait for the complete chemical analysis."

"All empty?"

"Well, not all . . ."

She looked up and stared him in the eye. "So it's possible that she had normal, pharmaceutical stockpiles?"

He shook his head. Nodded. "Yes, possible, I suppose."

She nodded, noting the components of the cocktail, then changed the focus of her questions. "Was this the only note?"

"Yes," he said.

She shook her head. He couldn't tell whether she was dissatisfied with his answer or the situation. "What else?" she asked, a tinge of nasty impatience in her voice.

He nodded, then shook his head; yes, yes, there was something more. How did she know? Knitting one detail onto the next, of course. His own declaration that it was a suicide was too positive. There was no equivocation, no room for doubt, therefore there had to be more confirmation of suicide than an ambiguous note. "Actually, there was a notification from a lab," he said defensively. "A medical test."

"Yes," said Maggie. "So? She was going for a new job. She took a physical. I knew that. What's that prove?"

"Prove?"

"We all take medicals. What's it prove?"

He looked away again, maybe for Sad Sam's support. He didn't know how to deal with her brisk aggression.

"Well, there's a reason, if you're looking for a reason . . ."

Maggie thought, Maybe cancer. Something terminal. But, no, that wouldn't explain the lunch date and the rosy sound of Cissy's voice. And it didn't fit Cissy's character. Cancer was treatable—a challenge. Cissy wouldn't cave in for a simple cancer; she'd get her back up and fight it. She'd be brave and have a positive attitude and probably win.

"I assume somebody checked with the lab," said Maggie in an abrasive, critical tone that flirted with insubordination. She didn't care. She owed her friend loyalty before she owed Scott respect.

Chief Scott turned away, disconcerted. "We checked with the lab," he said. "Yes. That was the first thing. Of course."

"And?" Her voice had risen. He was dragging this out. She didn't understand why he didn't say what he had to say and stop all this pussyfooting around.

He shrugged and looked at Sad Sam, who had already guessed the answer and had withdrawn into a deep, tactful silence. Chief Scott, meanwhile, had his back to the wall. He had no choice. "She was HIV positive," he answered quickly.

Maggie's belly turned over.

In her profession, Maggie had acquired the habit of putting one exploratory foot ahead of the other as she headed out onto uncharted ground. It was tricky, but essential in the art of detection. The only requisite was a kind of reckless tenacity. One thing usually led to another. Sometimes, she lost her way and found herself making pointless circles that led nowhere. But often enough, the incessant probing broke through the confused thicket and the territory became comprehensible. Not now. Maggie was not prepared for this account of Cissy. She was unsteady, reeling.

The lost, sick feeling reminded her of the first great emotional upheaval in her life. She could still remember the exact feeling—the wild denial she had experienced the night after Bobby Kennedy was shot. When she heard it on television, it broke the back of old, fixed beliefs—even for a seven-year-old—and laid the groundwork for a sad, permeating cynicism, which hardened in time into a permanent philosophical faithlessness.

There was something else. It was annoying, but true. A cop was like a priest. They heard the text and subtext of sin. At first, they thought that they were hearing it all, the farthest limits of depraved, corrupt behavior. But eventually, they discovered one more terrible secret: they never knew it all. There was always one last, astonishing bombshell.

Cissy was Maggie's best friend. She knew which men Cissy dated and only had to wait until the next morning to hear a lurid and giddy breakfast debriefing. She knew when the bubbles burst and the dates went flat. But there were boundaries beyond the sins of the confessional. Every life is, in the end, a mystery. No one reveals everything. Something crucial is always held back.

Nevertheless, she could not grasp it: Cissy Stone HIV positive? Unthinkable.

That was the wicked virus that struck doomed junkies and reckless guys and careless social butterflies, not normal people. Cissy was not a drug addict, she had not even had unprotected sex, or any sex for that matter, in a year. And even before that, she would only sleep with men with unblemished pedigrees. Period. Maggie was certain she knew that much about Cissy.

Nevertheless, Maggie Van Zandt had a quick, shameful, albeit human reaction. She wanted a culprit. It was the cop in her. She had developed the cop's brittle belief in social accountability. A strict, authoritarian voice was always there whispering that people determined their own destiny. This was founded on the rock-hard belief that said that if a person went through life in a cautious, righteous way, that person could expect an auspicious fate, given a certain fickle variable. (There were always the chance bystanders.)

In that first nightstick moment, Maggie wanted to believe that people got what they deserved. And Cissy had done nothing to deserve AIDS. She would later blush at the knee-jerk blame. The better angels would surface and admit that life wasn't fair; people didn't always get perfect justice. Sometimes they got random, undeserved grief.

But not yet, not in that early, angry moment when she was ablaze with a censorious fervor. She felt betrayed, and therefore denied the plain facts. Since Cissy fit none of the known risk categories, Maggie decided that the diagnosis had to be a mistake.

She gathered her shoulder bag and her purse, determined to prove it, to clear her friend's name. Chief Scott put himself in her face and stopped her. He turned to Sad Sam and said, "Wait outside, Sergeant."

"I know this is hard," Chief Scott said to Maggie after Sam shut the door behind him. "I know she was your friend."

Maggie nodded. "I don't buy the virus theory," she said firmly.

Scott put his hand on her shoulder and she looked down with disapproving scorn, as if he had touched her with something wet. He removed his hand quickly and spoke in a tough, unmistakable voice of authority. "She tested positive," he persisted.

She was one more insult away from tears, but wouldn't

give him the satisfaction. "I don't believe it," she repeated.

"For Christ's sake, she had AIDS!"

It was a slap that woke her from her dreamy denial.

"They don't make mistakes," he almost shouted. "Not on that." His voice became muted.

"I want to go there," she said.

"Okay," he said, trying to sound reasonable. "But wait. Listen." He held her arm and this time his hand was not soft or wet. Chief Scott had a surprisingly powerful iron grip.

"What?"

"Look, Maggie, this is a very bad thing," he said, shaking his head. "I know how close you were. Christ, I lost a partner in a shoot-out when I was a rookie." He shook his head again. "I haven't had a full night's sleep since."

She studied him carefully and wondered if he really ever was a street cop; she doubted that he had had a partner shot out from under him.

"You know what's going on now," he said.

"What's going on?"

He released his grip, but it still held. "The department is under siege, for Christ's sake! There are a dozen reviews by a dozen different agencies." His hand floated over his head, indicating the swirling, out-of-reach height of the investigations.

"So?"

"Don't play dumb with me. There's an election coming up and there's all kinds of pressure and . . . well, I just can't afford to lose one of my big guns."

"I didn't test positive, if that's what you're asking," she said angrily.

"No! No! Christ, you always jump in with both fucking feet. You know what I'm getting at."

"Spit it out, Chief. I wanna get over there before they zip up the body bag."

He swallowed and forced himself to push. "I hafta know if I can count on you?"

"What are you talking about?"

"I'm under a lot of pressure and I can't leave a homicide command without a leader," he said. "Can I count on you?"

"Can you count on me?" If anything made the world spin for Maggie, it was slowing down the speed of her thoughts to catch the petty drift of Chief Scott's question.

"You mean like, in a 'family leave' sense? Will I be in to work tomorrow?"

"Yes," he replied. "That's what I mean. I got too many outstanding Unsolveds and I need to know that I can count on you. Today."

She couldn't believe that it was just that puny. The little bureaucratic shit only wanted to make certain that she wasn't going on some long leave to grieve for her friend. He wanted to make certain that he wouldn't have to change the damn duty roster. She almost hissed back at him, "You can count on me, Chief. As much as I can count on you. Now get the fuck out of my way."

As he sat by the telephone in the private back office of the clinic where he worked, Eric Miller began to sweat. And he felt a tickle of phlegm in the back of his throat. Something. He couldn't tell for certain. A phantom sensation.

He still clutched the handkerchief. He walked out of the private office where he had made his call, took a drink of water from a paper cup, and went back to his work station behind the high counter.

"Berger, Marvin!" he called out, reading from the form on the medical chart.

A man in his midforties lifted himself miserably from

the chair in the waiting area. Marvin Berger was over-weight and had been sent by his doctor to see how much fat was gummed up inside his arteries. The doctor needed the big stick of a lipid profile to scare Berger into restraining his fat intake. But Eric had no doubt that after a period of remorse and lettuce-leaf penitence, Berger would dive headfirst back toward his fried, saturated fate.

"Sit here and roll up your sleeve," said Eric Miller, who was as expert in moving the traffic in and out of the serology lab as he was in finding a suitable vein and drawing blood. There was a new smoothness and sureness to the operation now that he didn't have to be careful about sticking himself.

"You mind if we use the right arm?" asked Berger. Eric could hear the apprehension.

"As long as I can find a vein."

One of the cardiac paranoids, thought Eric Miller. Keeping the left arm free for the unclouded sign of the big, fatal jolt. There was a whole subculture of men waiting for their first heart attack. Eric felt along the arm for the bulge of a suitable vein, tied it off, prodded the vessel to show itself conclusively under the layers of swollen tissue. He still wore two pairs of latex gloves, which was a reassuring precaution to the customers. It indicated that the technician was cautious and didn't want to catch a disease transmitted by blood. The implication was that the technician was disease-free. In this case, the implication was wrong.

Berger watched Eric carefully. He was, himself, a cautious, nervous man. Civilians had become like that in America's blood labs now.

Eric placed the tube in its honeycomb stack. He filled in the medical form directing readings for cholesterol and triglycerides and liver enzymes. He put on an elaborate show of crisp competence.

"Make a fist," he said in the flat voice of a professional. It was another display of his art. The patients felt themselves in expert hands when they heard Eric ticking off instructions like a drill sergeant.

Berger, meanwhile, never took his eyes from his arm. Except, Eric noted with some satisfaction, at that last second. When Eric's hand, loaded with the long, pointy needle, approached the vein, Berger turned away. It was always true. At the last second, they all turned away. There were some who were squeamish and could not watch any of it. Not the rubber Velcro strap being tightened around the muscle, not the search for the vein, not even the alcohol swab on the inside of the elbow. Even the real soldiers who kept a sentry's eye on the entire process—as if they suspected everyone of something dastardly, or at least assumed that the extra attention would defend against sloppy work—even the most alert could not bear to watch that dull, deep, savage instant when the needle was driven through the skin and punctured the vein.

There was no avoiding the distress. A needle was, after all, a childhood qualm, a tic of such intolerable, longstanding, and monumental dimensions that most people considered the aversion as normal as the blink at the introduction of an eyedrop.

Berger's reaction was no different. And Eric, in his new role of avenging educator, counted on the blind instant. It was at that second, when his victim turned, that Eric switched the pure, uncontaminated needle with the one he had hidden in his pocket.

The one in his pocket held a few drops of his own infected blood. As he drove it into the vein and heard the sigh of pain, he felt his own rush of satisfaction. He had transmitted the virus to one more innocent victim in that single heartbeat, exactly as it had been transmitted to himself. So quick, so lethal.

If he experienced any reservations about what he was doing, Eric drowned them out with the rationalization he had devised, which was that it took a few broken eggs to make an omelette. He was, he was convinced, doing good. He was educating the world about the malignant plague of AIDS. Not just the mushy television plays and docudramas about the poor homosexuals and junkies. No, he was teaching a real lesson. Anyone was at risk. Mr. Berger. Anyone. And so he chose his candidates carefully. No drug abusers. No homosexuals. No one who looked possibly sexually promiscuous. Only those sympathetic souls in low-risk categories were given his postgraduate needle.

six

It was almost evening, and Sergeant Sad Sam Rosen needed some more light to read his reports, but he was unwilling to touch the lamp beside the couch. He was sitting in Cissy Stone's West Eighty-first Street living room chewing on an unlit cigar, while Lieutenant Maggie Van Zandt ripped apart the apartment searching for a hidden clue. He didn't know what the clue was or what it would reveal, but he knew that Maggie had to find it.

Sam was glad that Maggie didn't want his help. He had a very strong aversion to handling dead people's things, which made it hard, him being a homicide specialist.

However, since this was not an official case Sam had no obligation to pick through the dead woman's haunted rooms looking for some jigsaw lead or indication of a crime. He parked himself on the couch and squinted as he read the parched police reports of other ongoing investigations by the fast fading twilight coming through the window.

The stabbing on West Seventy-eighth Street looked interesting. A young woman who was just breaking into publishing had been murdered in her own bed. There was a nice salacious touch: she was wearing an expensive negligee when she was killed. The other details were equally fascinating. She worked for Random House as an assistant editor—which meant that she got to hang around big-shot editors and famous writers. It was an entry-level job, which involved fetching coffee and fending off phone calls, but still it had its own glamorous cachet. Edie Severan, Sad Sam read between the lines of the first reports, was one of an army of eager Ivy League postgraduates who annually fell into the swank world of New York's literati, liberation and feminism and blatant sexism notwithstanding. She had private school credentials and aristocratic relatives and her own apartment in Manhattan at the age of twenty-three. She was killed viciously—one great efficient slash across the throat—and probably by a friend, judging by the unbroken locks and absence of signs of a struggle. Some misunderstanding on the limits of petting that got out of hand, he guessed. The murder was probably committed by another upper-class brat who was unaccustomed to rejection. He could envision the media frenzy already.

That would be a hot one. That would be high on Chief Larry Scott's Must Solve list. And it was close by. That was where Maggie Van Zandt should be, getting her puss on the tube, taking charge; that was the case she should be investigating, instead of conducting a maudlin lamentation over a dead friend.

In the background Sam heard the muffled angry sounds of Maggie picking up objects, slamming drawers, flinging open closets, muttering bitterly. Whatever she was looking for—assuming that she had something in mind—she apparently couldn't find it. She was having a temper tantrum.

The living room seemed oddly cold and inhospitable to Sam. Funny how quickly things change, he thought with detached although pained perspective. He had been in this apartment, this same room, before. Just recently, in fact. It had struck him then as a particularly congenial setting. At the time, Cissy was giving a dinner party and he had come to pick up Maggie. Cissy had handed him a soft drink and smiled as comfortably as an old pillow. She had generously neglected her guests to make Sam feel at ease, but no one had seemed to mind. It was, in fact, a long-standing quality of hospitality that was expected from Cissy, Maggie said. She had a natural urge to please.

Sam had remembered a bigger place, but it was a common miscalculation: rooms always seemed larger when they were swollen with noise and energy. He also remembered that the sounds of ice and laughter had tinkled musically together, the mood expansive and congenial. As he recalled, he had considered the apartment tasteful, very high class, very well kept, and inhabited thoroughly by the owner. It was the last time he had seen Cissy alive.

Now the rooms were shrunken. The homes of dead people were always like that for Sam—waxen, embalmed. The lifelike look only made the homes seem more dead. The objects and art, the furniture and books, were orphaned. Cissy's apartment had become a violated tomb and he felt as guilty as a grave robber. That was the way he always viewed the possessions of murder victims. His colleagues seemed to have grown a desensitized protective layer over their emotions as they ransacked the open purses or went through the private letters. He couldn't do it. Not without shame. When he had to, he studied the stacks of photographs, speculated about the unpaid bills, and delved through the checking accounts, but invariably he felt heartless afterward. The lost lives were laid out raw, without any possibility of a kinder version of the facts. Taking such liberties with the dead was accepted, maybe even proper, given the higher social need. Maybe the dead—

especially the murdered—had no right to modesty. But when he thought about it, Sam decided, no, even the dead, especially the dead, had a powerful claim to respect.

Maggie knew the routine. Cissy's body had been removed to the morgue, where there would be a quick and perfunctory postmortem. It wouldn't be very thorough because there was no point, and, besides, no one liked fooling around with the open cavities and toxic fluids of the seropositive. And there wasn't much new to discover. Cecilia Stone, aka Cissy Stone, had died of a self-administered lethal overdose of pharmaceuticals. Suicide was only a crime when it failed. The offense died with her. There would be a written finding that would make the point in roundabout bureaucratese, without dwelling too heavily on the guilt or sin or weakness that drove a woman in late youth to destroy herself. Since there was no evidence of foul play, the case would be marked closed. Everyone would be satisfied, all questions answered, all traces of what had happened would be buried with Cissy Stone.

But Maggie was not ready to lay her friend to rest. She prowled the apartment—an apartment whose features she knew by heart—in a state of war-weary fury. Why, she demanded of the empty rooms. Why? The unasked question was unanswered as she reeled from room to room, prying, poking, biting back tears.

The items and objects she had once found endearing and precious were suddenly hideous, grotesque, and putrid. The painting over the bed—cherubs and rosy maidens—was contaminated by what had taken place underneath. The chenille bedspread had turned into a shroud.

She opened a bureau drawer and smelled the perfume of the sachet, felt the silk of the neatly folded underwear. So carefully arranged, so orderly and fresh. The scarves at one end and the underwear at the other. So much time and attention Cissy devoted to the dresser, thought Maggie. Useless, wasted time now, she decided, uncharitably.

Her own life was never so orderly. Maggie didn't fluff and fold. She jammed her things together, one on top of another, hoping to be able to pick out a matching something in the bleary-eyed mornings when she dressed on the run. She was never matched or groomed or involved with fashion. She had nothing to regret about her priorities. What did it get you, all that effort and thought? she asked Cissy's tidy closets and empty rooms.

It was when she was sorting through the contents of a drawer in a small makeup table that she found a thick, hand-tooled leather notebook. On the front it said: *Cecilia Stone*. At first, Maggie felt a small twinge of hesitation at snooping on her friend; but she pushed that consideration aside and took the book. Unlike Sam she had long since come to terms with her rough, rude profession. She had grown used to going through the compromised pockets and ignoble possessions of dead people. It was part of the job, and she wasn't troubled by ghosts. She had persuaded herself that the deceased were beyond shame, and she was their last benevolent actuary. Not bad hands to leave it in, come to think of it. She carried around a shopping bag full of undisclosed disgraces and kinky secrets. They belonged to strangers, and she would tactfully, without any compunction, safeguard whatever could be protected. If she had to disclose the worst, it would be with what she regarded as a gentle mercy.

There was another motivating factor in her restless curiosity: she believed in a higher obligation, a need to straighten out the official record. Someone had to keep the books for society. Attention had to be paid. She did not believe in anarchy. Murder should be answered. As for the shock to her own system, she wrote it off as one more price of living within the boundaries of civilization. And it was educational.

She picked a page in Cissy's diary. *I have found another wrinkle*, it said in that familiar large script. The entry was on January 1—a Friday. An important milestone. Maggie sat on the edge of the chair in front of the makeup mirror and held the book under the light. *I am lonely in an erratic fashion. There are friends and there are activities, but I despair of ever finding the right man. Partly, this self-absorption is vanity and partly it's a coming to terms with reality. Soon my face will look lined and wrinkled, like a plowed field ready for planting. But it is not time for the cosmeticians, not yet. . . .*

The words had an odd sound. It was definitely Cissy's voice, but more formal, pitched to the eye rather than the ear. A solemn, serious, exposed voice. Maggie couldn't read any more. Not without bracing herself. She slipped the book into her tote bag, covered it with a fold-up umbrella, and went out into the living room, where Sam had chewed his way through his second cigar.

"You find anything?" he asked, looking up from his squad reports.

She waved her arm in the air and had a sad smile on her face. "No," she said wistfully. "Just some old sense memories."

He nodded. He was only being polite.

"C'mon," she said crisply. "Let's get over to that slice job. Where was it?"

"Seventy-eight and Columbus."

Maybe she's accepted the suicide, Sam thought. But then, knowing Maggie, he doubted it. She'd worry it some more, and if nothing turned up, she'd worry it a little more.

As they were riding in the unmarked black cruiser, Maggie stared out at the steamy streets of Manhattan in summer. They were filled with tank-topped women and sweaty men and the pace had slowed to match the heat. Maggie noticed a girl in her late teens walking lazily away from a bus. She had just come from the beach, judging by the towel wrapped around her neck like a horse collar. The girl was pink and glowing from too much sun, not concerned about the disarray of her hair. It was a depressingly deceptive image to Maggie—all that apparent, easygoing, casual health. Maggie knew that the girl with the burn had just increased her chance of skin cancer, to say nothing of turning her face into parchment before she was thirty.

"She didn't have it, you know," said Maggie, facing out dreamily, through the passenger window.

"What?" asked Sam. He knew.

"The AIDS virus," said Maggie, turning to stare at his profile. "Cissy never had it." She shook her head against the possibility.

Sam shrugged. "They say that these labs are extra careful," he said. "Hafta be about that."

She glared at him. "Forget seventy-eighth and Columbus. Hit a bookstore. Drop me off. Then get the forensic reports moving on the Severan thing. If you don't push those people it takes weeks."

Sam smiled. "Bookstore. Right. What's my motivation?"

"How about a pension," she answered quickly, feeling a surge of adrenaline as she began mentally making a list of things to check, areas to explore, closed doors to kick down to get to the bottom of Cissy's death.

seven

Between the Covers was located high on the refined end of Madison Avenue near Eighty-third Street. It was one of those dusty old book shops that survive on the luck of a long lease and the sentiment of loyal patrons willing to pay premium retail prices for the sideshow of a literate and opinionated owner who didn't mind losing a Grisham or Tom Clancy sale for the sake of art.

It was also a jungle, and the narrow aisles had to be hacked out daily lest the undergrowth of multiplying volumes swallow up unsuspecting customers. The thickets of fiction and nonfiction were broken occasionally by a restful arbor with a filigree metal bench, placed there by the same eccentric proprietor who thought that there should be nice, well-lit places in a bookstore to read.

The moment she walked in the door, with the little bell still tinkling in her ear, the shop reminded Maggie of a sloppy English maze; instead of topiary, the high hedges were Dickens and Rilke and Márquez. She snaked her way past the cash register—untended, which mildly incited her police sense of order. She found herself in the quiet dell of the philosophy section, fingering Wittgenstein and Spinoza, when she became aware of a live presence. It was a man. She glanced sideways and saw that he was in a noiseless struggle with a teetering oak of hefty texts. He had apparently been trying to remove a book from the bottom without disturbing the rest. It couldn't be done.

"I think you could use some help," she said, moving closer to brace the body of the pile of books.

But when his head snapped in her direction, his hand jerked, unseating the book that was acting as the fulcrum. First the pile swayed and she felt like she was watching a cobra. Then there was a low rumble as the avalanche came tumbling down, bringing other stacks down with it. Thick, thin, new, used—they fell in a heap. As she was ducking and weaving, Maggie cursed her own misguided urge to help the oaf who had set off the ruin. When the last book had beaned her in the noggin and she was up to her ankles in history and social sciences and poetry, a lovely hush settled over this portion of the store.

The klutz, meanwhile, who was one of those helpless professorial types in a bow tie and short-sleeved shirt, grinned at her. It was a completely guileless and winning grin that acknowledged the situation and placed it in the human condition. It was a conspiratorial expression, like a wink. God help her, she found herself grinning back.

Well, why the hell not? He was a good-looking man, even if he was a tad buttoned-down. Tall and distinguished with dimples in his cheeks and a mist of gray in his wavy hair, he reminded her of Gary Cooper in one of those thirties oddball comedies.

"I don't suppose we'll ever be found," she said, trying to wiggle her foot.

He looked down, as if he was just noticing that something had happened, and shrugged. "I've got some sandwiches," he said. "They say you can last for a long time on turkey and chutney sandwiches."

"I should really sue the son of a bitch," she said. "They should have a sign. . . ."

He perked up. "You're right. They should have a sign. 'No loud noises or you'll disturb the books.' "

"Are you hurt?"

"Just my pride."

She reached down and picked up two books and saw that there was no place to put them.

"Just leave it," he said.

He had a nice voice. She hated that. It was deep and soft and hadn't been used much. A pampered voice, and therefore probably a pampered man. She was all too familiar with the type. All he had to do was to clear his throat and waiters and women came running. Her voice had a different effect. It sounded like heavy traffic. Even her normal speaking voice sounded like grinding gears. It was the aftermath of a lifetime of uttering unanswered complaints. People fled from that racket.

He took the two books from her hand and tossed them over his shoulder, where they caused a secondary tremor in yet another pile.

"I am definitely gonna sue," she said.

He shook his head. Seemed serious, yet amused. "I wouldn't," he said in that same commanding purr.

"Why not?"

He sighed. It was a beguiling sound, sucking her closer. "Well, for one thing, you might win."

"That's the idea," she replied.

Again he shook his head. "Very bad idea. I happen to know that Mr. Between the Covers is as poor as a country mouse. You'd wind up owning the place."

She pointed her finger. "You're Mr. Between the Covers!"

"Jerry Munk," he said bowing, causing another book to topple onto his reddish hair. It was a good head of hair, she had to admit. It was thick and unruly and went nicely with the beard. He was a young forty, she guessed, catching his eyes, which had an intensity that was at odds with his nonchalant aspect. "Can I help you?"

"I'm looking for a book on AIDS," she said. "A primer."

"It's a big subject. You have a lot of advice and how to—type things, like *AIDS and the Health-Care System,* then you've got the Randy Shilts historical approach, and there are the painfully confessional-type books."

"I need to get a quick education," she said.

"High-risk date?"

Her eyes narrowed, like the metal gates shutting down on the glass front of a shop that was closing.

"Sorry, sorry," he said, plucking her out of the trap and leading her to the selection of books on AIDS.

"It's okay," she said, loading five books into a thick bag. "Touchy subject, AIDS. I'm trying to see why someone would kill themselves over it."

"I'm really sorry," he said.

After paying with her credit card, she stopped at the door and looked back at him. "I may need some more books," she said.

He smiled and said in that musical voice, "I've got a pile."

Professor Lauren Drake was working late, as she often did during the summer when there was no classroom urgency. It was all preparation and fidgeting, a writer straightening papers and sharpening pencils without the agony of actually having to write. She also enjoyed the prolonged quiet after the contractors and day laborers and the secretarial pools and academic politicians had left the campus. The smell of paint and plaster was strangely pleasant.

The lesson plans and reading lists were spread across her desk, along with a half-eaten turkey-roll sandwich from the cafeteria and a container of cold coffee, and her concentration was undisturbed. The tranquil atmosphere almost established the illusion of calm and clarity.

But she was neither calm nor clear-headed. After the afternoon meeting with the head of the history department, she was bitter and confused. Professor Henry Krauss, the aging head of the department who was on the lip of retirement, assured Lauren Drake that the coming term would be a period of painful crisis. Already there were signs of an ugly campus revolt. Waiting in ambush for the fall term to begin, Professor Krauss had been warned, were the activist student councils and committed ethnic study groups and sour Third World ideologues, as ready to monitor ticklish subjects as Orwell's thought police.

And in the modern, politically correct world, history was the touchiest subject of all. The weary head of the department informed his young professor that she had to modify her curriculum to reflect the emerging campus reality. At first she thought that it was a joke. But he was serious. He tried to sell the collaboration as a necessity, to ride out a seasonal squall. "It's one of those periodic winds, you know, like that McCarthy thing," he said over tea and lemon cakes in his paneled, book-strewn office. "In time, it will blow itself out. Meanwhile, we must endure."

Lauren Drake was thoroughly ashamed of herself for not storming out of his den, spilling the tea and lemon cake to demonstrate her angry opposition. But she hadn't, and in this late hour of the summer evening she was trying to replan the introductory world-history survey course without sacrificing accuracy or honor.

It was impossible. Professor Drake wanted to be careful and redress the long-standing insults to and neglect of Third World achievements and concerns, but even she had to admit that she was hopelessly Eurocentric. This was, after all, a Eurocentric country, built on European principles of Enlightenment; there was no reasonable way of submerging the importance of the Renaissance under the uncompromising, boiling revisionist agenda of the oppressed nations of Africa, Asia, South America, the Middle East, not to mention the fourth and fifth generations of America's own persecuted minorities. There was a growing intellectual knucklehead intransigence on this point—led by a vocal and rabble-rousing Black studies department—that insisted on twisting everything into the seductively wrong-headed "politics of inclusion." The upshot of inclusion was always exclusion, she saw. It made Lauren Drake seethe to think about it. Her discussions with advocates of this iron-clad faction always began with high hopes and vows of goodwill and ended in sullen resentment and slammed doors. She found no give on the other side, as they, no doubt, found none on hers. The whole struggle sapped her strength and drained her vocational appetite.

Still, she was a realist and was willing to bend enough to assign African, Hispanic, Chinese, and female writers to her students. What she was unwilling to do was to give any credence whatsoever to books that delivered only wild, enveloping indictments of White people and claimed that Europeans had no hand whatsoever (apart from the slaveholder's whip) in the development of Western culture, science, and the arts.

In the end, she would never surrender her conviction that Plato's *Republic* had more lasting relevance to the styles and beliefs of the modern world than the high architectural and mathematical feats of the Mesoamerican Mayans. Professor Drake was emphatically American and could not separate the English wars of succession from the Magna Carta and *The Rights of Man* from the Declaration of Independence. She was bewildered by the current topsy-turvy liberation movements that seemed intent on bringing on a new and ferocious intellectual tyranny.

It was clear, Professor Krauss agreed, that in the name of academic reparations, today's student could embrace any ignorant hypothesis. All across the dazed and confused landscape of academic America, colleges were surrendering the sword of intellectual authority to a cadre of anarchic, doctrinaire, and ignorant extortionists. And now she was expected to include these mean, weightless convictions in her classroom as if they were an authentic alternative to scholarship. Not possible. Lauren Drake felt that she was being called on to substitute one racist dogma for another. She shook her head in the empty office.

She heard the footsteps of a janitor, who looked in and saw her still at work, smiled, and said, "I'll be back in a little while, Professor."

It was a shock, seeing another human being when she had convinced herself that she was safely alone in her own universe. She felt obliged to say something. "I won't be long," she called after the janitor.

She followed the sound of his footsteps and the sloshing of his bucket to the next office. And then silence. It could have been a monastery instead of a college, Professor Drake thought, drinking in the muffled twilight. A Black man. Walking through the corridors of the White men's temples, scrubbing their floors, dusting their books. Someone excluded. Maybe his son was one of those obstinate students who wanted to overturn the syllabus, rewrite the texts, push open the monastic walls. The politics of inclusion. There was something to it, she conceded, but not scholarship; history was not necessarily fair, it was just the scroll of events. She turned to gaze out her window at the fading light.

From her window she could see a pair of students on the lawn locked in a long embrace. And the sight made her turn from her resentment at the department head's craven stance to thoughts of Edward. He had been in the back of her mind all along. When the student secretary told her that a man had called when she was in her meeting with Professor Krauss, she knew that it was him. The caller hadn't left a name or a number, but she was certain. Edward. Of course. Edward.

He had lingered in her memory since the one night they slept together. There was something about him, not anything she could define as classically romantic or even desirable, not in any knowable way. Nothing tender or intelligent or moving; no display of wit to speak of. Yet there was something exciting about him. When she put everything together afterward and tried to interpret her hasty and reckless interest, she realized that the "something" that stayed with her was a shadow of danger. It was funny because he hadn't seemed unsafe at first glance. He had seemed ordinary. Almost superordinary. Then he'd started to misrepresent himself—and the unshakable feeling that he was concealing dark secrets under the disguise of an ordinary man had left behind a vibrating tingle.

She remained behind this evening, she had to admit, because there was the possibility that he would call again. She was sick of the battle over the core curriculum. She would teach whatever the hell she wanted to teach and let the thought police come after her. She had her own edge of menace.

The buzz of the phone made her jump. She lifted the receiver too quickly—and held it without speaking.

"Professor Drake?"

"Who's calling?"

"Laurie, it's me, Eddie," he replied. He obviously recognized her suspicious voice.

She tried to sound casual, but he had dangled her feelings for too long. "Edward!" she said. The strain was evident.

"Hello."

"I've been thinking about you." She was speaking like

a car jolting and stalling from a faulty fuel line—too much and too little.

"Really?"

"Well, we never really said good-bye," she said.

"I've been thinking of you, too."

The line seemed to break as they both fell silent. The harmless admissions were explosive, excessive, and they retreated, like armies that come into sudden, surprise contact and pull back to reassess and redeploy.

"So," she said finally, breaking the awkward pause, "how've you been?"

It was then that his voice dropped below the ordinary conversational pitch and she became uneasy.

"Not so hot," he said.

She felt a bolt of fear.

"I've had some bad news," he said.

A cold shock moved up her spine. Why should he call her to deliver bad news? Why was it important to tell her? What was the point, her being all but a stranger? Unless she was somehow affected. These thoughts raced in fractions of time through her consciousness, erasing the earlier, erotic memories.

"I'm sorry to hear that," she said tentatively. Maybe it was money. Maybe he needed a loan. Whatever it was, it wasn't good news for her, either. Already there was a wall. She did not want to hear his bad news. She wanted to hang up and pretend that it had nothing to do with her.

"I had a report from the doctor."

Oh, Lord, she thought. Oh, Lord! This thing is coming at me and I am frozen in the light of something dreadful! There was no gently drifting away from it.

"I'm sorry," she said. She was almost resigned.

"Well, I thought you should know."

There was a catch in her throat. She couldn't speak. "What is it?" she demanded, pulling herself together.

"It's very serious," he said.

There it was again. She heard it. A false note. He was not sorry, and he was not sad. He was enjoying himself. "What is it, Edward?"

He resisted being rushed, dragging out the moment. "I'm afraid, Laurie, that my blood test came back positive."

"What blood test?" She was angry; she was not the sort of person who tolerated being toyed with. No, she thought. Definitely no. He was playing a savage prank. No one who tested positive for anything would sound that pleased about it. Unless he was a pyschopath.

"I thought you should know," he said.

"What!"

"The blood test. I'm afraid I tested positive."

Her voice fell into an ominous whisper. "What the fuck are you talking about? What fucking blood test?"

"I took a blood test and tested positive. HIV."

"AIDS?" She shrieked. The janitor came running, opening the door, and she waved him away.

"I thought you should know."

She lowered her voice again, trying to regain control. But there was a tremor of the earth shifting in her words. "Edward, we used protection!"

"Yes," he said, and she felt a provisional wave of relief. "But, you know, it's not foolproof," he said maliciously. "I wanted you to know."

"I can see that," she practically hissed. "But you did use a condom."

She had watched him put the condom on that overheated evening when most of her defenses fell. He had struggled with the package—she'd heard the tear and the slap of the latex. But then she remembered. He'd used the condom the first time. There was a second. An encore when they were drunk with relief and lying drowsy and content, cupped in each other's arms. There had been a second act. It was a sleepy embrace, hardly worth counting after the first, according to the moral accounting of her youth. She didn't remember a second condom.

"Of course I used a condom," he said.

"Both times?"

He didn't answer.

"Where can I get in touch with you, Eddie?" There was now a distinctly hysterical undertone in her voice.

He was evasive. "You know, you can imagine. This thing has . . . well, my life is over. I'm sure you're okay. I just wanted you to know about it. To be fair."

She was frantic, but she could hear the satisfaction on the other end of the phone. There was no choice—she couldn't grab him through the phone—but she tried to impose an artificial normality to her question. "Eddie, if I have to reach you, though, where can I call?"

"I'm moving, trying to get my life in order. Hospital tests, treatments . . ."

Don't scream, she told herself. Keep at him. Calmly. Then she heard another voice on the line, breaking in. "Gotham Medical Lab!" said the voice.

"I'm on this line!" Eddie snarled.

The last thing she heard was the click as he slammed down the receiver. She held on to the phone and began to weep. The tears grew into large, open-mouthed sobs that once again brought the janitor running; he stood in the door while she howled into the dead receiver.

eight

EARLY, WEDNESDAY, JUNE 30

Jerry Munk had been trying to read a book about the fifties, a singularly wooden and uninteresting decade. In hundreds and hundreds of dry, dusty pages, the author attempted to imbue life and meaning into a wearisome progression of dull detail. But like its topic, the thing was a snooze.

The famous and celebrated author had assembled most of the pertinent facts and applied some far-fetched and tortured theories to the events and come to the absurd conclusion that the fifties were really a pretty spectacular and riveting moment in the story of our times. But the most significant fact to Jerry Munk was that the fifties couldn't keep him awake. This surprised him since the book was busting out on best-seller lists all over the country before pub date.

The only explanation was a depressing peculiarity of modern publishing, which was that people did not always buy books to read. Books were often bought and treated like good intentions, retired to dusty shelves after the initial burst of fire.

The usual literary standards—which should have dismissed this book as a graduate thesis whose conceit didn't quite work—counted for nothing. There was the steamroller effect of the celebrity author and public opinion, moved by the sheeplike reviewers. It was being snatched up by A-student types and limp social drones who would go off the deep end praising its industry and merit. (All that sweaty effort had to count for something.) In chic parlors and uptown restaurants, obedient clusters of trendy clucks, who turned like weather vanes into the latest cultural wind, would discuss the air-filled theories and the social weight of Elvis Presley and Marilyn Monroe, as if such things really mattered.

And still, no one would actually read the thing, which was in truth unreadable. They would display it, allude to it, comment on the sophomoric insights, but no one would bother to plod through the cement text. They didn't have to. Because they would never come face to face with anyone else who could possibly contradict them.

Munk wasn't sure he wanted to help the promotion by carrying a lot of copies at Between the Covers. He had just finished reading a truly praiseworthy book that illuminated the Middle Ages. It was brilliant and made that remote and garbled epoch seem exciting and coherent. That was a book deserving of fanfare. That was also a book that had only a bare cult following, all of whom actually read it.

Still, for purely commercial reasons, Munk was being forced to fake enthusiasm. He had wasted the whole evening attempting to follow the slow, plodding prose; he felt a tug at his eyelids, like someone bringing down a window shade.

Munk was, therefore, fast asleep in his Greenwich Village apartment (with the full weight of the fifties on his chest) when he heard the air-raid sirens go off. He knew immediately what it was. The Russians had finally delivered their sneak attack. According to the established Civil Defense coaching, he was supposed to dive under his desk (if he was in school), repeating the protective mantra, "Duck and cover!" Somehow—and he had never quite understood the mechanics—this was designed to defeat the thermonuclear force of the Russian bombs.

The strange part was that nuclear war was not his threat. By the time he'd started kindergarten in 1956, school officials had stopped scaring the short pants off kids with the threat of nuclear attack. Never had Munk actually experienced nuclear fear.

Which is why, at the twentieth century's stroke of midnight, with the Soviet Union in shambles, the sound of an air-raid siren seemed so curious. The next surprise was the blinding light. Where the hell did that come from? In his sleepy, sedated state, he found a logical explanation. It was the air burst of the Big One, which came at the exact instant that he dove off the bed in order to assume the defensive attitude while uttering the magic mantra, "Duck and cover!" It took a moment to connect the events and appreciate the fact that what had really happened was that when he'd cannonballed headfirst off the bed, he bashed his skull on the wooden floor. This was no doomsday nuclear attack, after all, just a dumb, defensive misfire.

As he gradually regained his full senses, Munk realized that the siren, which was still pealing, was in reality the downstairs bell to his apartment. He looked at his bedside clock. It was 2:30 in the morning. He was perspiring and afraid. He staggered to the front window where, twenty feet below, he saw a woman leaning on his bell. She looked up, and he recognized her. It was the woman from the store, the one upon whom he'd loosed an avalanche of books.

She might be unhinged, he thought. Drugs, liquor, or

books, same thing. It didn't take much provocation nowadays to undo the strings and bring out the oddballs in the middle of the night. He thought of the wild man of Ninety-sixth Street and all the other urban rogues, beggars, villains, and terrorists whose chief occupation seemed to be to make New Yorkers jittery.

But then he remembered something else: he recalled a very powerful attraction for the somewhat crusty and indisputably flaky woman on his doorstep. All the other, riskier possibilities faded in importance.

He buzzed her in and watched her rapidly climb the groaning staircase to the second floor. It was an old house, and the banister jiggled under the pressure of her hand. She moved quickly, but cautiously, looking up and back, aware of her surroundings, and then she stood in front of Munk, who had thrown a ratty old bathrobe over his summer pajamas. His smile was somewhere between dread and a greeting.

Having come this far, neither seemed certain of the next step. Neither of them spoke as they stood in the hallway; they just swayed and measured each other and took shallow breaths.

"You have to be a real asshole to buzz me in like that," she said finally.

"That's some charming gift you have for small talk," he replied. "Real winning."

She shook her head angrily. "You live in New York. You always ask for identification. I don't care if it's your mother. What the hell's wrong with you?" She had an edge in her voice, but it was soft in the center.

He nodded, agreeing. "My mother has no identification. She was born before they had such things. She does have a bad attitude."

She shook her head and looked at him with pity.

He nodded. "Okay, you're absolutely right. Let's see some ID."

She paused. "I don't have any."

He smiled. "Does anybody have custody of you?"

"I dropped my ID in that compost heap of a store you run."

"Never mind. You look okay."

"I need my ID," she said through clenched teeth.

"I suppose waiting until I open would be inconvenient?" he replied.

She glared at him.

He nodded. He understood. "I once had a blanket like that," he said. "I couldn't sleep without it."

"You sleep alone now?"

He thought about offering her coffee, but Munk wasn't ready to change the terms. Right now he had an advantage of sorts, although he couldn't say what or why. "You're a cop, right?"

She didn't really look surprised. She was accustomed to being "made" as a cop. It did bother her a little because it excluded high-fashion model, talk-show host, and corporate CEO, and that was bad. Of course it also excluded secretary, office ornament, and tough-talking waitress, and that was good. "It shows that much, huh?"

He shrugged and ushered her into the apartment. She sulked past him. "You're a cop," he said. "For one thing, you found me. I'm not listed."

"Yeah? What else?"

He held out his hands, palms up. "You're out on the town at three in the morning—that makes you either homeless, a psychopath, a hooker, or a cop."

She nodded.

He wasn't finished. "You talk like a cop. You walk around like you own the place; you bang into things like it's their fault. You look at me like I did something wrong and you're just waiting to pounce on me and read me my rights. Unless I am badly mistaken, you have a gun in that purse. I can tell by the way you hold it."

"The purse? How do I hold it?"

"Like a gunfighter."

"I hate that Sherlock Holmes crap," she said, dropping onto the couch, surrendering at last, although she was not sure to what. "You got any ID?"

"Would you settle for instant?"

He saw the confusion on her face.

"Coffee," he said.

He walked into the kitchen. Through the open door, as he started to make coffee, he noticed her looking around, taking in everything. The apartment was neat, in a cluttered sort of way. He had a cleaning service once a week. She had obviously expected a rat hole, like the store, and was now taken down a notch by the paintings and the small, tasteful sculptures and the neat racks of video tapes and well-kept books. The surfaces were clean and well tended and the glass on the pictures was clean.

"You gay?" she asked, shouting so that he could hear. It wasn't asked in any malicious or offensive way, although it might have been taken as an insult because of the neighborhood and the state of the apartment and his obvious solitude and her presumed occupational bias. He decided to be forgiving and assume that she simply wanted neutral information. It was her nature. He came to the conclusion that she was rough, but true, like some fact-seeking missile.

He stepped back into the living room, the coffee jar in one hand and the spoon in the other, and fixed her in his gaze for a moment, just enough to make her feel the energy of his reply. "No," he said softly. "I'm not gay. I am competent. A lot of people confuse that with homosexuality. It's a bad linkage. I am just a guy trying to make a cup of coffee at three in the morning for some fruitcake cop."

* * *

They rode back uptown toward his store along Madison Avenue after the coffee. It was surprisingly comfortable. She settled into his company as if they'd been together for a long time. Friends—it was not past that. In fact, she was scouting him for Cissy. She was still scouting for her dead comrade. Some part of her knew that the behavior was loony, but some other segment of her mind remained decisively in a state of denial.

He would be good for Cissy. Good looking. Poised. Well read. A man who made literary allusions and dropped educated puns and would fit nicely into a charity dinner. She could still pretend that Cissy was alive and preoccupied with getting on with her life. What was hard was to erase the memory of the diary entries, which made her knees weak when she read them. It was an activity she could only take in small doses, like donating blood.

February 1st:

So many boorish men. Who needs it? Rather go to a movie with Maggie. She's busy these days with her new assignment. I miss her. Still, not lonely enough to really feel sorry for myself. Betsy asked me to tea. Imagine her calling it tea? Well, that's Betsy. She affects tea and I play along because I like cucumber sandwiches and English posturing. Then she had to invite that nasty Martin. Hands-under-the-table Martin. God, he makes my skin crawl! You'd think he'd take the hint (the creep!) when I cut his finger with the knife. . . .

Betsy said that she knew of an opening at Boulevard Magazine. But do I want to work for those people? Such silly, self-loathing Jews! I'd have to go around all day speaking in Yiddish, just to remind them that we were all Jews together. Comes along another Hitler and we're all in the ovens again.

I'd love a job, but my, my, my, my, how they would wear me out. I may have to cash in some bonds, but I don't think that things are that desperate that I have to take that Queen's shilling. Oh, well, who am I to complain?

Cissy would have liked this man, Maggie thought. He'd have taken her mind off of her dwindling bank balance.

"It is a very big deal, losing your badge and ID," she said by way of explanation. "Not as bad as losing your gun, but they can bring you up on charges."

"What if it's not at the store?"

She turned and glared at him. He obviously had a hard, cynical side.

"I'm not going to think about that."

He thought about her. She stirred his interest, no doubt about that. There was a physical side of it, and there was an undeniable and indefinable heat. She put him in a sweat.

But that was a hesitation. He had spent ten years as a hard-core journalist, poring through records, questioning official versions, and it had given him a dark lens of mistrust about authority. Especially cops. People with guns made him nervous. Still . . .

"You . . . uh . . . seeing anyone?" he asked.

"No," she said quickly.

He was stung by the prickly nature of her answer. But he persisted. "You date?"

She smiled at him. "You should have met Cissy."

nine

Detective Sergeant Sam Rosen knew who had planted the note in his locker at the Seventeenth Precinct station house. There weren't that many suspects: Bannion and Queen. They would deny it, but no one else had their devotion to heartless pranks.

He'd found the note in the morning when he reported for duty; it had been slipped through the crack of the locker door. Just a tiny scrap of paper, with a swastika at the left-hand top and a Star of David at the right. Not much to launch a chill up his spine, but enough. A reminder that there were always enemies.

He crumpled the paper as if he was guilty of something and stuck it into his pocket. In a way, he felt guilty of not facing the bastards down, even if he understood that there was no profit or sense in that approach. They would only deny it and then make him look stupid by putting on an exaggerated show of indignation. How could he suspect such a thing—from his pals, no less? And everyone in the precinct would know that they had done it and gotten away with it with a slapstick disavowal.

He didn't even mention it to Maggie. What was the point? He was hardened to the Bannions and the Queens, or, at least, as hardened as one gets to locker-room persecutors. Besides, she was coping with Cissy's suicide. When he tried to talk to her about the Edie Severan killing, she rolled her eyes as if she couldn't be bothered. But he knew that he had to protect her against her enemies, of which there were many. She had to pay some heed to the Severan case.

He would try not to mention the note to Bannion and Queen when he debriefed them about the Edie Severan murder. Plant a minor doubt that maybe the paper slipped through a hole and he didn't see it. But he knew that he couldn't carry it off. He was too hotheaded, in his subdued, restrained fashion.

He had to question them about the murder case because they were the "catching" detectives. Maggie had to know the details when she was called in to brief her superiors since the case was starting to generate important media heat. All the tabloid and local television and radio crime jocks had jumped like rabbits at the ingredients of a steamy and ritzy killing. Pretty girl, good family, savage killing, a city teetering on the brink of bedlam. That was the theme of the coverage on the second-day stories.

BEAUTIFUL, GIFTED AND SLICED UP LIKE SALAMI! That was the afternoon banner headline in the *New York Post*. The story read like a pitch for a TV movie: The gorgeous child of a Midwest poet and farmer, the grandchild of a Depression-era populist congressman, cut from ear to ear in her own bed by an unknown maniac. And he's still out there stalking our prize lovelies, was the unwritten text. Of course the underlying assumption behind the story's big appeal was that Edie Severan, like many an unsuspecting innocent flung into the fleshpot city, was lured mothlike to her death by the irresistible flame of sin and lust. It was an urban morality tale played on the broken record of the New York City's echoing and reechoing crime reports.

Some of it—enough to make the headlines plausible—was true. Edie Severan was the child of a second-rate farmer who once wrote a volume of third-rate poems. The poems were, however, good enough to land her a job in publishing. Her grandfather had served a single term in Congress during World War II, where he stole enough money to buy the family farm in Lincoln, Nebraska. So much for the particulars.

The real art came in the retelling by the newspaper poets. All the facts were airbrushed to make a more sentimental, heart-tugging, and lurid tale. The cynics would see from the photographs that Edie Severan was plain. She had a thick nose, thin hair, and a receding chin. On any street in Manhattan she would have been passed by without a second glance. But newspapers and electronic editors regarded it as an act of kindness (a gesture that conveniently worked to their advantage) to bestow beauty on murdered girls. Who was going to challenge it? In the popular ballads of tabloid outrages, female murder victims were always beautiful, men victims were always cut down on the lip of success, the killing was always senseless, and police were always searching for answers.

How or why Edie Severan was killed was, at this stage, still a riddle of many parts to the detectives of the Manhattan North command. Not that there was ever much variation. Sam understood the routine. The murder would fit into one slot or another, but he knew the outlines: she was found dead in her own bed, and the reasons were probably unbearably trite and, in the end, unimportant. She had been available when some lunatic had gone off the deep end. All they had to do was find the right lunatic. That shouldn't be too hard. The city was crawling with them.

Usually, there was a quick arrest of a jilted boyfriend, a

delivery boy on parole, a janitor who'd vanished in the night, a midnight pickup in a desperate bar. Such crimes were cleared up with a little shoe leather and the selective use of some rough questions with implied but unmistakable threats. When it counted and the downtown chiefs took an active interest—when the detectives felt the combined pressure from the newspaper columnists and the politicians and the chiefs—the beefy cops bore down on the witnesses and onlookers and invariably hammered out results. Rarely did a big case loiter long enough to become an unsolved mystery.

Sad Sam needed a forbidden cigarette. He stood outside the precinct cupping the cigarette, feeling guilty and waiting for the two catching detectives; they would fill in some blanks on the murder story. Technically he was their superior, but in the homicide detective command, rank and titles were never strictly enforced. Maggie said that she preferred a ''collegial'' atmosphere. But then she didn't have to contend with Bannion and Queen's Nazi emblems crawling into her locker.

He watched the car approach and was reminded again of why he disliked them so much. The hubris was unbearable. They could actually make a car swagger, he thought, watching the slow progress of the sedan. All the other traffic had to bend and get out of the way as the unmarked cruiser—a cop car that fooled no one—crept along, using the middle two lanes. It reminded Sam of a small-town bully pushing everyone off the sidewalk.

Riding up front in the unmarked cruiser, their eyes slit half open like speakeasy peepholes, were the two detectives. They were wearing their plain, dead-giveaway suits and the sleek, bloated look of men who had just finished a heavy meal. Joey Queen was driving. He was only thirty-two, but with his brush-cut hair and growing paunch he could have passed for forty-five. Bannion was the senior man at thirty-nine, and the great misfortune of his life—apart from the fact that he had married a good Catholic girl out of high school who endured sex by clenching her eyes shut and muttering prayers to the Virgin Mary—was the fact that his crew cut was thinning out like a defoliated forest.

The car stopped at a slant, blocking another car from leaving. Detectives Second Grade Matty Bannion and Joey Queen came slowly, sumptuously out of the cruiser, front doors swinging open in unison. They hitched up their belts together—a menacing signal that they hauled weighty and loaded holsters—then looked around wearily, skeptically, as if they might run everyone in just for the hell of it. They never looked at Sam—a point of honor—automatically taking up defensive flanking positions.

"Sooooo," began Matty Bannion, rocking back and forth on the balls of his feet, sweeping the low rooftops in the distance, "if it isn't Sergeant Rosenberg. My man!"

"What's the deal, home?" asked Joey Queen, examining the opposite rooftops in the same dull fashion. They acted as if they were always expecting an ambush.

Sam shrugged and replied with an acid laugh; he wouldn't give them the satisfaction of showing cramps. "You guys!" he said, shaking his head. "You gotta quit leaving me love notes."

Bannion looked at his partner with a skeptical expression. He didn't want to admit much. Then he smiled. "I believe in communication, Sarge," he said. "That's the key."

"Yeah," echoed Queen.

"You gotta let people know how you feel about them," continued Bannion.

Sad Sam replied with a sorry laugh. "Oh, I know how you feel."

"I don't think you do, Sarge," said Queen. "Why, we

was just talkin' about your holiday comin' up. You guys always have holidays. You know, Rosh ha-something.''

"We celebrate Rush Limbaugh," said Sam, smiling. "He's our god."

"No shit?" said Bannion. "I didn't think you people believed in God. I mean, not a real God."

"Yeah, the ACLU," said Queen. "I always thought that was your temple or church or whatchamacallit."

Sam led them into Maggie's office; he didn't want them sidetracked. The clues and blood specimens and fingerprint scans were floating between the forensic labs, the state computers, and the coroner's office. But Bannion and Queen had been there supervising the squads that would fan out in the neighborhood and pick up the jungle rumors. They would track down recent vagrants, listen to pet theories, press to see if Edie Severan had a nasty boyfriend, if anyone had heard or seen anything. There was always a laundry list of technicalities that included or excluded possibilities.

"She was a fuckin' nun," said Bannion, running through his notebook. "No boyfriend. No men. No parties. No visitors. She didn't smoke, drink, or fuck."

Sam was sitting on top of Maggie's desk. Bannion and Queen were spread out in front of him on metal and false leather seats.

"You talk to her co-workers, her boss at the publisher?"

"On the phone," said Bannion. Queen nodded. "We're going up there after we type up some fives."

Sam nodded. He wanted the DD 5s to show Maggie. They would include all the pertinent details, all the interviews.

"What've we got, as far as manpower?" Sam asked.

"Five teams," said Bannion.

Sam shook his head. He was operating on nerve and

intuition now. If he guessed wrong, it would be his ass. But he felt certain that he was right. "Not enough," he said. "Let's jump into the pool on this one."

The police department had graded lists of manpower pools. Manhattan North could draw for a big case from the city's entire 500 homicide specialists. First they took manpower from the closest portions of the borough. Then, if they needed more, they spread out and drew in gold-shield homicide specialists from the entire borough, then the outer boroughs. In a pinch, they could raid the 4000 other detectives assigned to burglary or narcotics or precinct squads. They could form a task force and turn loose an army of plainclothes detectives, if the case was big enough.

"The lieutenant wants this thing blanketed," said Sam, assuming powers that would ordinarily be reserved for a deputy chief, not a lowly detective sergeant.

"So what've we got, half a borough?"

Half a borough would strip the 100-member homicide command. They would assemble 25 2-member teams.

"No," said Sam, advancing far out on the limb. "We're gonna use fifty teams. We want at least a hundred shields out there. After you do the fives, start skimming the boroughs and we'll have a meeting here"—he looked down at his watch—"after lunch. Say three."

"You want a hundred guys in here from Queens and Staten Island and Brooklyn and the Bronx, you better make it four," offered Bannion, starting to feel the case growing unmanageable.

There was something unsettled and Sam was aware of it. Bannion didn't want to bring it up.

"So that means Maggie's gonna run it?" asked Queen finally, drawing a hot look from Bannion.

Sam nodded. "The lady's gonna take it over."

"So where the hell is she?" asked a flushed Bannion.

"She's downtown with the chiefs now," said Sam.

* * *

On the phone, as she was waiting to be summoned to the high chiefs' meeting at police headquarters, Maggie listened to what Bannion and Queen had told Sam. When he related Bannion's opinion that the victim was a virtual nun, Maggie agreed to upgrade the case and order a full-court press. She thought, A nun wearing a sexy negligee? No way! She told Sam that she'd be back soon, hung up the phone, and resumed her place on the hard, wooden bench outside of the fifth-floor conference room.

The weekly gathering of high police chiefs had been underway for an hour when Maggie was called from the waiting room, where low-ranking members of the department were reminded by the stern, spare setting of the power that they confronted and the ordeal that they were about to undergo. It was, she thought, not unlike the windowless rooms where they broke suspects.

Smoke from cigarettes from four of the six men hunched around the table created a smoldering, hellish cloud. The paneled walls and long, heavy table and acoustical damper added to the chamber's claustrophobic and vaguely menacing quality.

Chief of Detectives Larry Scott pointed, and she took the assigned place at the center of the table, while all the chiefs leaned on their elbows, bent closer, and held her in the sniper scope of their critical gaze.

"You are aware, Lieutenant, of the murder of Edie Severan?" asked Chief of Patrol Arthur Warren. It was intended to be an insulting question. Rough sarcasm was the operating technique of the chiefs. Chief of Patrol Warren was a tall man with a thatch of white hair crowning his black face. He had worked his way up through the maze of police-department racist hostility by adapting an attitude of unyielding and degrading tenacity. It had left him bitter, and scowling in a lifelong quest for revenge. Of all the groups, interests, factions that competed with his own race for recognition, respect, and a slice of the American pie, women pissed him off the most. It was his opinion that they had no business at the occupational end of a nightstick.

Lieutenant Margaret Van Zandt, no stranger to routine male animosity in the paramilitary police department—or even the exaggerated resentment of a downtrodden black man who felt cheated out of the full measure of restitution—did not allow herself to be drawn into an emotional firefight with Chief Warren. Besides, she admired his fury. He had earned it, the old-fashioned way.

"I am taking charge of the case, myself," she said.

"I will be in overall command," chimed in Chief of Detectives Larry Scott, the yapping terrier for this group. Everyone ignored him.

Chief Warren glared at her and blew a long stream of smoke across the table in her direction. "Where do we stand? Do we have a suspect? A hunch?"

"Chief, I have a hunch you are going to burn out a lung."

Scott looked murder at her.

"I mean *my* lung," she shot back calmly, waving the smoke out of her face.

"What about the murder?" asked Chief of Operations Frank Mancini, a fussy member of the police department's upper echelon. Mancini was a peacock of a cop who had his uniforms custom made by a British tailor. There were a number of such high-level showpieces—recruiting-poster cops who looked superb on parade and whose glittering, polished image gave heart to the embattled citizens. Mancini tried to make up for his limited intellectual gifts by studying hard and consistently supporting the traditional sentiments of his superiors, but Maggie knew him to be a plodder, slow to recognize a subtle shift in the social sands and incapable of useful introspection.

She shrugged. "I'm assembling a task force," she said. Scott looked surprised.

"It won't be a quick one, I think."

"No, uh, chance that we have a serial killer here?" asked Mancini, always overcautious and redundant in the face of any kind of resistance.

She hesitated. "Always a chance, Chief." She held up her palms.

Chief Warren, who was chairing the meeting in the absence of the commissioner, turned a page in the briefing folder. He looked up and frowned. "You are still here, Lieutenant?" he asked sharply. "You should be out catching someone."

It took her a moment to recognize that she was dismissed, collect her things, and leave.

"Next item," she heard Chief Warren say as the door closed behind her, "July Fourth. Security. Enforcement. Possible terrorist actions. Possible defense . . ."

ten

Full Blown Rage / 105

THURSDAY, JULY 1

He missed Leon. Harry Graham was a big man, with a big man's bulk and sweep, but he confined himself to a narrow sliver of the king-size bed in his Brooklyn Heights apartment—leaving room for Leon to come home. The habit of grief did not diminish, he had discovered dismally, gradually. It had been eighteen months, long past any reasonable boundary for a reconciliation, but at bedtime Harry always left some space, like a light burning for Leon. And every morning he felt a sharp pang when he found that he was still alone.

On this particular summer morning he lay there for a while and then he sighed and lumbered to his feet and looked out of the sixth-floor window across the East River at the dramatic Manhattan skyline. It would be a warm day but the clouds were low, a patchy arch over the city, which struck out toward the heavens like a great, glittering splay of spokes and spires. Naturally, he thought, there was a distinct profane arrangement to the skyline, something reflecting the strange, irreverent, overbearing tribe who lived there and raised up all those haughty towers.

It should have been an exhilarating sight, but nothing looked or tasted right these days to Harry Graham. He watched the quick speedboats cut across the paths of the slow ferries and felt nothing. It should have clicked, made him smile—something gleeful was happening. But without Leon the harbor was only a dry selling point on a rental agent's checklist. Beauty or charm or fast capers by yapping motorboats in the harbor only added an unwanted texture to his heartache. For anything to count, he had to talk about it, to point it out, to admire it—even silently—with someone. With Leon.

Maybe it would never be behind him. Maybe this was a lifelong ache and he had better get used to it. A year ago, when he'd first moved to Brooklyn Heights, he was uncertain about the wisdom of changing boroughs. He was afraid of leaving the known sanctuary of Greenwich Village where he could at least mourn among familiar landmarks and in a society that was at least sympathetic. In the Heights, he might be letting himself in for more backlash, more sudden loss of attachments, more emotional alienation. He wasn't sure that he could face so much change alone. But in the end all the arguments were outweighed by a powerful instinct that dictated the rearrangement of the furnishings of his life.

His first night in his new neighborhood was spent in an anxious sweat of doubt and disorientation. As the moving van unloaded his things, he noticed that everyone looked wholesome and walked with what he read as a kind of nonchalant, midwestern confidence. They didn't look like the nervy Manhattan misfits, who moved like boxers. This Brooklyn of quiet brownstones and well-tended tenements—kept at a safe distance from the disturbing slums by a defensive ring of thick cinderblock courthouses—was a foreign land.

But on the second day, when Harry ventured out of his

apartment on Cranberry Street, he was struck by an astonishing phenomenon: his neighbors acted as if he was just another resident. They smiled and said hello and welcomed him to the community. He found himself enveloped in a leafy tranquillity that even he, in all his urban, gritty, and cement ways, could not resist. There were trees and single-family homes and squads of chatty nannies. It was a nineteenth-century postcard setting. Lonely walkers—as long as they didn't appear menacing—were accepted without conditions. Harry even took to eavesdropping on the couples planning families and vacations and career moves. It gave him an odd sense of belonging, as if he had entered a tastefully roomy, gently noisy, and incessantly busy family.

But it wasn't all Norman Rockwell charm. The nearby cluster of courthouses, with the attendant traffic of villains, made that clear. At lunchtime the courtrooms emptied and the pitch and pace of the main streets changed. Glib lawyers in off-the-rack suits chattered like carnival barkers at dazed parents who would, before the day was done, put up their hard-won homes to pay the hammering, clockwork legal fees to defend their sullen, hopeless children.

On weekdays Court Street was a vast, daffy commotion of cultural diversity—a bazaar of colliding, jostling, lurching, babbling humanity. In ground-floor shops, Orthodox Jews in garments out of the Middle Ages delivered with Talmudic clarity spiels on state-of-the-art computer hardware. On the corners, standing with otherworldly patience, the Jehovah's Witnesses tried unproductively to pass out literature. They were immune to the devout rejections. They seemed to have a far loftier acceptance in hand.

By eight in the morning, a fleet of minivans would arrive in a howl of peeling rubber, double-park, then drop off tables and chairs, along with a dizzying array of goods and wares. Black merchants in African robes set up folding tables warped with mutinous literature or exotic herbal cure-alls; Arabs swaddled against desert sandstorms set up their stands, which were terraced with sumptuous dry goods, baubles, and gadgets—all of shady origin and dubious authenticity. The designer names on the so-called designer hosiery were misspelled, the electronic gizmos often did not have the functioning parts inside, the jewelry was paste, the gold watches were guaranteed to keep time only for a day, the silk scarves were a blend of synthetic fabrics, and the latest craze in plastic toys would break on the subway ride home.

Nevertheless, there were stalls and markets that delivered concrete value. They were laden with roasted nuts, heaps of fresh fruit and spices, and discount books. From high metal rolling kitchens, the air was perfumed with shish kebab and hot dogs and sauerkraut.

Harry adjusted to all the shades and moods of his new neighborhood in an outer borough. He managed to come up with strategies to make life endurable, twisting through the dense crowds like a dancer before plunging into the subway, then sensibly avoiding the express train and taking the local to Manhattan. He could have saved time with the express, but time wasn't the issue. The express was always a clenched fist.

On the local Harry watched the passengers slide in and out of the trains without ugly pileups. There were even occasional shows of civility. The words "Pardon me" were uttered, provoking smiles that broke out like blushes. Maybe it was the fact that passengers on a local train had a shorter train life. They were there for one, two, or three stops, then gone.

Yet the local had a downside. The slower train attracted the reeking, increasingly quarrelsome beggars.

There was no room or patience for them on the express. New Yorkers had grown weary of the wretched and dishonest song and dance about sudden homelessness brought on by cruel circumstance. It was plain that the destitution was usually brought on by cruel addictions. When the spare change dried up, the veiled threat-tactic ("I could be robbing your house but I'm trying to go straight") backfired. Hearts hardened in the cold summer of the early nineties.

On this first Friday of July, Harry was due to arrive at work at noon. He had just settled himself into a corner seat on the "R" local when a man came wobbling through the car, loudly proclaiming himself to be a wounded Vietnam veteran. He wore a torn and smudged overseas army cap. It was a size too small. And it had the remnant of red artillery braid running around the edges. A prop, thought Harry knowingly. The beggar was tall and bony and had a bad attitude. "I am homeless," he said indignantly, holding out a mangled cup. A few coins rattled at the bottom. Out of his mouth wheezed a sour mist. "Wounded twice." He looked down at his side, as if that was proof enough of his story. "Metal pin in my hip." He tried to maintain contact with the slippery eyes of the passengers. "Now I gotta sleep on a damn subway bench!"

Yes, well, thought Harry, that much is probably true; he doubtless did have to sleep on a hard subway bench. Harry felt a slight twinge of sympathy, which was mixed with resentment. He knew firsthand how it felt to be wounded and forced to carry eternally inside his body fragments of blasted metal. Almost a quarter of a century earlier he'd been a crewman in a medevac helicopter. He had flown into a hundred hot LZ's and lifted out of the nightmare firefights more than his share of bleeding men. He, himself, had been wounded three times in the process. There was an unrecovered enemy bullet floating somewhere near his pancreas. He bore his scars—both visible and un-seen—without complaining. And so as he watched this man with the ill-fitting army cap, red braid running around the brim, he felt a moment of rancor before the onset of pity. The beggar was not even thirty—too young to be a soldier in the sixties or seventies. You had to be chasing fifty to have been in Nam. And real veterans didn't shake a cup like a grenade in the face of an old broken medic.

But Harry didn't care that the man was lying. Because it was his nature, Harry fished inside his pocket and pulled out a dollar bill, handed it over, and accepted the beggar's gratitude. The homeless were an army and they had their own war to fight; Harry recognized a shattered trooper when he saw one.

He turned away and glimpsed something reflected in the window as the train flashed through the dark tunnel. It was a weary, middle-aged man. It was himself. Well, he thought, we're getting gray. The Vietnam veterans are showing age. Or maybe he was just missing Leon.

Maggie Van Zandt was in a bad mood. First, they made her wait for fifteen minutes—sat her down on the plush couch outside the office of the big-shot publisher, asking with thin disdain if she wanted coffee. The manner of the receptionists was intended to convey the long-suffering tolerance of people with more urgent business; Maggie and her sergeant were simply two more pests after some-thing. There was also the matter of the reports that she had read about Jack Fox and his habit of taking on pro-tégés. Then, while she was building up a nice head of steam over the smug corporate insolence and the warn-ings of her superiors about pressing too hard on the big-shot publisher, she felt the first shocking evidence of a toothache. A tenderness that was not quite pain, but would be. She was rolling her tongue around inside her mouth, trying to pinpoint the exact tooth that was in distress—her face contorted so badly that Sergeant Rosen was about to ask if she was all right—when one of the secretaries whispered that Mr. Fox would see them now.

Maggie's expression was mild—a professional disguise—when she was ushered into the sanctuary. The book-publishing big shot just sat there in Mandarin silence and reached tepidly across the desk to shake the fingertips of the police detectives.

It was a tactical mistake on Jack Fox's part. He made Maggie mad. You'd shake, she thought, if I could get you in a windowless room and sweat you. If I could sit you down in one of my own metal chairs and let you finger the jagged surfaces of a police desk, let you see the guard blocking the door—in case you had any ideas that you were free to come and go—then turn my own blunt silence on you like a rubber hose. Then you'd shake like a leaf, she thought. Especially if you knew what I know.

It was the arrogance, or maybe it was the pulsing tooth. Or possibly the command that came down from the chief of detectives that she should conduct the interview, herself—discreetly. Jack Fox's rank made it a matter of policy that a relatively senior police officer interview him about the murder of Edie Severan. After all, the executive editor of a major publishing house was entitled to his perks and pride. This was a man who had exclusive use of a company jet and dined at the White House and regularly kept Hollywood celebrities (to say nothing of senior police detectives) cooling their heels in his outer office. There were tastefully ostentatious tributes to his high status everywhere Maggie looked: Pre-Columbian pottery on the shelves, authentic Picasso lithographs on the wall, two devoted secretaries standing sentry outside of his door.

Maggie didn't breathe. She took it all in. There was not

a speck of dust on the polished surfaces of the dark teak desks and high bookcases, which were laden with best-sellers that Fox had personally pressed into America's face. There was not a loose piece of paper floating out of the empty In or Out baskets, not an unholstered pencil rolling across the desk.

Strange, thought Maggie. For a publisher. She had pictured something messier, more chaotic. Loose manuscripts and flying memos. Ideas erupting like rockets. But not here. So much compulsive tidiness, so much systematic order—it was unnatural. Wrong. Like coming upon a bloodless battlefield. Where was all the blood? The signs of life? It made her suspicious. A certain level of eccentricity was useful, she supposed, among the exceedingly quirky clan of intellectuals who inhabited publishing. But this neatnikhood went far beyond a few odd traits.

All she saw was a small man perched in a high leather chair wearing a crisp white shirt, an expensive tie pulled to the top button like a noose, and a suit jacket that was cut to fit the contours of his runty body. His tanned face—which appeared to have been painfully pinned back tight—showed no expression beyond a backlight of fixed contempt. She squinted and leaned on the desk for a better look. He grimaced, as if she had violated something. But he had the light arranged behind him so that it blinded anyone sitting in the guest chair. She was not there to be inspected. It was supposed to be the other way around. Maggie got up and walked behind him, all the time watching his effort not to flinch, and pushed the neck of the lamp away, moving its light out of her eyes. He seemed relieved that he was not going to be touched. She took a perverse satisfaction in the reaction: an instinctive fear of the police. Everyone knew it in a voluptuous, sensual way, from jaywalkers to serial killers. They always expected to be slammed against the wall, patted down, and cuffed, she observed. Even big-shot book publishers who had their own planes and dined at the White House. Police touched some remote trigger of guilt in everyone.

"I didn't know her; I don't know what else I can tell you," he said when she resumed her seat. His voice was low, a whisper. Intended to make others bend close and listen. He knew all the tricks of a little man to dominate, gain attention. His hands were in constant, supple motion, gliding over the surfaces of each other, never quite touching, but maintaining a kind of air cover one over the other. Finally, he reached out and touched a desk button, and one of the secretaries appeared instantly in the doorway.

"Coffee?" he asked Maggie.

She wondered if he had offered coffee to the first detectives who had conducted the initial interview on Wednesday. No, she doubted it. That was a perfunctory interrogation, before they knew of the deeper connection. Just two dull detectives covering all the bases. That wouldn't require ceremony.

Maggie nodded. "Black," she said. "No sugar."

"Tea," said Sergeant Sam Rosen. "Black."

Jack Fox blinked, and the secretary was gone. A man who could command with his eyes like that, Maggie concluded, had to be a liar. This was someone who left no trail. No promises in words, or on paper. A nod, a gesture, nothing that could be counted as evidence. She'd hate to work out a contract with him. The stark communication explained the empty desk and carefully stage-managed office. Jack Fox was laying the groundwork for deniability.

"What time do you usually get in?" asked Maggie.

"Six-thirty," he replied, nodding. "I find that I get more done," he said. "No telephones." He glanced over at the sleeping console on his pristine desk.

"Too early for me," said Maggie.

"Not me," muttered Sam, sarcastically.

Jack Fox just narrowed his eyes, showing attention, maybe a judgment, but not necessarily revealing anything.

"I wouldn't want to live with anything I decided before seven in the morning," she said.

"No, of course not," he said with a dusting of contempt.

It took no time at all for Jack Fox to corroborate Maggie's first rough impression that he was nothing more than a cultural zombie. So powerful and so barren of important aims. He published celebrity books that sold well and said nothing. His views were empty and his utterances trite, yet given weight by a hungry mob that had no one better to glorify. Maggie had come across these burnished zombies before—lamps that gave off no light, stoves without heat, carcasses without life. She felt a moment of pride in her own worthwhile profession.

Maggie's tongue, meanwhile, was making big lumpy jawbreakers in her mouth as she hunted down and tested the sore tooth. It was only a half-conscious assault, and Sam Rosen leaned over and whispered in her ear, "You okay?"

She nodded. She was fine. The whispering was good; it gave Foxy something to worry about. It took her a few seconds to connect Sam's question to her tooth predicament. She thought he was playing the game. That's when she called off the search.

Then Maggie stopped playing the game. She reached into her wide shoulder bag, pulled out her eyeglasses, a clipboard, and a ballpoint pen. She read through a sheaf of DD 5s. "Did you happen to see the deceased on Monday, the twenty-eighth? The day she was killed?"

She peeked up from the clipboard, watching the effect of the word *deceased*. It was always sharp. Sometimes it cut through an array of defenses.

He took a fraction of a second to answer. "I didn't know her," he said.

Something in the pause. And the voice. For a second, it was unsteady. But then he clenched and grew strong. "Could have met her, but then there are so many young women."

Maggie made allowance for the fact that everyone gets nervous around a murder. She knew that old tales of horrifying injustice fall across innocent stories like shadows. But there was something off about Mr. Fox's twisting distortion—and she was certain beyond all doubt that she had him rattled and he was hiding more than an innocent lie. He put too much effort into seeming cool, she thought.

She leafed through the reports, giving him time to brood. Sam took the coffee and the tea from the secretary, who floated in as if on air. He put Maggie's coffee cup on the desk. She reached over and took a sip and groaned as the hot liquid found the inflamed tooth.

"Too strong?" asked Jack Fox softly.

She shook her head, coughed, and said, "Perfect."

Fox nodded and pushed himself back away from the light and moved his hands, one on top of the other, resuming the wringing pantomime.

"You happen to know a good dentist?" asked Maggie, in a different, less official tone of voice. It threw Jack Fox into confusion.

"Uh, yes," he said. "Matter of fact I have a very good man."

" 'Cause I got this killer toothache. . . ." she held her palm against her cheek, still uncertain exactly which tooth was out to kill her, but certain that she felt the rumblings of a big dental bill.

He pressed the button again. "Sheila, write down Dr. Raphael's name and number for the detective," he said.

"Lieutenant," Maggie corrected him, smiling crisply. "Worked hard to get that grade."

"For the lieutenant," he amended into the intercom. Then, to Maggie, "Tell Dr. Raphael that I recommended you. He doesn't take on new patients."

She had lulled him. He was using his power and position and creating a ledger of debts and favors now. Familiar territory. "Maybe you saw her in the halls," said Maggie, pushing a picture of the dead girl across the desk.

His head snapped back automatically, then he leaned forward deliberately and picked up the photograph. It was a crime-scene shot of the fresh body. He studied it for a few seconds and then handed it back. "There are so many . . ."

"Yes, I know. But this one worked here and passed through the halls and came into your office and maybe you saw her, or, rather, let me put it this way: Maybe you noticed her?"

The smile on his face was plastic. He didn't appreciate her rough, bullying interrogation. She was baiting him and he knew it, but he had no choice. This was not a meeting with his senior editors in which he dictated everything from the agenda to the tone. She was in control and now he was squirming in his seat.

Sergeant Rosen handed her a report; it was a device they used when questioning witnesses. It gave Maggie an advantage: a sidekick with a thick portfolio of extra ammunition.

She read the report that Sam had handed to her. Or rather, pretended to read it. She knew it by heart. "I got a report here that says you took her to dinner," said Maggie, looking up quizzically, as if she couldn't reconcile the facts. "Four Seasons. That same night she was killed. Not Moe's Diner—The Four Seasons. Very high profile. So unless you are in the habit of taking strangers to dinner in the limelight, we definitely have a problem here."

"Lieutenant," he began, then stopped.

"Yes?" she asked.

Sergeant Rosen performed his role and leaned in closer to emphasize the importance of the answer.

Jack Fox's mouth opened and closed. He looked away and she let the pause linger, like a finger on his windpipe. Finally, he said, "I always have dinner there. I often run into someone from the office. It would only be polite for me to ask them to join me." He felt the chaos in his story and stopped. "Perhaps I should speak to my attorney before we continue."

Maggie nodded. "We're not arresting you," she said, and watched the blood drain from his pampered face. "But, good idea, by all means, get in touch with your attorney." She began to straighten up her papers and reports. She paused and looked him full in the face. "I should make it clear: we're not talking libel law here. I recommend a lawyer familiar with criminal law."

His face was pale, and his eyes rolled around his head in panic. But he remained silent.

Maggie and Sam gathered their things in a flurry of efficiency. "We will continue this at the Manhattan North Detective Command headquarters," said Maggie, handing him her card. "Have your lawyer get in touch with my sergeant. At your convenience. I expect to hear from you, or your attorney, sometime soon. Today." She smiled, but there was no warmth in it. She didn't offer to shake his hand as she marched out. She left Jack Fox—the hot-air balloon—totally deflated, a little rubber man lost in a big chair.

At the reception desk, Maggie took a folded note from the secretary: the name of the dentist. She wondered if she could afford Dr. Raphael. Then she rolled her tongue over her tender tooth and decided that she could.

eleven

Cissy's diary lay open on the desk. Maggie sat back, as if getting too close would be a breach of etiquette. But then she couldn't help herself and bent closer:

Wednesday, June 9:

A callback. Finally! Two more high mucky mucks in tiny little offices with no windows. The Style Editor was a fashion atrocity; everything expensive—designer outfits that frighten, colors that clash and saucer-sized glasses. She had very firm opinions, until the other guy—her superior—disagreed. Then she suddenly got a strained expression on her face, like, "Did I say that?", and dove for a cigarette. (She stopped herself before lighting up—apparently, they do not approve of smoking at the Times.)

I wanted to tell Roger—the superior muck—that with his salary and important title, he should definitely have a window and maybe even a sofa. Nobody at the Times seems to have a place to rest. What do they do for a nap? But you do not tell these people such things. They are wise beyond human comprehension. You may offer criticisms, but only if you acknowledge first your miserable inferiority, and then follow up with the actual cringing critique (calling it a critique is one way of scolding the gizmo). Above all, you must couch it so that it sounds like flattery. They're all Jewish mothers!

Still, I was a good soldier and sat up straight and made tasteful, tactful conversation about how sad it must be not to work for The New York Times. In a wild burst of recklessness I ventured an opinion that the fashion section was, well, a tad dull. The Style Editor had a stroke. Her face froze with horror and she struck a match and applied it to the tobacco, which meant that the poor thing lost her head. I couldn't back off. Yes, dull, I said sadly. Not always. Just on certain days. Roger smiled when I suggested that fashion and style should be somewhat adventuresome, and yes, insolent. An exalted aesthetic implied adventure, I babbled, completely committed to a totally looney and absurd speculation. Then I did something smart. I shut up. This seemed to please Roger, although who knows? He had a little noncommittal smile on his face. They don't laugh. The best they can manage is a tight little ironic smile. This is going to be very hard if I hear a belly-buster and let one loose.

Maggie was smiling, lost in Cissy's diary. The air conditioners were on full blast at the Manhattan North Detective Command headquarters and the sound was like a blanket shutting out all the shouting and bells of the daily business of a hectic police command. Then she heard the door to her office open and looked up.

"He's got three consiglieres with him," said Sergeant Rosen. His head swiveled behind him, indicating the conference room. Maggie was still mesmerized by Cissy's voice. She could actually hear it in the notes. It was a comfort to immerse herself in the diary—Cissy was still alive in there.

"Jack Fox," said Sam Rosen, who saw the book and understood that he would have to retrieve his boss gently from her enchanted, delicate state. "He came in with three partners in Rosenzweig & Wharton. They're in the conference room now. The chief's in there, too. They're waiting for you."

She nodded, took a slug of cold coffee, clearing her head. Then she looked out of the office window across the rows of desks; it could have been any office engaged in any enterprise, except that the men and women in shirtsleeves and blouses also wore heavy shoulder holsters, which swung like loaded sacks, patting their comforting lethal potential as they bent and turned and talked and typed and went about the routine business of processing reports, witness interviews, and arrest warrants. At the far end of the bay were the curtained-off windows of the plush conference room. Not the plain, peeling, windowless backroom coffins where the usual suspects were tossed like carcasses to linger before being rudely interrogated. Where she would have preferred to take Jack Fox.

"Rosenzweig & Wharton? They do takeovers and become Supreme Court justices. I didn't know that they handled criminal work," said Maggie, pushing the diary into the top drawer of her desk.

Sam Rosen shrugged. It was an eloquent shrug, she thought admiringly. Sam could tell a whole story with a pitch of his shoulders. Now he was informing her, in his subtle, unspoken way, that three gunslinger partners from the law firm of Rosenzweig & Wharton could handle anything.

They were tucked cozily in the fragrant conference room, with fresh water pitchers and coffee containers on the twenty-foot-long table; there was a lawyer on each side of Jack Fox, with one more behind him to whisper in his ear. For good measure Chief of Detectives Larry Scott sat on the far flank, laughing too loud at a witty remark by one of the lawyers. No mystery which side the chief was on, thought Maggie, taking up a chair opposite Fox, who wore a different linen suit than the one he'd worn this morning. He wore the same impenetrable expression he'd stuck in her face when she first entered his office.

She had to fight off the urge to show how much she didn't like this man. She wanted to test him the way cops do, push him with little suggestions and accusations, see him explode. Find out how the chemistry worked with someone accustomed to vast deference. Show him the weight of all the locks and guns and an insinuation of force—let him know what he was up against, within the boundaries of fair play.

She settled in the seat opposite him, in his face, and put on her no-nonsense tortoiseshell glasses. The papers and reports were tilted at an angle so that he could see the official police department headings, recognize the serious turn that the situation had taken, yet couldn't read them. Then she pulled her chair closer to the desk and—just her luck—banged her right knee.

"Oh, shit," she said, looking down at the rip in her panty hose. The sharp pain came a fraction of a second later.

"Are you all right?" asked the senior Rosenzweig & Wharton partner, Thomas McCord. The others murmured some technical expressions of concern. All except for Fox, who sat there as if he had planned it and was now enjoying her pain. And Larry Scott, who looked annoyed that one of his officers could be so publicly clumsy.

She groaned because she had lost the psychological advantage. And now she felt something wet run down her leg. When she glanced, she saw a thin trickle of blood snaking toward her good summer shoes. She had cut her knee on the sharp table edge. Now there was nothing she could do to stop the blood and save the shoe, or, for that matter, her dignity.

"I'm fine," she said, smiling and turning to her notes.

Sam Rosen leaned over her shoulder and handed her a handkerchief.

"I'm okay," she whispered.

"Take the hankie," he insisted, and she saw that she had blood on her hand. She wet the handkerchief, cleaned off her hand, and pressed the linen against the knee.

"I take it that this is an informal meeting," said the senior partner, McCord, silkily. He was one of those charmed men who look better at sixty than they do at forty. The silver hair suggested good judgment and the creased face implied experience. The voice was that of a knowing mediator, someone who could settle any dispute, if only everyone exercised a little flexibility and common sense. The smile belonged to a someone accustomed to winning. Maggie decided that she didn't like him, either.

"Informal? No such thing, Counselor," she said, staring down his smile with her own.

McCord looked over at the chief of detectives—they had an agreement.

"You know, Lieutenant, I think we can keep this on an off-the-record basis," said Chief Scott, looking back and forth between McCord and Maggie.

Her eyes were on fire. "I don't think so, Chief," she said, shaking her head emphatically.

The chief looked savage. He got up dramatically and walked over and sat next to her and whispered in Maggie's ear. "What the fuck is going on here? This is a very important man. You're acting like he's a suspect."

She bent low and turned so that only Chief Scott could hear her. "This very important man lied to me and my sergeant this morning," she said in her official, departmental don't-fuck-with-me voice. "He lied about his knowledge of a homicide—a homicide! By doing that stupid thing he placed his own ass high on the list of people that I would call suspects." She waited a pause. "Lying is not something that a completely innocent man would do."

"Are you accusing Jack Fox—"

She held up her hand. "I'm accusing him of lying." She blinked. "Nothing else. So far. He was with the dead girl on the night she was killed. He was with her in a conspicuous restaurant. A lotta people saw him. Then he lied about it. I wanna know why. Maybe he ran into her by accident—I doubt it. But I have to press the man about the contradiction. Now, I would appreciate it if you would let me pursue this in my own way."

The attorneys and Fox were five feet away. All they could hear was the rustle and rasp of urgent whispers, and all they could see was the face of the chief growing ruddy and red while the face of the lieutenant remained composed.

"Are you telling me to leave the room?" asked an astonished Chief Scott.

"I don't give a shit if you go or if you stay, but if you interfere with me, I will take this matter further," Maggie replied softly, returning to her reports. The implication was clear and Chief Scott did not want to risk that confrontation. Better to catch her when she was clearly in the wrong. Knowing Maggie, he wouldn't have long to wait.

"I'll stay," said the chief, who was beaten for the moment. "But you are dancing on sharp knives."

When she looked up, she almost smiled. For the first time, she saw a squint of alarm upon the countenance of Jack Fox.

It was a neighborhood of second chances. The laboratory where Harry Graham worked as the chief medical technician was thus ideal, from his point of view. It was remote, and therefore difficult to reach by public transportation.

He walked thirty-four blocks from the subway at Fifty-ninth to Ninetieth Street. Perfect for a man seeking a second chance. True, it was possible to hit a closer subway stop and chop all but six blocks off the walk, but Harry liked to approach things gradually, softly, allowing them to emerge. And every day this fragment of Manhattan—north of Eighty-sixth Street and south of Harlem—came upon him like a surprise.

The laboratory was on East Ninetieth Street, and as he turned east and headed toward York Avenue, Harry tried to soak up all that second effort that seemed to expand the atmosphere. He could feel it, all around him; it was evident in the immaculate streets and the well-tended stoops and polished brass. There was an unmistakable burst of fresh energy in the air.

In his romantic way, he imagined that it came from the ghosts of all the blue-collar immigrants who had come pouring out of Europe at the turn of the century, escaping compulsive military service or famine or class oppression, and established their own ethnic enclaves. And with them, the castoff German or Italian or Irish workmen brought Old World habits of art and craftsmanship; when they built their tenements—fifty-foot-high blocks of cement—they included ornamental cherubs and Greek cornices. And the fire escapes were filigreed with intricate steel fretwork.

Almost a century later, in the housing-boom market of the eighties, flea-market connoisseurs scooped up bargain tenement apartments, tucked them away in the same way that the old immigrants sewed their savings into mattresses. The old structures were now occupied by seasoned, settled natives who were, for the most part, on their second marriages, raising their second families, and inhaling the sweet second wind of thriving middle age. The neighborhood had never been famous for being stylish, but it served as a kind of no-man's-land between uptown spunk and downtown swank. Even the old tenements, like the citizens who worked so hard to maintain them, had all undergone some reconstructive surgery. The structural nips and tucks were evident, as were the layers of paint and the odd, metal air conditioners that stuck out of the windows like the old milk boxes in which people kept the dairy fresh before refrigeration.

Gotham Medical Laboratory was two steps down from the sweltering street in a damp basement, below one of the restored tenements that had been broken up into three-room apartments. Only a discreet white sign identified the clinic—a commercial blotch—in the basement on the south side of the street. The building was shaded by an elm tree whose leaves suffered a yellow blight from the heavy traffic off East River Drive. For Harry, the tree had become one more heroic symbol of survival.

In addition to the revived energy, Harry also felt an unmistakable raw, edgy anxiety. Lately, the residents were disturbed by the ever-growing number of homeless drifters who prowled the city, from soup kitchen to soup kitchen. The more aggressive homeless found the West Side of Manhattan more congenial, with its sympathetic, left-wing guilt. But the quieter, in some ways more annoying, beggars came across town, to rest among the fastidious, fussier natives of the East Side. They sat crumbled like deflated balloons in doorways and on street corners holding pathetic, hand-lettered signs proclaiming their hunger and disease. The occasional coins, invariably dropped from a safe, sanitary height, fell into the outstretched cups like stones—synthetic charity.

Still, everyone tried to keep to his or her place. The residents walked with implacable blindness past the silent beggars while Harry groped for his proper berth. Sometimes he emptied his pockets, and sometimes he marched past the outstretched cup with a trailing sense of shame.

The employees of *Gotham Medical Laboratory* arrived in staggered phases, between seven and noon, braced and starched, carrying bags with coffee and sweet rolls. It was a cheerful place to work. At least it was for Harry Graham, who was determined to give this second life a chance. Except on the days when he saw himself sitting outside on the sidewalk, holding up a gray, hand-lettered cardboard sign.

It was warm that noon as he hurried east on Ninetieth Street, and when the temperature went past a certain point, when moisture broke out on his skin, he was back in the war, coming down into a hot LZ. He could still hear the bullets whacking through the thin metal of the chopper, he could actually see the soldiers running bent in their Groucho sprint with the burden of the wounded in the low-slung poncho. He could remember the texture and feel of the rubber poncho as he reached down to help bring the wounded soldier into the medevac. The weight of the soldier was always a surprise, maybe because it was always a shock that the boys he pulled up with strength he didn't know he had were so young and so blasted apart. Sometimes the poncho would tilt and blood would pour out like rainwater.

Usually, the young boys were dead by then and he would turn and look for someone else to pull to safety in that rough jungle triage. In the distance of his tortured memory, through the storm of the helicopter rotors, he would occasionally hear a sound from the litter. A cry. Pain. Life. He was still astonished, after all that blood, after all that time, that life could endure so much punishment. The really disgraceful fact that Harry couldn't shake, the little detail that made it come back day after day, whenever some little something triggered a reminder, was how vivid it all was. How exciting. Until then, his life had been an ashen and remote exercise. He had endured childhood, attended school, achieved grades, won diplomas, carved out a career. But that was going through the motions. There, in the war, when he was up to his knees in blood and gore, he felt the bare pulse of life. He reached down and pulled men back from the brink of extinction. Nothing rose to that majesty, nothing could match that suffering. After Vietnam, coming out of the closet had been a small, puny matter. And losing Leon was really not as tragic as it felt.

"Listen," began Eric Miller as Harry was putting on the white coat with his name tag clipped to the pocket, "you happen to know anyone with AIDS? I mean, personally?" His head was down and Harry could not see his eyes.

They were not close friends, not even close co-workers. They shared work space and were polite to each other, but Eric Miller was not the sort of person who asked for or offered confidences. Still, there was an urgency, maybe even desperation in the question, and Harry considered talking about Leon.

twelve

Maggie sighed, shut the door of her office, climbed back behind her desk, and stifled her inflamed emotions as she violated the raw entries of her dead friend's diary:

Thursday, June 10:

   Maggie wants to go shopping with me. She has a wardrobe crisis. Nothing fits her. It's a bloating thing or a seasonal thing or a gender thing. More likely it's a whim thing or an envy thing or some damn thing. She has to do everything that I do! So she's going shopping with me. Why does a police detective need outfits from Saks? If I was a police detective I'd be picking up stuff at Macy's or A & S. Or more likely the Banana Republic. I tried not to be bitchy and said fine, come along, but I really wanted to be alone and nurse my exploding anxiety and migraine terror in peace. What the hell does Maggie have to be nervous about?

   I didn't mean that, please God! I am turning into a terrible shrew. Maggie has every right to be tense, what with having to hang around all those rough and evil characters (and those are just her colleagues!) The poor woman even has to schlepp through life with a loaded gun strapped to her side. That's got to be a real nightmare—finding suits that are cut to hide a holster and still look flattering! Saks must have a shoulder-holster department.

Fashion isn't the only tricky problem. She has this other cross to bear: me. Not an easy responsibility, Cissy Stone. I am her millStone. I try not to be, Lord knows, but I am. I need her presence and aura and most of all, her respect and affection. She's so damn plucky and confident! And, frankly, I'm getting a little cranky and weak in the knees from this long financial and emotional drought. No job, no man, no money. Sounds like a blues song. Oh, well, I'll get some outfits, finish up with the annoying medical exam (they make you go all the way up, then all the way across town just to get a simple blood test); then I'll embrace the appropriate anatomical parts at the sacred 43rd Street shrine, and my life will return to the same, safe sluggishness of plain old middle-class, middle-aged angst.

What if they find a lump!?

Maggie shuddered, shaking off the surge of sorrow and anger that came crawling up her back like a pair of talons. It wasn't easy, even though she had a talent for maintaining self-control. From the clinical one-way mirror of her profession, Maggie had disciplined herself to lifting the skirts of the dead and seeing all of life's lewd, unspeakable, and savage secrets. Nothing surprised or shocked her, or so she thought. Lieutenant Van Zandt was no stranger to the midnight lust of ordinary people who harbored uncontrollable leather fetishes, or dreamed frightful dreams. From her perspective, life was messy, erratic, and vivid. Under the mild canopy of everyday existence lurked volcanic rages, shameful urges. How could she be offended by the wild, far-fetched cravings of her fellow creatures? And, in the end, it was only sad, never personal. The inescapable fact was that the people with whom she shared that kind of intimate, decisive contact were all strangers.

There was also one last detail: she had the ultimate advantage. Life. And so, like a priest, she forgave the faraway dead.

But this was different. This was Cissy. Her friend—her best friend—and the voice that came at her from the open grave was astonishingly unexpected. Not ugly or angry or evil. Not even unrecognizable. Just . . . unexpected. It was all too human. Just hard to swallow: brave Cissy, wracked with pain and spite—Cissy on a human scale—was alien. It was a voice she had heard often from behind that expert one-way glass of her occupation, not unlike the sound contained in the daily detective reports, farewell notes, and reflections of the remote victims of an unceasing tabloid storyline. Only now it was not something detached, or only technically interesting; it was Cissy. She didn't want to read what lay in the diary pages ahead. But of course she knew that she wouldn't stop. Not now, not with her instincts awakened and aroused and pushing her to find a different—a plausible—explanation for Cissy's death. Not in midstream.

Suddenly, she looked up and Tom McCord was standing in the doorway, his hand knocking on the wood frame—softly. She hadn't heard him open the door. He was smiling. It was a petitioning smile. It took her a moment to connect the shrinking man on her threshold to the same inwardly calm and polished and urbane sophisticate she had left in the conference room.

After Chief Scott stormed out in the midst of the interrogation, it had been a crisp meeting, and she had been all tough cop. "I want to ask your client some questions, Counselor," she had said, addressing McCord; she'd made a tactical decision to ignore Jack Fox, thus knowingly and maliciously ratcheting up the pressure. "I have some . . . inconsistencies in the versions and reports about the homicide of Edith Severan; I'd like to clear them up," she said, flattening her voice. "Before this goes too far."

At the word *homicide,* she noticed a small jolt of fear ripple through Jack Fox. She continued. "Your client is here voluntarily. He's not a target of any investigation." The muted steel in her voice made them all bend closer, squint as she laid out the terrain. "I know that he knows that he has every right to remain silent, but keep in mind, he's being asked to cooperate—merely cooperate—in a serious police investigation of a homicide. Again, I stress the word *cooperate.* Nothing more." Everyone in the room was aware that there was a clear, ensnaring implication in her tone and careful choice of language; they all knew that Fox's failure to cooperate would count heavily against him in whatever lay ahead. When Maggie was finished, they all nodded—the three lawyers and even the disregarded client.

Then she gathered up her notes and reports and left the four men there in the conference room to talk it over. She pictured them clustered and sweating together, the lawyers spelling out the pros and cons and Jack Fox sitting cramped, tight-lipped, and frightened. It was a pleasant image for Maggie.

Now, twenty minutes later, lost in Cissy's diary, she looked up to see the suave chief counsel at her door. "Come in," she said, waving McCord inside. "Coffee?"

"No, thanks, Lieutenant."

She felt the smooth stroke of fresh respect in his manner. It was a nice summer breeze. Must be a tough thing for a senior partner at Rosenzweig & Wharton to stoop for a mere police lieutenant.

She put Cissy's diary back in the drawer and locked it. Then she took a swallow of her own cold coffee, which had sat on her desk for an hour. It tasted wonderful.

"So, what's it gonna be?" she asked, motioning for Sergeant Sam Rosen—who had been waiting outside—to join them. Sad Sam came in quietly and took a seat behind McCord, who now knew in no uncertain terms that a witness was present. This was to be formal.

McCord shook his handsome head and issued a curdled laugh. "You got a law degree, Lieutenant? 'Cause if you do, I'm prepared to offer you a junior partnership in my firm starting today."

"You know, a remark like that, it could be misconstrued," she said ambiguously.

McCord had a twisted smile; he didn't even look alarmed. He shook his head. "Look, I'm way out of my depth in this," he said. "All I'm saying is that we need someone with criminal experience on this. We're bumpkins when it comes to crime." He swung his hand behind his head at the conference room. "We handle mergers and takeovers and libel threats." He ran the same hand through his silver hair. It was a very disarming gesture. Maggie decided that he was probably a nice man—a good companion. She nodded. He went on. "These guys," and he gestured again over his shoulder, "well, let's just say that we could tell you more about the tax rebate possibilities of contesting a criminal charge than the plea-bargaining precedents that go into sweetening the deal."

"So your guy wants to plea-bargain?" she asked.

He laughed. "You should definitely get a law degree." He shook his head in admiration. "No, frankly, Lieutenant, this man is guilty of nothing except maybe big-time arrogance." He smiled conspiratorially. "I hope that this is off the record." He looked around, checking with Sad Sam, who smiled back reassuringly. Sam understood that kind of commercial appeal. So did Maggie. McCord went on. "I'm pretty certain of my man. I grant you, he's not likable; no one likes someone who runs a big company.

Hires, fires, makes and breaks people. No one likes that kind of man. Ruthless, no matter how gently it's done, and Jack's not gentle. No argument about that. But murder?" He shook his head. "It would ruin his manicure."

She nodded. She wasn't certain that she agreed. It takes a certain deadly, sharklike quality to cut a budget; she regarded crunching numbers as another way of crunching people, only a little more abstract. Like dropping bombs on people you don't see. That same trait can be as cold and lethal as a knife, she thought. She looked down at her notes. "So you don't feel competent to represent him?" she said.

"Not against you."

"Okay," she said, looking up with a nod. "Go get competent counsel and I'll get a law degree."

He bent closer, out of Sam's earshot. "You mind if I ask you something?"

She looked at him. He was blushing. "You, uh, free for lunch sometime?" he asked softly.

There was a wedding ring on his finger. "Sometime," she said coolly. He turned an even deeper shade of red, nodded, and left. Sam's eyebrows were raised like a flag when they were alone. If he hadn't heard the invitation, he'd guessed it. He didn't speak above the arched eyebrows.

"Shut up," said Maggie, who watched the commotion as the well-tailored group left in a tight little band.

They marched Jack Fox out to his waiting limousine like a French prisoner, a lawyer on each side and McCord protecting the front, ready to swat away the cameras, if there were any. There weren't. There should have been, she thought. Where the hell were the tipsters who popped up for every subway mugger? Jack Fox was still too dangerous, she guessed. He was a wounded lion and even the tipsters must know that a wounded animal is far more dangerous than a corporate shark.

Still, she saw with satisfaction through the occasional breaks in the swarm of shielding limbs that Fox had gone completely pale. Good, she thought. How many bleached bones had he shoved out of his office into the cold? Then she made herself comfortable behind the desk, put on her glasses, and descended into the files of the Edie Severan murder. She did not like making quick assumptions about the wrong villain. She wanted to be certain.

Sad Sam was coming down the stairs heading for a coffee break when he saw a young delivery man from a florist standing at the magistrate's desk. The delivery man, a Black youth wearing a back-to-front baseball cap, held a large bouquet of roses in his right hand. He held the hand high, like a soldier in enemy territory showing that he carried nothing dangerous, that he meant no harm. Sad Sam stopped and watched from a distance as the delivery man struggled with the desk sergeant, who had a dead-fish expression on his face as he listened to the youth attempt to explain that he had come to the precinct to present the outsized bouquet of eighteen roses to one of the detectives. The desk sergeant waited silently after each successive detail: that the flowers were ordered, paid for, and were a routine business event in the life of a floral transfer (given the admittedly unusual destination of a police precinct).

Sam recognized the sergeant's method. It was the silence of the backroom bully; a tactic used to break nervous suspects. It was a universal sign of hostility. Sam remembered a similar encounter in Paris—he had seen that same lifeless stare when he tried to speak French.

"You got some ID?" asked the desk sergeant finally, breaking the nervous rambling.

The delivery man fumbled in his pocket and produced a laminated card. It had his picture on the front, which attested to the fact that he worked for Futterman's Florist

Shop. It was signed by Jack Futterman. It was a cheap thing, a device manufactured in one of the private ID shops in Times Square that catered to tourists (faking FBI membership) or urban desperados (faking welfare status or citizenship). But in this case it was a homespun attempt to stave off what had undoubtedly been the interminable hassles and exclusion faced by the young Black man from White doormen and security guards in the world of corporate and residential racism.

"Anybody could make up one of these," said the police sergeant, turning the slick card over and around, as if he would unlock some secret chamber and discover a cache of crack in a hidden crevice. Meanwhile, an audience had sprung up in the bay of the station house—uniformed police about to go on or off duty who stood smiling, arms folded, savoring the embarrassment of the delivery man and enchanted by the notion of a working cop getting a delivery of roses. Cops were, by nature, nosy creatures charmed by gossip.

"Lemme just leave 'em here," pleaded the youth.

The sergeant shook his head. "Can't take a chance," he said, looking down from his high perch. "Could be dangerous. How do I know that these are not explosive flowers? People send letter bombs. We gotta be careful."

"Yeah, could be an explosive bud," chimed in one of the uniformed cops.

"That's right, Sarge, I heard about someone sending poison candy," said another of the uniformed cops.

"That was to a desk sergeant," said a third, this one a white-haired veteran unable to hide his glee.

"Someone in the midnight shift got a crush on you, Sarge?" came an anonymous voice from the rear.

The sergeant flashed a deterrent frown at the audience. "Who did you say that these flowers were for?" he asked the youth, deflecting the remarks.

The youth looked down at the floor of the bay, his head shaking back and forth.

"You better tell the sergeant before he calls the bomb squad," said a rookie standing too close to be ignored.

"Lieutenant Van Zandt," replied the delivery man.

"Oh, it's Van Zandt," said the veteran in the bay, nodding his head.

"Van Zandt!" repeated someone among the observers, meaningfully.

"Well, that happens; female detective bosses," came a knowing voice.

Someone else: "Could be a new thing now, with our female cops. You know how a perp is gonna try to, you know, see if they can knock off some of the charges. Appeal to our better nature. 'Course in most cases, they offer, like, a piece of pizza."

There was a rumble of suppressed laughter under the banter. Any minute, it could break.

"I never get flowers," said the veteran.

"You probably get the wrong perps," said another veteran, falling into cop-comedy banter. "I personally prefer the candygram guys."

"Yeah? How can you tell?"

"You can tell. A look. If they rub your leg. That's a big tip-off."

Sad Sam decided to stop the show. He pushed his way through the crowd, took the delivery boy under the arm, led him to the stairs, and pointed out Maggie's office. He watched him run up the stairs like a messenger from Marathon, holding the flame of red roses aloft.

"Hey, Sarge, you better sign for that guy!" said the youthful cop. The others saw Sam's angry expression and backed off.

Upstairs in the homicide lieutenant's office, Maggie was disturbed. She had been studying the crime-scene photographs of Edie Severan's bedroom. Something was wrong, she thought, comparing the angles of the shots and the details one by one. She studied them with the assumption that she was missing something in plain sight. Then she saw it. There was not enough blood. The woman was supposed to have been murdered by a savage knife attack and yet there was only a minimal, discreet amount of blood on the bed. Where the hell was all the blood? She jotted a memo to herself: *Check the postmortem. This may be more complicated than a knifing. She would have thrashed around, died messier.*

The kid bearing flowers came through the door and she dropped the pencil, her face bursting into color like the roses. She felt everyone watching as she emptied a metal wastebasket, poured in some water, and used it as an improvised vase. The flowers looked lost and skimpy in their makeshift home. Then she sat down and read the attached note.

Have dinner with me—Jerry M. PS: I assume you know my number.

Dinner. Cissy's man. She picked up the phone with an angry expression on her face. Her voice was hard. "Yes," she told the answering machine. "I'll pick you up at seven-thirty."

Outside the station house, Sam followed the young delivery man, who couldn't seem to get away fast enough. He grabbed the young man's arm.

"What's up?" said the youth in a voice rising with irritation and exasperation.

Sam tried to speak. He took in the backward baseball cap, the glittering rows of gold chains hanging halfway down the youth's neck, the diamond stud in his ear, the undone sneakers—marked down all the differences between them. Then changed his mind. It was the smoldering eyes of the young man. There was a long, burning fuse in them.

Sam meant to soften the experience, tell the kid that the boys were just having a little fun and that it didn't mean much. But he couldn't. For one thing, he didn't believe it. For another, the kid knew that Sam was disqualified and full of shit. Sam shook his head sadly and walked back into the station house.

thirteen

FRIDAY, JULY 2

Lauren Drake was determined to find Eddie Barnes. All she had to go on was his name and the name of the clinic she had heard on the phone when someone else picked up an extension. Gotham-Something-Something-*Clinic.* Her fingers trembled as she ran down the page of the telephone book and found a *Gotham Medical Laboratory* on the East Side of Manhattan. Just looking at the listing made her mad.

She came to the clinic in the morning and stood outside behind a yellowing elm tree trying to decide how to attack the problem of confronting him. She stood there for twenty minutes in the dank swelter of intense emotion, behind the inadequate refuge of the tree, before she lost her nerve and fled like a thief. What finally drove her off was the sudden realization that she didn't know what the hell to say when someone answered the door. She got as far as imagining ringing the bell—she pictured that much—and then someone would answer. Then the frame went blank.

The more she thought about it, the more uncertain

she became that she had the name of the clinic right. Had she heard Gotham when that son of a bitch called? It sounded like Gotham, but it could have been anything; the name turned to mush as she repeated and repeated and repeated it in her mind. Gotham. Gotham. Gotham. Gretcham. Gritchmar. Gray-sham. She felt like one of those careless students who showed up completely unprepared for a test, expecting to bluff his way through.

Whether she had it right or not, she still had to decide what to say. Should she act confident, casual, bold? She didn't know. Should she just ask to speak to Eddie Barnes, as if she was certain that he worked there and was waiting inside? Think, she told herself. Make believe this is a seminar and you are the senior proctor. But she had not even come equipped with a good excuse for asking about Eddie, and she felt weak in the knees. Someone was bound to ask what her business was, and she did not have a plausible answer.

She couldn't just blurt out that some guy whose name she barely remembered—a man she had picked up at a party (let's face it) and then slept with in the most casual, cavalier, brainless act of her life—had called her up from a phone in a clinic that sounded like Gotham and announced with strange and malicious, barely supressed glee that he had tested HIV positive. It made her woozy just summing it up. She pictured herself standing there, like some nineteenth-century lithograph of tragedy, a wronged, abandoned woman with a nameless baby in her arms. In a way, it was a true image, only the baby was a wildfire virus.

Well, what the hell, she was allowed to feel tragic and act flustered. Given the lethal provocation, that was certainly understandable. If she didn't ask the most coherent questions or lost her poise, if she seemed on the verge of hysteria, that was understandable. People panic under deadly fire. If she got some detail twisted, well, that, too, was within the boundaries of her peculiar predicament. She was at a disadvantage.

Hard to keep a lid on the anger. Every coil and curve of the story had her boiling. The bastard had even hung up too fast, before she could press him or maybe appeal for sympathy. Lucky that someone had picked up that extension phone and revealed the name of the clinic, if she'd heard right. God, let it be right! It had to be Gotham; it was a thin line to follow, but it was all she had to prove that she was not raving.

Then she had an interesting thought: What if Eddie Barnes himself answered the door? She would just launch herself at him, leave the ground and fly into his face and rip apart his flesh. She would kick him in the groin—a fitting target—and bite any part of him that came within range. Even thinking of it, imagining the salty, bloody taste of revenge, made her feel a little better. Maybe not the most dignified approach, but certainly within her rights. Let a jury try to kiss off that provocation! She had a good cause and her blood lust was up. At the moment, she didn't care if it was infected blood.

Of course, he would probably become defensive and uncooperative if she assaulted him. And much as she hated to admit it, it was essential that he cooperate. She had to find out the exact state of things. Uncertainty was unbearable. She had to know if he had been double-tested. Was it a reliable test? Was he serious?

She realized that she would have to put on a convincing show of generous amiability. She rehearsed a speech:

"No, no, I am not really upset! Of course I'm a little upset, who wouldn't be, but I understand. You were embarrassed, but you did the right thing by calling me. This is a great social problem that requires vast understanding from everyone, so you have to understand my concerns!

We must all behave rationally, sensibly, tenderly; we must all find some way of dealing with whatever it is we have to deal with. Be supportive. We're all in this together.''

Would she be able to smile? She gagged. She was not absolutely certain that she would be able to stop herself from plunging her nails deep into his eyeballs. She couldn't swear. So she retreated. She turned and walked away from the clinic and tried to cool off.

Later, after a long, late breakfast and an extended and aimless ramble up and down the East Side of Manhattan—with none of the blinding uncertainties or reservations settled—she came back to the clinic and rang the bell. She found Harry Graham alone; the rest of the clinic staff was apparently out for lunch. Harry seemed calm and sympathetic.

"I'm supposed to meet someone," she said softly. She kept her voice within tolerable limits and asked him straight out if he knew of a particular young man, and she mentioned his name: Eddie Barnes. When Harry raised an eyebrow, as if to ask why she wanted to know, she said that Eddie Barnes was a student in one of her classes—she was a college professor—and needed her help for reasons that she had sworn to keep secret.

Harry nodded and asked what this Eddie Barnes looked like. She drew a blank when she tried to describe Eddie. The truth was that she couldn't picture him, although she could hear his voice, the hateful sound when he'd called and told her that he had AIDS. He sounded almost happy. That she remembered vividly. Clearly. It was, perhaps, the most convincing part of the conversation between them.

"He's . . . about thirty," she said finally, as she stood at the clinic's front counter with Harry in his white coat and mournful, sympathetic eyes. A student? Thirty? She was twisting the strap of her handbag, whispering so that none of the clients waiting on a long wooden bench for a blood test could hear. They looked worried enough. "He's just ordinary," she said. "Blond hair, blondish. Medium build."

She realized by the wavering tone of her words and by the patient tolerance of Harry's expression that she sounded wild and unbalanced.

"What was the name again?" he asked mildly.

Her back stiffened. She had mistaken the question for an insult. "My name is Professor Lauren Drake," she replied primly.

"I meant his name," said Harry as if the ambiguity was all his fault and the confusion was a natural mistake. He had a forgiving and soothing manner.

It took her a moment to recover. Then she nodded. "Barnes," she said. "Edward Barnes. He's no taller than five seven or so."

Harry waited, thinking, then shook his head. "No one by that name works here." She thought that she heard in his hesitation another answer. She heard something. He was hiding something. Maybe not hiding, but he was being cautious.

"What about clients?" she asked, not wanting to push.

"I really couldn't tell you, even if I knew," he said gently. "It would violate privacy."

"Privacy," she said. She nodded. Of course. She understood. People had rights to privacy. Her unusual circumstances might test that rule—not many people had someone wielding a positive-HIV hammer at them—but she couldn't explain that to Harry. She couldn't spell out the full range of emotional contortions that a little phone call had put her through. A valid exception to the delicate privacy rules, she thought. There was another thing: the whole situation was terrifyingly eerie. She felt as if a loaded gun had been cocked and aimed at her face. All she had to go on to support her high level of fear was the sound of his voice—the delicate sadistic undertone—and the odd circumstance. Why the hell had he called? She would almost prefer ignorance, she thought.

None of this could be easily explained to a stranger, not even a sympathetic soul in a white jacket who looked as if he wanted to help. She thanked Harry and left behind her phone number. She had tried to make her quest seem ordinary and harmless. A lost boyfriend. No big deal. She didn't want to alarm or alert him prematurely. But, of course, she had been unable to conceal the desperation and the frustration.

As she walked away, sobered by the face-to-face confrontation with Harry Graham, she tried to plan a more effective strategy for finding Eddie Barnes.

The woman's visit left Harry unusually agitated. Professor Lauren Drake was clearly not some deranged crank looking for a phantom lover. She impressed Harry as a clear-eyed woman of some substance, judgment, and common sense. Although he recognized the stress. She was definitely chasing something specific and hazardous. And he was sure it was someone and something real, but he was not sure what it was.

Harry and Eric were in the lounge of the blood clinic drinking tea. No one could overhear them, although Harry was aware that Eric kept looking around, checking for eavesdroppers. Eric was folding and opening a fresh bulletin on the latest improvement in latex gloves to keep the retrovirus at arm's length. Precautions were always a big topic in the clinic. Gloves, carefully covering cuts, avoiding contact with any bodily fluid, recognizing lesions and open wounds—the safeguards were drilled into all the employees like kindergarten lessons. There were always new defenses, but it was guerrilla warfare, and the advantage lay as always with the offense, with the unseen virus.

The numbing fear about AIDS that had infected the

medical profession since the virus emerged in the early 1980s felt like defeat. Not that the fear was ever uttered. Not in those terms. The medical world's arrogant, upbeat convictions suggested that even the most complex problem could be solved, given the proper application of reason and deduction. Science was, after all, irresistibly and inevitably logical, marching forever upward and onward.

Except for this virus. There was something overwhelming and mystical—something almost beyond reason—about AIDS; it had cracked the crust of the medical conceit that anything was susceptible to science. Harry detected the astonishing shift in the wind by the unsteady eyes of the professionals whenever the topic was raised.

In the end, they were all at risk and they were all aware of that fact, even if they openly and noisily complained about public ignorance and spoke bravely about the overblown danger of contracting the disease.

There were subtle and overt signs of just how deep the uneasiness had gone. Too many sleep disorders had been reported among clinical blood technicians. Tempers were not reliable. And the turnover in the field had become a hemorrhage. The ones who stayed fretted over every detail. Lab technicians read their medical insurance plans like scholars, looking for loopholes, stipulations, provisos that would hurt them if the worst came to pass. As if they could protect themselves from the toxic virus by a turn of phrase. As if a health plan could guarantee an immune system!

"You afraid of catching something?" said Harry Graham when Eric asked again if he knew anyone who had AIDS. It was a flip comeback. Not like Harry. He regretted it instantly. But the business of handling blood as if it were radioactive waste had become so fraught with dread that a toll in mood and temperament was inevitable. Everyone was obsessed and worried. Even someone with Harry's dependable, sober-minded character and demeanor devised strategies for avoiding the topic.

Miller shook his head, his eyes downcast. "No more than usual," he said.

Graham didn't believe him. He detected in Eric Miller a sad undertone, maybe even a harrowing resignation. Something had made him ask Harry the question. It was not in keeping with Miller's hostile, deterrent armor. Harry didn't like Eric Miller. No one did. But for the first time since they had begun working together, Harry felt something close to sympathy for him.

"I knew one or two people," said Harry.

Miller looked up. He had not expected an answer. Harry was not the sort of person who confided. Everyone in the clinic knew—or assumed—that Harry was gay. Not that he advertised or admitted it. He said simply that he was a bachelor and everyone knew what that meant.

"He had AIDS? Your friend?"

Harry didn't answer right away. He remembered it like some pretaped football game that he watched over and over, again and again. The outcome never changed, no matter how hard he rooted.

How could he tell this one, a person as emotionally brittle and cold as Eric Miller, about someone as sympathetic and supple as Leon? he wondered. There was no chance of compassion. And Leon was as private as anyone could be in an age of indecent vulgarity and cruel Outing.

They began, he and Leon, as a kind of discreet conspiracy. They met at a political fund-raiser. Harry was standing at the bar in the grand ballroom of the Hilton Hotel, waiting for a glass of the red liquid that was being passed off as punch. Out of nowhere, the mayor's legislative liaison expert, Grady Myers, approached him, a shrewd look of open appraisal on his face. He stared at Harry brazenly, audaciously, flirtatiously. He was measuring Harry Graham, judging him, taking long guesses about him.

"Will you get one for me?" he asked Harry, indicating the glass of punch that had just been placed in Harry's hand.

It was an approach, a coy tactic, but nothing crude or ugly. Certainly thrilling. And Harry responded. He smiled back and handed the mayoral aide his own drink and asked for another. The signal had been understood, accepted, and given a favorable reply. They had, in an instant, sized each other up and agreed that they were both available and desirable homosexuals. It was, in its fashion, a sweet and romantic tryst.

"Harry Graham," he said by way of introduction.

"I know," said Grady Myers. "You are a bleeding-heart liberal supporter. The reliable backbone of the elite shock troops in our staunch political army." He smiled winningly. "My name is Leon."

Harry was confused. That was not Grady's name. He knew his name. He recognized the young man. "But aren't you Grady Myers?" he said. He knew him from the political gossip about the up-and-coming young aide and the newspaper photographs. Myers wasn't famous, but he was known.

Myers shrugged and nodded. "Maybe. But that's not the name we'll use," he said, already making assumptions about the durability of their relationship. "You'll call me Leon," he said. It was a tender command and Harry was drawn to the adventure and settled intimacy of being admitted to a false name.

Harry's homosexuality had been a lifelong fact—he recognized it, admitted it when he had to. But it was barren. The sexual encounters were sterile, mechanical, arid of any deeper feeling. He had never fallen in love.

With "Leon" it was different. There were a few

lunches and some sweaty afternoons in Harry's apartment, and gradually the sexual attraction mutated into something else. They fell in love during a vacation in France when they rented a house in a town called Beauvais located in the foothills of the French Alps. It was summer. The air was fragrant with ripe fruit, and the fields were purple with flowers, which gave the area a sense of enchantment.

The section of France was not Provence, not discovered or fashionable enough to make them self-conscious of being American or gay or in love. There were ancient towns and rare restaurants sprinkled through the hills where the natives did not mind patrons who spoke English and sat silently content over cognac, drinking in each other.

They drove to Orange and Avignon and strolled through the Roman ruins, and no one bothered about the fact that they held hands. They shopped on market day and cooked together and each meal tasted like a delicious conspiracy.

After three weeks, they came back to America and it was like dropping a precious piece of crystal. Everything changed. There were still trysts, dinners, and lingering phone calls. But this was New York City, where they were known. They could not hold hands.

The worst part was Leon's wild streak. He vanished every now and then, without explanation. He said that it was business, politics. But Harry didn't believe him. Finally, after conventional nagging, Leon admitted Harry to his secret life. He took Harry to the Mineshaft, a gay bath and bar. Harry was thunderstruck, although he was aware of the rougher forms of sex. At the main room of the Mineshaft they both shed their clothes. It was compulsory, said the manager, who looked like a pirate.

Harry was astonished to see the floor writhing with

men groping and sucking in combinations of four and five. Along the walls were piles of towels and vats of petroleum jelly and grease to assist the men sliding in and out of each other. The room groaned like a ship in heavy seas. In the middle of the room, one young thing hung from a leather harness that looked like a complicated trapeze. It was designed to expose maximum backside. Another man caressed the youth's face with one hand and stuck two, three, four fingers through the anus, then worked his fist up into the groaning, weeping, delirious youth. The man drove his arm up the youth's anus with sweaty, frantic abandon, cursing and swearing his love to the total stranger.

Leon saw the horrified look on Harry's face. "You know," he said, touching Harry's arm, "it's a kind of ecstasy. I love it."

"You do that?" asked Harry, nodding at the wild pulsing of the two men.

Leon didn't answer at first. Then he said in a strange, distant voice, "The boys, they're really quite flexible and it's very nice."

"With who?" asked Harry, looking around. "Do you do that with someone in particular?"

"Boys." Leon shrugged. He tried to explain. "It doesn't matter who. It's better if you don't know. It's the exotic intimacy, you see." He shook his head and laughed, then grew serious. "How can I explain? You reach inside deep, you know? You think, well, maybe I'm going to hurt this nice little boy. But he's begging for more. Screaming for it. And more. And more. And before you know it, your hand moves higher and higher, until, my God, it's almost up to your elbow."

His voice was hushed as he tried to convince Harry. "You know, Harry, when your hand is up so high and the boy is still pushing against it, you can feel a great rhythmic

tempo. The pounding of real, raw sex! And then you realize that you are actually feeling his heart. Literally! It is
beating in the next chamber, you are almost touching his
heart. The only thing that separates you from his heart is
some tissue.''

Harry saw the glow on Leon's face and came to per-
plexing and difficult conclusions.

That was, in fact, the end of them. Harry had no interest in such rough sex. Afterward, Harry insisted on the use
of a condom, (it was a hopeless insult), and Leon had
more and more absences. One day Harry came home and
found a farewell note. Later, he learned through a friend
that Leon had AIDS. By some miracle, Harry still tested
negative.

Of course, he couldn't explain this to Eric. Even
though he was certain that Eric had a good reason for asking, and somehow he knew that Eric was the person for
whom Professor Drake was looking.

But he was not prepared to unburden himself about
Leon, although he was willing to ask about the woman.

fourteen

He was sitting on the bed, dressed and waiting, when Maggie rang the bell. Excessive punctuality was an old lead weight with Jerry Munk. Before he became a bookseller, Munk had been a staunch newspaper hound who never missed a deadline. Now deadlines were no longer critical, but the antique habit of getting ready early remained; his clock remained set half an hour ahead of the rest of the world, which is why he found himself on the bed, brooding and moist with uneasiness, when the front doorbell rang.

Paradoxically, it was, he concluded, the dread of what lay ahead that made him rush to wait. Frenzied with the details and preparations, the final goal blurred and he was ready before he knew it.

No, he did not look forward to engagements (he couldn't bring himself to think of them as dates), and when he managed to get himself entangled, he invariably left himself enough time to brood and sink and fret as punishment.

Anticipatory remorse was what he called it. It began

the instant he made an appointment. Somewhere ahead lurked the terrible prospect of a relationship, and with that came the awful certainty of failure, doom, and sorrow. For he was, in his overheated imagination, already at the end, breaking up, before it began. That's how it was with Munk; the ending came first. He skipped the lighthearted, happy, fresh opening part, he ignored the delightful intermezzo and arrived early—his unshakable custom—at the gloomy, terrible finale, with its bitter fights and thundering silences and sullen recriminations.

And so with a grave sigh and an overburdened heart he lifted himself and headed reluctantly toward the door to stop the bell and start with the misery. What was I thinking? he asked himself. Dating a cop!

He hated cops. It was the anarchist subtext of his life. He had been indoctrinated at antiwar college rallies, then during the counterculture New Journalist days of his early career, to believe that cops were ruthless Cossacks, sadistic bullies who came mindlessly charging into the middle of everyone's life, swinging weighted clubs and spilling innocent blood.

How would he get through a long meal with a cop? All the questions. It was always a test, that first meal, or an interrogation. With Maggie, he was ratcheting up the process. She would be expert at the interrogation. And he made a perfect suspect. Sweaty and nervous and wracked with vague, nonspecific guilt. Maybe she would respect his right to remain silent. No, she was a cop!

This is what he thought as he dragged himself across the room. But when he opened the door and saw Maggie standing there—her hair flying in all directions, her lipstick worn away, her suit wrinkled and buttoned wrong, a whole soul in utter disarray—he smiled. He recognized at once a fellow traveler in the slow, awkward lane of the socially dysfunctional.

She was glowering back at him, obviously in her own low state of distress, and that only made him smile harder. Then she smiled back grudgingly and he opened the door wider and she came sideways into the apartment.

"This is a big mistake," she muttered, and his heart sang.

"Some wine?" he asked.

"I don't drink," she said. Then, "Okay, I'll have a snort of scotch. Make it a big one. A double."

"What do you drink when you do drink?"

She gave him a scorching look, which made him blush. Her antics made him nervous; she was switching and twitching in all different directions. He took a glass and started for the kitchen to fetch some ice for her liquor. She stopped him.

"No ice," she said, pointing to her jaw. "Toothache. I really don't drink; it's medicinal."

Quicksilver, he thought. Tricky, but not without appeal. In a blinding instant he knew for certain that there was no key to cracking her secrets. Maggie Van Zandt was a tangle of lightning and sparks, and he would go on forever trying vainly to figure her out. In that same flicker of insight he realized that they were old friends already. He wondered if she knew.

She downed the whiskey quickly and shuddered.

"God!" she said, flopping onto the couch with a casual familiarity that touched him in an aching way that made him dizzy.

"Dentist?" he asked.

She shook her head. "Next week."

"Can you eat?"

"I can always eat," she said. "I got shot once and I had a hamburger in the emergency room while they were stitching up my arm."

"I once bit my tongue," he said.

"Good," she replied.

He laughed.

She got up quickly and looked around. "Where?" she asked.

For a second he was confused, then he pointed to the hallway. "First door on the right."

She came out of the bathroom ten minutes later remarkably transformed, looking fresh and wearing new lipstick, with her jacket buttoned correctly. Her hair was under control and her outfit seemed less creased. The barbed official mask had been replaced by soft and agreeable civilian textures and she was, if not beautiful, attractive and impressive. A change had come over her. Except for the investigating, penetrating eyes. They remained on duty.

The reservation was at a small French restaurant in Midtown on Sixty-second Street, down a few steps from the street, where the maître d'—Robert—fussed over Munk and led them to a choice banquette in the rear where the lighting was dim and the atmosphere had a subtle romantic cast. A waiter called him Mr. Munk and left a platter of toasted country bread with sautéed onions on top and Maggie groaned as she bit into a piece.

"You'd better take care of that," Munk said, indicating her tooth.

She shook her head and said, "Hunger." Then she attacked the menu with enthusiasm. They had salads and soup and broiled fish, and if Maggie's tooth bothered her, she didn't show it. Her appetite was good. A big appetite suited her, he thought, watching her take big portions with pleasure. No dainty, stammering forks for Maggie Van Zandt.

He ordered wine and it medicated her tooth as well as any uncomfortable silences that fell like crumbs between courses. They drank the wine, sitting side by side on the banquette, staring out straight ahead, yet managing to study each other, peripherally, intensely. Their mutual awareness of the moods and expressions of each other was heightened by the indirection. It was one of those moments that swarmed with clashing sensations—electrifying and yet strangely peaceful.

"You're working on a big case?" he asked finally.

"Yes," she said. "Big case. Boy, I wish I had a cigarette."

"I didn't think anyone smoked anymore."

"I don't. And I don't drink," she replied quickly, emphatically.

"I had no idea that toothaches were so unhealthy."

She gave him a crooked smile. He didn't look—he could sense it.

"So," she said at last, "you want to know how I became a policewoman."

"No," he said, pouring tea. "Not particularly. Unless you want to tell me."

"Not particularly."

There was a small murmur of conversation drifting in and out of his ear from the other tables, nothing that you could track or follow. It was an after-dinner sound, an enjoyable, pleasant, musical whisper, just soothing enough to heighten the atmosphere and not loud enough to disturb. It reminded Munk of a discreet piano in another room.

"I'll tell you how I stopped being a journalist," he said brightly, as if he was about to start telling a joke. "I did tell you that I used to be a journalist? Past tense."

He looked over, and she nodded and looked up. She was curious. "You did. What kind of a journalist? I can't picture you running around with a crew, annoying people and sticking microphones in people's faces."

"I was a bad journalist."

"That's a relief."

He nodded. "Yes, terrible journalist. Not electronic, though. Not that bad. I was a pencil pusher. A newspaperman. I was good at it, matter of fact. Not great, but pretty good. My only real trouble was that I hated asking questions."

"I'd say that was probably a career drawback," she said.

He nodded. "Definitely." He shook his head, laughed. "But I couldn't help it. I just felt stupid asking people how they felt about suffering a major catastrophe. I mean, how are they supposed to feel?" He turned in his seat and she was staring down at her wineglass, ignoring the tea. She shook her head. It was eloquent. "What's the point of asking an idiotic question like that?" he went on. "Besides, in my experience people don't really know how they feel. Or else they lie."

She took a breath. "I have experienced that very same phenomenon in my own chosen field," she said.

"Well, yes, maybe, but on the other hand, in your chosen field, people are inclined to tell you the truth. Eventually. You have much a bigger stick," said Munk.

"Not really. In fact, I'd guess that both have the same exact size stick, when you think about it."

"A gun? A pencil and a gun?"

She shook her head. She was still staring at the wine, contemplatively.

"It's not the gun," she said softly. "Although there is that possibility in the back of everyone's mind when they get in that windowless room. But it's not the gun. That's not why people spill their lunch."

"So why do they, as you so elegantly put it, spill their lunch, given the fact that it works against their best interests and they are advised to keep quiet?"

She shrugged again and picked up the wineglass. "It's very simple," she said. "They don't want to disappoint us. They want our approval." She looked him full in the face. There was no smile there, only a bleak and unaffected honesty. "That's really a much bigger stick."

He shook his head, unconvinced. She saw that and spread out her palms. "Look, when you interview someone, it's roughly the same business as when I question someone. You are a figure of some authority. You can't put them in jail, but you can put them on television. . . ."

"Not television."

"Okay. Not television. In the newspaper. Same thing. You can offer them media."

"And you?"

"I am the police. An official. Police have a certain proportion in the eyes of a civilian. We carry weight. In most cases, people want us to like them. Or admire them. Or respect them. Or maybe even just recognize them. A very human thing. You know what I hear when I have them in a windowless room? Not out loud, not spoken, but you know what I hear? People pleading, 'Don't think I'm one of them; I'm not one of those filthy hairbags.' " She sighed. "We trade on that very human desire to be liked."

"You, maybe."

"We all do. Me. You. We pretend that we are taken in, but we have opinions. We think that they're squalid hairbags." She shrugged again and smiled ruefully. "We are professionals and we fake interest. But we're really detached. I'm not saying you—I've never seen you—but I've seen reporters fake orgasms of sympathy."

His voice cracked. "You make it sound pretty ugly."

She shrugged. "Hey, that's how it works. You want a story, I want a perp. Listen, Munk, they have no reason to talk to us. Their best tactic—when it comes to their own interest—is to keep their mouths shut. Yet they talk. They want our approval. . . ."

"Or forgiveness," he offered.

"Or that," she agreed.

"Only we're not in the business of forgiving."

"No?"

"We're detached."

She nodded. "Priests, cops, nurses, and reporters. All detached and saintly. All pulling out fingernails for some greater social good. Actually, we are in the business of betrayal."

Yes, he thought, she was right. Distant priests. Only there was a romantic myth that he could not easily dismiss.

He looked around, not that he thought anyone was listening. "I didn't hate it all that much. In fact, I loved it. Or at least part of it. I loved poking around the edges and finding a real good story. Pulling back the covers and seeing who's doing what—what makes things tick. The best part—I loved telling a good yarn."

"So how come you quit?"

He shook his head. "I guess that I just couldn't get used to that other stuff, to being a pest."

She nodded. She understood. They were old friends.

"No," he said in that deep, rich voice after a moment's pause, "I could tolerate that part. I could stand the humiliation. It was something else."

He took a deeper breath. "There was one particular story," he said. "A kid killed in a school-yard shoot-out. Teenager. Routine stuff, really. The take on it was—no big deal, one less gang-banger. I was working late, just happened to be in the office after polishing off a profile of some ditz actress peddling her latest crap movie. The story came in on deadline and the city editor walked over to my desk. I was free. Fair game. He asked me to help him out. Make a quick call for a reaction. Well, we were on deadline. I didn't think about it. Just a quick call. Get a fast no-comment to stick in the middle of the story and I'd go home."

He could see her bending closer, growing more inter-
ested. The waiter placed a fresh teapot on the table.

Munk smiled a melancholy smile. "So I made the call
and got this chirpy voice on the other end. Island accent. I
should have known from the way she answered—musical. I
went through the standard apology for calling at such a
time and asking for a comment. You know, 'Is this Mrs.
So-and-So and is So-and-So your son?' And the music went
out of the voice on the other end of the phone. She said,
'What for, man? What I want to make a comment for?' So,
not thinking, I dumbly answered, 'Because of the tragic
death of your son.' That's when I heard the phone drop. I
didn't realize that they hadn't been notified yet—the parents. I was breaking it to them. All I heard was the phone
drop."

"You got too close to the flame," she said. "Happens
to cops all the time."

She was harder than he was. She had made the calculations and he was only working it out, still. Munk shrugged
and took one last mouthful of wine. "I quit. Walked
around for three days and then bought a bookstore. It
seemed a nice place to lick my wounded hide. A place to
write a book. Perfect place to write a book, in a garden of
books."

She thought for a moment. "Are you writing a book?"

He paused. "I will," he said.

She looked up and caught the waiter's eye. "You
wanna split this?" she asked Munk.

It was a sensible marriage. That was Jack Fox's editorial
opinion of his twelve-year union with Betsy Fox. She was a
sensible woman from a sensible background who helped
her husband lead a sensible life.

She was forty, but didn't look it. Elegant. That's the way
people described her. She never spoke above a whisper,

and she never smiled too hard. Such exertion made her beauty brittle. Already there were lines around her mouth and her eyes from the strain.

Jack noticed, understood the mechanism, but did not mind. It was enough for him that his life ran on schedule, that the clockwork grouping of social events, vacations, travel were planned and executed with a kind of effortless precision. He accepted with reflected pride the fact that everyone admired Betsy's taste, style, heroic responsibility. She kept up appearances no matter what. Her outfits were always in vogue, yet somehow vaguely formal; she managed to keep her shape slender and her grooming impeccable. She worked at the maintenance of her body with the devotion of a martial arts black belt. She spent an hour every day at rigorous exercise, she starved herself with a half grapefruit for breakfast, a salad with no dressing for lunch, washed down with half a glass of diet cola, and skipped dinner entirely unless she was the perfect hostess at one of her perfectly planned dinner parties. And still, in spite of all of that labor and expense, she struck some chord of undesirable and remote sexlessness among those men of their class who were sensual scorekeepers.

But her best feature of all, as far as Jack Fox was concerned, was that his wife placed no unwanted demands upon him; she recognized that he had a grueling work life, reading and editing and catching in the wind the fleeting whiff of topical culture.

Not that she had any interest in it, except for the fact that it kept Jack busy and therefore gave her the privacy she had come to cherish. She picked her lovers carefully, requiring discretion above all other qualities, and did not inquire if Jack had any important outside interests beyond the obvious: raw power, wealth, and the fawning attention of a worshipful constituency. She assumed that he dallied—her word—with any number of the cow-eyed graduate English majors who came under the sway of his empire year after year.

So after his interview with Maggie and his lawyers, when he came home all pale and trembly to their expensive and sterile pied-à-terre in the luxe Trump Tower, when he went straight for the bar and poured a tall glass of whiskey and drank it down, only blinking his bloodshot eyes in concession to the whopping slug of liquor, then collapsed in a French Provincial chair—almost cracking the wood—without a word, his wife was a little unsettled.

She spoke in her usual husky voice. "Is there something wrong, dear?"

He was staring straight ahead at the fireplace, at the antique andirons they had shipped back from France on their last vacation. A book had gone legal, she guessed. Some author had committed an embarrassing and costly fraud and the publisher had to make good. Or, perhaps, a critical report from the financial wizards indicated that they were in for some belt tightening. Maybe some firings. She dismissed that possibility. That wouldn't upset him, she thought.

"Betsy," he said in a tremulous voice, "I'm afraid I have some bad news."

She didn't like the sound of that. It had the ring of real trouble. And he was not looking in her eyes. He was proud of the fact that he could stare down anyone. His not looking in her eyes sent up a flare.

"No, no," she said. "I'm sorry, Jack, I haven't time now. I've got to be in a decent mood for the fund-raiser. I'm on the committee."

He nodded. Let her go, he thought. Let her have her last moment on the committee. She would feel the earth move under her feet soon enough.

fifteen

Sergeant Sam Rosen took a deep breath after climbing the steep staircase that led to the Manhattan North Homicide Command. The huge room looked like a battlefield.

Thin plumes of smoke from cigarettes rose into a dreary, suffocating cloud that hung over the bay. Teams of detectives—moving like exhausted soldiers drawing on their last reserves of energy—were assembling reports, matching stories, collecting clues: methodically putting the death of Edie Severan into the configuration and patterns of a standard murder investigation.

Sam thought, Always like this after a long day on a sizzling tabloid murder case. A big, complicated investigation was a beast; it had to be wrestled to the ground, tamed, and ultimately broken. So far, the killing of Edie Severan was still a wild, loose thing. The strain of the hunt showed.

The bay spilled over with battlefield debris. In the heat of an urgent case, detectives behaved like combat infantrymen. The little things like housekeeping and grooming and wastage didn't matter. They kept going on cigarettes and coffee and fast food. Paper containers with cold remains and dead butts were strewn like spent shell casings across the surfaces of desks, chairs, cabinets, and even the floor. Half-eaten sandwiches, discolored apple cores, and crushed pizza cartons spilled out of the garbage cans.

And yet, underneath the weary performance, a subdued excitement was detectable. Something was happening. In spite of the nerves and exhaustion, a sense was growing that parts of the puzzle were being matched, corners and crannies were coming into focus, clues were being assembled and labeled—a case, a picture, a version was taking shape.

The squads had fanned out into the city during the day and now, back in the nerve center of the investigation, were double-checking stories with their colleagues, examining the accounts to see if one alibi agreed with another; they were scrutinizing neighborhood maps to see that all of the buildings had been covered, all of the stores and shops canvassed, all of the casual passersby questioned, all of the neighborhood regulars and area denizens—eyes on the street, like mailmen and shop owners—were interviewed and reinterviewed. The same ground had to be covered and re-covered because people forgot, or lied, or needed a trigger to remember the slippery details of daily life. Some of the detective teams were assigned to keep track of the tenants who had been home, others were sent back to catch the ones who had been absent when Edie Severan was killed or when the police came around to ask. It was all systematic, all carefully complete, all part of a proven method.

As they reassembled in Manhattan North headquarters, setting figures and testimony down on paper, Sam was conscious of the sulfuric stench of cigarette smoke. He shook his head. Too many cops smoked. They blamed the high pressure of the job, but he knew that it was something else. A primitive belief in macho magic. Coupled with a pathetic kind of defiance—scorn in the face of danger. Detectives—male and female—in hard, active homicide commands agreed that it was unmanly to quit smoking. (If you couldn't cope with tobacco, how would you perform as a backup in a gun battle?) They had to know unknowable things about each other. And so they illustrated their unproven valor with cigarettes and rough talk and swagger. The show never impressed Sam.

The traffic inside the bay had a certain muscular tone. The detectives pushed aside chairs on their way to a filing cabinet; they smacked open the door to the squalid bathroom, they hit the keys of the typewriters too hard and developed migraines staring at conflicting, copious reports. They snarled into telephones, lit up too many times, and sprayed each other with aggressive, battlefield humor. Limp suit jackets hung over the backs of chairs—a symbol of the sagging spirit. Under the fluorescent light young faces had grim shadows.

Sam Rosen was a veteran of such moments. The members of the command were not ready to quit yet and they weren't very productive, but still they kept at it. Sam slid between desks, making his way to a spot by a window where Matty Bannion and Joey Queen were passing written detective reports back and forth as if comparing baseball cards. They had called his beeper, summoning him to headquarters. A subject. They didn't want to say more, except that he might want to be there when they questioned the subject again. They didn't have to elaborate. He had called Maggie—pulled her away from her dinner—then rushed over to the precinct. It was possible that he had heard from Bannion and Queen the distant sound of a crack in the case.

But as he approached the desk of the two catching detectives, he slowed down. Neither showed the typical nervy itch of cops sitting on a solution. They were in the middle of an intense cop quarrel about something dumb. Married bickering, Sam called it. How to start a barbecue, where to get good pizza, how to tell from a look if someone was a stickup man or a burglar. (Your average burglar is shy, the locker-room wisdom went, on the other hand your stickup man is a social creature and likes to interact with people.) Such arguments were as pointless and routine with cops as breakfast nagging—vocal flailing and pontification about something that seemed trivial on the surface, but hiding in the folds of the chatter a cultural Rosetta stone—dense social opinions, and ancient grudges.

"Sinatra," said Bannion decisively.

Queen shook his head. "Wayne Newton," he said.

They were passing the reports while they argued. "Ask the sarge," said Queen.

"Sinatra," repeated Bannion, looking up, nodding at Sam.

"Hey, Sarge, maybe you could settle this—Who's the greatest entertainer?" asked Queen.

"Very subjective," said Sam, smiling, spinning a chair around and sitting backwards.

"C'mon, Sarge," said Queen. "Don't give me that crap. This is a fair question and calls for a fair answer. There's only one Wayne Newton, am I right?"

"I hope so," replied Sam, nodding emphatically.

"You don't like Wayne Newton?"

Sam shrugged. Bannion smiled triumphantly. "Even he knows. Fig Newton's just a puffy, overgrown kid with oily hair and bad pipes," said the thirty-nine-year-old detective with the thinning crew cut. "Tell him, Rosen, gotta be Sinatra, am I right?"

Sam smiled and shrugged ambiguously. "Sinatra's good. But, well, he's not my cup of tea."

They both looked annoyed, as if they were entitled to a better, more forthright answer than that.

"Okay, who's your cup of tea, who's the best enter-tainer?" asked Bannion, his voice thick with sarcasm. "Jane Fonda?"

"No, no," interjected Queen. "My guess is that the sarge likes Whoopi Goldberg. Am I right? Tribe thing."

Sam shook his head. "No tribe thing. She's not Jewish, you know."

"Goldberg? C'mon, you're full of shit," said Queen. "She ain't Black, either, am I right?"

"Let me put it my way, she's no Wayne Newton."

"Okay, Sarge," prodded Queen. "I'll make it simple: Who do you want to entertain at your thirtieth?"

Sam was amused. He thought for a moment. "You promise you won't laugh."

"Promise," they both agreed, rolling their eyes.

"Well, I'd say Ex–Vice President Dan Quayle would be my first choice," replied Sam, skimming through a pile of reports.

"I told you; he's being an asshole," said Queen. "For-get him. Let's keep this an intelligent conversation. Christ, Quayle!"

"No, I'm really serious," said Sam without looking up. "If I was going out, at my thirty bash, that's who I'd have to entertain at my party. The Honorable Dan Quayle, ex–vice president."

"What the fuck are you talkin' about?" said Bannion, disgusted. "Quayle don't do nothin'! We're talking about entertainers."

Sam looked up and grinned. "Says you, he don't do nothing."

"What about Sammy Davis Junior?" Queen asked mali-ciously. "He was definitely a Jew and at least he does some-thing."

"Not anymore," replied Sam lightly.

"Quayle!" said Bannion. "You know . . ." he sputtered, "you guys just won't leave that poor fuck alone. Anybody can screw up a few speeches and stuff."

"How'd you like to take a spelling bee?" suggested Queen quickly.

"I'm surprised at you," said Sam, addressing them both. "I wasn't joking. I would really love to have him entertain me, as he always does, with his unique insights and interesting opinions. He's a brilliant entertainer. The man just gives and gives and gives. Talk about Wayne Newton! You ever see how Quayle smiles the minute they put a camera on him?"

"Fuck you," said Bannion. "Gives and gives! I got something to give you!"

Sam was not finished. "Dan Quayle has given this country something it has lacked for a long, long time: a good laugh. How many politicians have given us nothing but groans? Nixon. Clinton. But Quayle, my God! He could say almost anything and make you fall down laughing. You never knew what was going to come out of that mouth next. Just that 'losing one's mind,' that quote alone, will live long after the three of us are dinner for worms. Remember when he wanted to learn Latin before he went to Latin America? That's inspired. Steve Martin could not do better than that."

"Fuck you, Sarge, we're trying to talk sense here," said Queen.

"Okay. I was just, you know, trying to help out, calling your attention to one of America's great surreal politicians. . . ."

"Don't listen to that liberal, phony, intellectual shithead; let's talk business," said Bannion, not really annoyed, enjoying, in fact, the demonstration of the spectrum of Sam's politics. He picked up a batch of detective reports that had been laid aside. "Why'ncha read these and we go in and talk to the lady." He handed Sam the reports.

"I think we should wait for the boss," said Sam, taking the reports. "I hit the beeper."

"You hit Bruce Springsteen's beeper?" said Queen.

Bannion smiled. "Not that boss," he said. "He means George Steinbrenner. That boss."

Sam shook his head. "Actually, I was referring to William Marcy Tweed. That Boss."

The room grew smaller and smaller the longer Carol Sinclair sat there. Alice in Wonderland, she thought. The dull, peeling green walls were institutionally grave, and created an overpowering feeling of insignificance and pessimism. No, the room did not grow smaller—she did.

She wondered if that effect was intentional, if interrogation rooms in police precincts were deliberately kept shabby and stark and vaguely menacing to suggest hopelessness and defeat to innocent civilians and suspects. Were the police thinkers that shrewd?

Her first impression of the detectives who brought her in was of clumsy, insensitive men—thick-witted and hamhanded. But she could have been wrong. Gradually, as they drew her out, as she found herself backtracking and twisting out of little traps she never even suspected were being laid, as they revealed a depth of intimate knowledge about her life and work, she perceived a dangerous cunning intelligence operating against her. The detectives stalked and sniffed and circled around her relationship with Edie Severan with unsuspected skill. Did those seemingly oafish and heavy-handed louts actually engage in subtle theatrics and deftly manage props and astutely arrange staging to achieve an entrapment? She was perplexed, and that, too, seemed another level of concern.

Well, she didn't have to talk. It wasn't compulsory. She could go into the Miranda shelter, stick a lawyer between herself and the cops. But that would imply guilt. That was, of course, their great secret mental trick. You could sit on your rights, you could get stiff and technical and call for a lawyer—that was within your rights. But they were also conscious of your fear of declaring war. If you haven't got something to hide, why are you hiding behind a lawyer? It was an insidious and unspoken stick.

Just cooperate, she told herself. Carol Sinclair wanted it done, settled. She wanted to explain, clear the air. After all, she was an articulate woman. She should be able to talk her way clear of this.

No, she was not ready to call for a lawyer. Better to avoid that. You didn't want to get them mad, not those beefy men carrying guns and smoldering with dangerous possibilities.

Suddenly the door opened and an old, bent man came in. He carried a large, black plastic garbage bag. "I thought the room was empty," said Max Gross, the precinct janitor. "They're supposed to leave the OCCUPIED sign on when it's not empty." He smiled at her. It was the first friendly gesture she'd seen since they'd brought her in two hours earlier. He studied her for a moment. "Well, you don't look dangerous." The old man then shuffled over to the desk and turned over the wastebasket into the black garbage bag. It was empty but he did it anyway. Then he put the can back, smiled at Carol Sinclair again—an expression of solidarity, one inmate to another—and left.

When she turned back to the desk she saw a Baby Ruth candy bar. Was this another prop? Her mind raced with possibilities. They could have doped the candy. She was hungry, but could she swallow? Was the old man a young cop in disguise? Were they testing her endurance? She was beginning to crack. She felt it. The little smile from the old man had an exaggerated impact. She was too grateful for the small blessing. It was understandable. After all, she was alone in this barren room without an ally.

Again the door was flung open, and the sound of metal

on metal was like a shriek. This time in marched the two dull detectives who'd first brought her to the precinct. Their faces were blank. Then came a third man, a large, Black detective who nodded at her, as if he was a helpful presence. Psychology again, she thought. A Black detective to break a Black witness. Finally, in came the woman. She almost smiled. Now they've got me surrounded, Sinclair thought.

The men took positions around the table; they were close in, with their chairs blocking her in case she decided to make a break for it, as if that was a realistic prospect. More games, she thought. The woman detective took the seat across the desk. She opened the folder with some official-looking documents inside. She was in charge.

"I'm Detective Lieutenant Margaret Van Zandt," said the woman, looking up from the folder and across the table at Carol Sinclair, whose first impulse was to reach out and shake hands. Then Carol stopped herself. This was not a social occasion. They were not meeting for drinks at the Peninsula Bar. This police lieutenant was not trying to sell her a book. She was trying to nail her for homicide.

The lieutenant was an impressive woman, Carol Sinclair thought. Not physically imposing, but dominating all the same. She looked like someone who picked apart the loose threads of weak stories, someone who didn't tolerate nonsense. She would probably have made a good researcher, guessed Carol Sinclair. There seemed to be a tireless, bulldog air about her. On the other hand, that would make her very dangerous in a quarrel, thought Sinclair.

"You've been read your rights," she said.

The breath stuck in Carol Sinclair's throat. Somehow, when the first two detectives read her her rights, Miranda had seemed airy, unreal, a technical detail. But when the female lieutenant began to repeat the police mantra—

"You have the right to remain silent, you have the right to counsel; if you cannot afford counsel one will be provided. . . ."—somehow that stuttering salvo of conditions had the feel of metal.

"Yes, yes," she said.

"You are an editor," continued Van Zandt. It wasn't a question. They were past questions, Carol realized. The lieutenant had the DD 5 sheets spread out in front of her, looking at the reports right to left, left to right, and then up at Carol Sinclair with those hard, penetrating eyes.

The two original detectives—Bannion and Queen were their names—looked smug and menacing. They were hovering, waiting to pounce, clearly enjoying her discomfort. They knew what she was going through exactly. The Black detective (she heard the lieutenant call him Sam) seemed troubled, sympathetic. Well, he would understand the fear and turmoil experienced by a Black suspect in a sealed room full of White power.

"I edit books," she said.

Van Zandt nodded. She picked up a slip of paper, put it closer to the light. "Children's Division," she said.

"That's right."

Carol Sinclair, at the age of twenty-eight, was an impressive woman herself. The old defenses kicked in. She had faced down executives—the worst were women—to get where she was in life. She could handle bullying cops, she told herself. She would simply explain to this woman in painstaking particulars, using slow, careful sentences, that there was no reason for them to bear down on her, to suspect her. She was innocent.

On the other hand, there was a nagging memory in the back of her mind: a traffic cop who'd stopped her for speeding. He'd stood over her, listening to the long unraveling of her complicated explanation, never interrupting, his face frozen in certainty, his mind long made up, the ticket already written in stone before she was even pulled over. The worst part was, no matter how futile it was—and she'd known that with certainty—she couldn't stop herself from babbling. People were always trying to wiggle free, and cops were always filing away somebody's lame alibi. They listened to so many that they grew a professional crust of disbelief.

Still, as Carol Sinclair faced Van Zandt's frozen expression, she was not ready to throw in the towel. She was innocent!

"The Children's Division, that's on the ninth floor of your office building?" asked the lieutenant.

"Yes, it is."

Van Zandt was slow, methodical, reading the reports, asking questions as if Carol could help her figure out the puzzle. She made it seem as if she was calling on the help of an expert to guide her. There wasn't so much menace as there was charming guile.

"The divisions of your company are pretty tightly compartmentalized," Van Zandt said. "I mean, you wouldn't have any business dealings with someone who worked, say, on the twelfth floor, in the executive wing, would you?"

"Of course I would. There are always meetings and conferences. It *is* one company. We're all part of the same company."

The lieutenant nodded, put down the report. Smiled aggressively. "Ms. Sinclair, I'm not going to play games with you. You know that I know a lot more than I'm letting on."

Carol Sinclair felt the fear crawl up from the floor. Her scalp tingled. She nodded.

"You knew Edie Severan."

At that moment, Carol Sinclair considered stopping the whole thing and demanding her own lawyer. But she didn't. She couldn't. She was committed. She had already answered so many questions that to stop now would only make matters worse. Besides, she was convinced that she could talk her way out the door. In spite of the fact that there was a tape recorder going and she had been properly warned about compromising herself, she thought, as many people under the same circumstances wrongly think, that she was better off talking.

Most of all, she didn't want to make all those people with guns and police badges mad.

"She worked for the same company. I spoke to her. She was new. . . ."

The lieutenant put on a pair of reading glasses and pored through her notes quickly. Then she looked up.

"You were friends," she said flatly, reporting a matter of fact. "You had lunch together, often."

"That's true. . . ."

"Sometimes you went out together for dinner."

"That's true. There's nothing wrong with that. There's a social aspect to any large company."

"So how come you told detectives Bannion and Queen that you only knew her casually?" She nodded at the two bulldog detectives, who were savoring Carol's misery. "You had to be prodded to remember her name. How come?"

Carol Sinclair wanted to clear that up. It was a lie. A little one. She wanted to erase the lie as soon as possible, before it became perjury, or part of the official, written record.

"I was afraid," she said.

She didn't realize that it was already official. She was an established liar, therefore a legitimate target.

Van Zandt slipped the glasses on and off, as if playing with the safety catch of a loaded gun. "There was more than simple friendship there," she said.

"I, uh . . ."

"According to a report from an eyewitness, you were seen kissing Edie Severan. There's another report, of a note of an intimate nature. Which we found in her apartment."

Carol Sinclair was, by now, turning to the other detectives, flushed with fear. "We were friends," she said, feebly looking for support. The Black detective smiled, but it held out no offer of help. It was a sad smile.

"That kiss. It was not a girl-to-girl peck." The lieutenant leaned across the desk as if she was confiding something. She said, "It was a passionate, mouth-to-mouth soul kiss. Full tongues." She backed away and looked down at the report. "In the stairwell of the library," Van Zandt continued. "You were seen."

"I'm a married woman. . . ."

"This was"—Lieutenant Van Zandt had her glasses back on; she was reading from the report—"on the afternoon of the murder." She took off the glasses and stared hard at Carol Sinclair, demanding an explanation.

"It wasn't a big thing," insisted Carol Sinclair, her voice breaking.

The room was dense with the hush.

"Did your husband agree? Did he think it wasn't such a big thing?"

"My husband?"

Van Zandt looked down again. "James Sinclair," she said. "Your husband."

"He didn't know about it."

The lieutenant smiled. "You sure?"

Carol felt the sinking, woozy cloud of her mistake. She had been wrong. She couldn't talk her way out of it. She was enmeshed in her lies. She should have kept her mouth shut. But it was too late. She kept talking.

"I didn't kill her," she said in a voice that split apart. "I loved her."

* * *

Outside of the sealed room Maggie asked, "Where's the husband?"

"Upstairs," replied Sam. "In a holding room."

"What's his story?"

Bannion flipped over the pages on a clipboard. "Thirty-nine years old, veteran of the Gulf War, runs a computer consulting service." Then the detective smiled. "And, oh yeah, he's got a record. Man cut somebody. With a knife."

"Lemme see," said Sam, taking the clipboard and reading the rap sheet. "That was ten years ago," he said. "He was being robbed. The guy was defending himself."

"Yeah, but he still used a knife and he still cut somebody, and we got a murder victim who was cut with a knife. You could make an argument that he was defending his marriage when he stabbed Edie Severan."

Maggie shook her head. "Cut it out," she said. "This is way too soon to start this shit. Let's talk to the man and let's get her on record, as far as she will go."

"You think?" asked Sam when they were walking for coffee.

Maggie shook her head and growled, "God, I'd hate to let the Fox go free. What's the story with the postmortem?"

"Not in yet."

Then she had another thought. "Get me another inventory of the Severan apartment," she said. "Everything. Sheets. Towels. And count the silverware. I want a count on the silverware."

sixteen

At seven-thirty on Friday evening, Harry Graham and Eric Miller were beginning to shut down the clinic for the long July Fourth holiday weekend. There was one more client left, and after that they would be free for three days.

They were both there because the policy of the lab was always to have at least two people stay late. One alone was not considered safe, not from the swarm of addicts and desperados who systematically stripped New York City to the bone like piranha. There were no drugs on the premises, but the name—*Gotham Medical Lab*—was enough to suggest a target. Besides, crime was no longer reasonable.

Nothing was reasonable. Especially not in New York City after dark.

Crime had gone crazy. Even empty buildings were judged ripe for vandals. They ripped out plumbing and wiring and sold them for pennies. A furnished office with medical equipment was in the center of the bull's-eye. There were computers and televisions, stereos, and even the laundry and the carpets, not to mention the great stock of bandages, ointment, medicines, and syringes.

Possessions were replaceable. But lately the world was learning that there was something far more vulnerable and irretrievable at risk: a sense of security. After cleaning out the registers and the pockets and the shelves, after snatching the handbags and wallets and watches, after taking all of the tangible items that there were to take, modern criminals took revenge. They spilled lives wildly, carelessly, gleefully.

There was no protection against this furious tide of incidental cruelty. Not even meek submission fended off the onslaught. Offering no resistance offered no protection, nor did the fear of getting caught. The bandits were reckless beyond all sanity. They staged brazen carjackings in full daylight, spraying bullets promiscuously, leaving corpses like candy wrappers in the street. Citizens were not just mugged, they were mauled and left for dead. Sometimes they weren't even robbed, just killed.

The collapse of tolerable public behavior was blamed on the outbreak of crack or the abuse of liquor or the persistence of racism or the aftermath of childhood neglect; there was a geometrically exploding number of excuses on the increasingly absurd laundry list of unhealed social wounds to explain the heartless conduct. The villains, feeling molested and battered by fate, declared themselves immune from accountability, entitled to retaliate and kill at random.

But it was not burglars and vandals and sociopaths who made the hairs on Harry's neck bristle that Friday evening. It was a strange, unexpected, and sinister stillness inside the clinic. Not that the clinic was ever noisy. On the contrary, it was usually subdued, with people speaking in polite whispers, as if in some lesser state of consolation. No, this was a thicker, weightier hush, and Harry felt an uneasy danger in it. Something was going on inside that silence. He could sense it. A premonition of something bad. But maybe it was just a phantom sensation, maybe it was nothing, and he tried to shake it off.

The client in Treatment Room One was waiting for a series of blood tests. He was sitting tensed up in the chair that looked like a high school desk with the wraparound armrest; his chest was heaving and in spite of the excessive air conditioning a line of sweat was visible on his brow.

Harry felt sorry for the man. There was always that emotional divide: the technicians walked through the day professionally detached, in a state of remote calm, while the clients pulsed and blinked and fretted with solitary alarm. Harry saw that the client was just another middle-aged man, a little overweight, who had hung his suit jacket carefully on the hook on the door. The sleeve of his monogrammed shirt was rolled up and a Velcro band was tied around the bicep; his right fist was clenched to pump up the vein and his left fist was clenched in fellowship with the right. He was pale with the effort to appear brave.

The tests were being carried out by Eric Miller, who was fussing in the drawer, moving around between the tubes and his own locker, getting on a fresh pair of rubber gloves, labeling the vials, laying out a needle. But in a blurry instant, Harry saw something in Eric's hand movements that was furtive. Not something discreet to spare the client's feelings, but a quick flash of hand, as if to conceal something forbidden. He noticed it when Eric was standing near his private locker. Then Eric looked up and saw Harry watching him and he moved, putting his body between the open locker and the door, concealing whatever it was that he was doing.

Harry was puzzled, but he walked away. He went into the vacant administrative office to finish up a pile of last-minute paperwork. He didn't like to leave behind unfinished tasks. Or unanswered questions. The administrative office, unlike the crisp, clean treatment rooms, was a quiet, private sanctuary with a plush carpet and wooden panels and a bottle of liquor hidden behind a medical text. Harry sat at the desk, unable to focus on the insurance forms. He was convinced that Eric was doing something very wrong. Why else would he take such pains to hide it?

Then Harry heard the outside door slam—the departure of the client. It hadn't taken long for Eric to complete the procedure and for the client to make his escape. Then he heard Eric yell through the empty office that he was going to wash up, time to quit.

"Okay," Harry called back. "Be through in here in a minute."

Listening like a blind man to sounds outside the door, Harry was jolted into action. He had to know what Eric had been doing in that treatment room. He heard the bathroom door close. He waited until he heard the water running. Then he opened the top drawer of the administrator's desk and reached in the back where he knew he would find the master key to the lockers. He pulled out the box with the key in it, opened it, and took the key in his hand. It burned. He was aware at each stage that he was trespassing on very dangerous ground.

Taking a deep breath, Harry got up and started toward Treatment Room One. As he moved through the darkened office, he kept looking around, as if something might leap out at him from the shadows. The whole office was dim, with only the last rays of sunlight slipping through the blinds, although bright lamps still burned in two of the treatment rooms. The large waiting room was silent. He felt the floor move and heard the boards creak as he made his way across the waiting room toward Treatment Room One.

Toward the light he moved, slowly. When he stepped into the glare of the treatment room's lamps and brilliant overhead track lights, it felt as if he'd been caught in a searchlight. Harry was perspiring and he kept looking around; his heart thumped inside his chest and his hand fumbled when he reached out, trying to insert the master key into Eric's locker.

He'd left himself an escape route—the door to his own adjoining office was open. If he was caught, he would say that he got confused, he thought it was his own room and the locker was open. It was a weak excuse, but it was an excuse.

Breaking into Eric's locker! This could end badly, he thought. He might be fired. That was the least of it. Most of all, he was physically afraid of Eric. There was something sinister and unpredictable about him. It was his eyes—a flat, dead expression.

Harry didn't know what he expected to find inside the locker. He only knew he had to see. Still, it was Eric's locker, a private place, and he felt the shameful jolt of breaking a powerful taboo. Poking his nose into someone else's business was completely out of character; Harry was someone who respected the privacy of his fellow workers. Nevertheless, he was determined.

In the back of his mind was the woman—the professor. She was desperate to find Eric. It had to be Eric. He'd thought so at the time, although he hadn't said anything.

If he thought about it, Harry couldn't name a reason for his boldness, for plunging ahead like a madman, risking his job, his life. It wasn't just that Eric was strange, or even the fact that Harry disliked him so much. It wasn't even the stealthy movement at the locker, although that was the triggering event. It was an inexplicable prod, a certain knowledge that there was something to be found out. There was also a whole range of attitudes and behavior that convinced Harry that Eric had a sinister secret.

Then Harry thought, Well, I could be wrong; maybe it

was the homophobic tendencies I detected. He shook that off. It didn't matter. He had to know.

The locker door made a screeching sound when he finally got the key turned and pulled the handle. It wasn't very loud, but any noise struck fear in Harry now. His breathing was shallow but, he thought, audible. At first he saw nothing unusual. An extra pair of shoes, socks, a shirt. A spare lab coat hung next to a sport jacket. There was a collapsible umbrella on the bottom, along with a pair of rubbers, next to a copy of *Penthouse*.

He stared for a moment, convinced that he was missing something, that the explanation was staring him in the face and he was too panicked or too dumb to notice. Then he started to close the locker door. But he paused, opened it up again, and looked harder. It had to be there. He would not get another chance.

He looked near the top. There was a shelf under which hung Eric's street clothes. It was a small shelf, meant only for a wallet and some modest personal items. There were a few pens, some stamps, Eric's wallet, a splatter of change and some subway tokens, a few bank-deposit receipts—nothing unusual, nothing abnormal. It was at eye level and Harry lifted himself for a better perspective and squinted in. Toward the back of the shelf, he saw it.

A needle. It was not fresh. The protective cap was half off. It had been used. Why would anyone put a used needle back in a locker? He didn't touch it, just stood leaning forward on his toes, trying to see if there was any trace of narcotics in the barrel of the needle. There were a few drops of blood, but nothing else, no suspicious viscous fluid that he could detect.

Still, Eric was a drug addict! Who else left bloody needles lying around a personal locker? It was peculiarly satisfying, this discovery. In a bizarre way, it even made Eric touchingly pitiable. There was something appropriately sinful about finding that Eric was a junkie; it fell within the bounds of common misbehavior. Lots of people were junkies these days. It didn't take a monster to be an addict. Just a weakness of character. It even made Eric human.

Having thus felt that reassurance, Harry knew it wasn't true. Eric Miller was not a dope fiend. First of all, why would he be fumbling around in his own locker with a bloody needle when a client was in the room? Second, if Eric was a junkie, he didn't need to reuse old needles. He had access to the supply closet and its hundreds of fresh needles. No one would question a few missing.

Harry stood there, frozen. He tried to picture Eric as a junkie. He couldn't. There were no drugs on the shelf, no signs of an active drug addiction in his behavior. No junkie cunning. No money problems. No roller-coaster moods. No cryptic absences. No wavering job performance. But most persuasive of all, Eric just didn't fit the psychological profile of an addict. He was a control freak, not a chemical abuser. He was a right-wing soldier, not a slave to Morpheus.

He could recall times when Eric had exhibited a brittle contempt for the addicts who came to the clinic. It would be merciful, Eric had once said in an unguarded moment, if we gave them all a dose of curare. Just enough to end their misery with one lethal surprise.

At the time, even though Harry had told himself that his co-worker was kidding, he had shivered. But now he didn't think Eric was kidding.

Still, he thought as he stood in front of the open locker, there was that possibility. Eric could be a junkie. Anything was possible.

Carefully, slowly, Harry shut the locker, exaggerating in his mind the sound made by the scraping of the door. He looked around, then locked the door and left the room. He could still hear the water running in the bathroom.

He felt safe, but confused. He still didn't know what to make of that bloody needle in Eric's locker.

Then he began to concentrate on the woman, the professor, who had come searching for someone, someone who fit Eric's description. That had been bothering him all day. He went into his own office and sat behind his desk. She had had a definite purpose. There was something important—something malignant—behind her pursuit. His hands were trembling.

Suddenly, without much more thought, he decided to settle it. It would be easy enough to do. Just ask her. In spite of her transparent duplicity about looking for a student, Harry thought that she seemed somehow dependable. There was something sturdy in her manner and her eyes. He decided to confront her. At least he wasn't afraid of her. But he didn't want to expose himself too openly. He wanted to find out why she was looking for Eric before turning over his co-worker. Above all, he didn't want to arouse Eric's anger.

What was her name? Then he remembered that she'd left behind a card with her home phone number. It was still in his wallet. PROFESSOR LAUREN DRAKE, CITY UNIVERSITY OF NEW YORK. The home number was written in pencil under the name. He didn't hesitate. He made the call. The water still ran; Eric was still washing up, so he had time.

"Hello," said the starched voice on the other end of the phone. Harry didn't recognize it and almost hung up.

"Hello," said Harry, trying to keep his voice down. "Is this Professor Drake?"

There was a pause. "Yes," she replied hesitantly. "This is Professor Drake."

"This is Harry Graham at the *Gotham Medical Laboratory*. I'm the clinical technician you spoke to today."

Again, that hesitation. "You were here earlier looking for someone," he pressed. "One of your students."

The voice on the other end of the phone lifted in relief. She grasped the situation. "Yes, yes, of course," she said. "I forgot. Your voice was so low. I couldn't hear you. I'm sorry, I was working on something. No, actually, I was sitting here brooding about my problem."

Harry faltered. He was not sure that he was doing the right thing. Should he speak to Eric first? Was his first obligation to his colleague? No, he decided, he would not get a straight answer, and he was afraid of what he might provoke. Better to find out exactly what was at stake. There was no breach of loyalty in checking it out first. Eric would have his chance when Harry knew more about what was going on.

"I'd like to talk to you," he said.

"Fine," she replied, brightening more. "Great. Where? When?"

He had already decided. "There's a coffee shop at York and Eighty-sixth Street. Meet me there in an hour."

He turned and reached up to the wall and took down the group picture of the staff—Eric's face was there, blurry but identifiable—and put it into his case.

"Uh," she paused. "Make it an hour and a half," she said. "Might take some time to get dressed and across town."

"Okay," he said, looking at his wristwatch. "We'll make it about nine."

When he hung up he noticed that the light on the five-line telephone console stayed on for a second. Maybe not even that long. Just a flicker, just long enough to weaken his knees. Someone had been listening in.

After he hung up the extension in Treatment Room One, Eric ran on tiptoes back into the bathroom, turned up the water full blast, then sat on the lip of the tub and surrendered to a wave of self-pity. He wept. Not open, sharp sobs, but a broken spill of emotion. He had been betrayed. Again. The two of them were on the phone together (he'd recognized her voice instantly), plotting against him.

The sadness turned to anger.

As if he hadn't suffered enough! As if he had not been the victim of exactly that faction—miserable fucking faggots!—who had murdered him and were now persecuting him. Not bad enough to inflict a lethal viral infection, not bad enough to be condemned to die by ass-fucking scum and dope fiends who didn't give a shit about anyone or anything except their next fix, now he had to endure treachery!

They had no right! No fucking right! First they had killed him and now they tormented him! Well, they wouldn't get away with it.

Not Harry, not that cunt teacher! And to think, he'd even tried to be nice to her. He'd tried to warn her. Hadn't he called and delivered a clear warning that she could be at risk? He didn't have to do it. He could have let her just find out during a routine checkup.

Now she was trying to track him down. For what? To punish him, to attack him, to gloat?

He bit his thumb. "She probably wasn't even infected," he muttered. What were the odds? A million to one. They had only fucked once. Once! He was the one who was going to die!

He shouldn't have called. But no, now that he thought of it, better to have called. Better to plant a little dagger of fear in her cunt heart. He could see that now that she was stalking him! At least he had that satisfaction. He had heard that sweet intake of air when he told her. He heard the silent shriek when he uttered the word *AIDS*. The sucked-in breath was the intake of death. Good! He was glad that he had told her.

Oh, how he wished he could guarantee that she had been infected. "Don't you read the fucking ads," he muttered aloud. "That's good. Fucking ads. Don't you know about safe sex, bitch cunt fuck!"

Now they were meeting, plotting, arranging his destruction, as if he wasn't doomed already. Well, he wasn't going to be the only one to die. He had seen to that already with the contaminated needle.

It had taken time to sink in, that he was going to die. Ever since he'd found out that he tested positive he had been living in some twilight of denial and anger. Couldn't be true, he told himself. He felt too good. Just a little cold.

But now he saw with a terrible clarity that there was no way out. It was not a bad dream, reality was not negotiable. It was inexorable. And he believed it. He was doomed. And deranged. He saw that, too. Whatever was making him do what he was doing, it was out of his hands. If he acted crazy, it was on behalf of some higher, more potent force. The understanding made him, somehow, calm. And dangerous.

There were things that he could do. He could act. Not by taking AZT or ddI, or any of the other poisons that only postponed the inevitable and made the drug companies rich. He could take whatever life was left to him and use it. Do something worthwhile. Teach the real bastards, the ones who went around as if life would go on forever, the ones who spread the deadly curse in the first place. Like Harry. Like gay Harry.

No, it was a real advantage, when he thought about it. He had nothing to lose. He could act with impunity. He wasn't going to die gasping for air in a high hospital bed with tubes coming out of his withered, broken veins. He was going to be there at the end, with his full faculties, a righteous avenger. Maybe he couldn't defeat the virus, but he could tear up the night. All he had to do was to get some breathing room. He laughed, thinking how little real breathing room he had left.

And it pleased him to think that he was not going to die alone.

He wanted to laugh and cry.

"You okay?" called Harry through the bathroom door.

"Fine," replied Eric, pulling himself together, reaching for the instrument that he kept now in the pocket of his lab coat. "I'll be right with you."

seventeen

There was a single word written on the page for Thursday, June 24, in Cissy's diary:

AIDS ?

Maggie stared hard at the bleak journal entry, as if she was trying to break a tricky code. She studied the message for a deeper, unexpressed meaning; she was convinced that she was missing a final, unambiguous clue to her friend's death.

The handwriting was steady and the letters were clear, although they were larger than the letters on the other pages. Well, she thought, the hideous and brutal implications gave them added dimension. After the word there was a space and then the puzzling question mark:

AIDS ?

Did the note question the diagnosis, or merely admit the possibility of AIDS? Did it challenge fate? Was it a gesture, the raising of arms to heaven in ferocious protest? Maybe it was a simple dispute, a summons to whatever God kept track of human paradox and pain to defend one more insult.

AIDS ?

A word that struck the heart like ice.

Maggie had an interesting afterthought: Could a word kill?

Technically, it was not even a word. It was an acronym. Acquired Immune Deficiency Syndrome. Maggie had to recite it out, to see if she remembered what the letters stood for, to make certain that she got it right; for some reason it was important that she not be ignorant on the subject. Four letters grouped together that packed an unalterable wallop.

Obviously, concluded Maggie as she moved the diary back and forth, trying to find the correct focus, Cissy did not believe the HIV-positive finding. Maggie deduced that from the fact that her friend had written it down, committed it to her diary, made it official. If Cissy believed it, she would have been too stunned or too ashamed to make any notation. Anyone who accepted it, or put any credence at all in it, would have been too wobbly from the news of her own destruction to register the immense seismic shock in an ordinary log.

No, what had probably happened, as Maggie reconstructed it in her professional analysis, was that Cissy had received the lab report, been appropriately staggered, but didn't believe it. Well, how could she? It wasn't possible. Cissy was Miss Careful, Miss Perpetual Optimism, Miss Sunny Spin. Cissy would never give in to dark fatalism and simply embrace the worst possible tidings. In her case, denial of the negative side of life was not an evasive tactic, it was an ingrained way of life.

Still, Maggie shivered, trying to imagine the moment when her friend took the telephone call from the lab— what was it? *Gotham Medical Lab.* She would make her own call, find out some more details. She needed some ground to walk on. Something more substantial than the invented remembrance of her own friend's terror. Cissy would have taken the news with a tinny, hollow laugh, she would have tried to sound casual as she arranged for another test. Even Cissy wasn't immune from that dread. The results, she would have said in her best haughty, dismissive tone, were obviously mistaken. It had to be a blunder in the lab. We will have to do the test again. That would have been Cissy's public reaction.

She turned a page and saw that the entry for Friday, June 25, said *Gotham Lab, 9*. There was that name again. That would be the retest.

Maggie's own reaction to the results would have been different. She would have believed it. No question. Not that she had any risky history or remote cause for such a belief; believing the worst was just her nature, it was the moving part of her own chronic pessimism. Poor Cissy.

On the other hand, Maggie didn't think that her friend had been overly worried—not to the point of paralysis—at least not judging by the steely diary entry. The hand that made that solitary notation didn't look as if it had been struck by something fatal. It was not the journal entry of someone with five days to live.

But to be told you had AIDS! Maggie couldn't picture what her friend had gone through. A whiff of perdition. It couldn't help but launch aching, mortal fevers. It would summon forth an instant memory speed-search of careless moments, reckless behavior, forgotten liaisons. Friends, acquaintances would all be reevaluated (as Cissy, when the news broke, would be reevaluated by everyone who knew her); everyone would be weighed on a different scale. Every contact, every encounter would be revisited with a somber and suspicious new perspective. No one was absolved. Blame and guilt and suspicion, all incubating like the virus itself.

For an instant Maggie got sidetracked, speculating

about who could deliver such news. How, exactly, would you make that particular phone call? Maggie had no idea. It certainly could not be done glibly. This was nothing to be dealt with by someone—like herself—with rough hands. It was a subject requiring the most exquisite, transcendent sensitivity. Mere doctors or priests—people whose business was to console the conventionally dying—were not qualified. This call required a higher order of spiritual enlightenment; it called for understanding surpassing all understanding. Someone who embodied a saintly forgiveness.

And yet someone had to deliver the news without inflicting more pain. She couldn't imagine anyone who could perform that little trick.

The clumsy efforts of those tactfully unfit were all too evident in the appeals to common sense splashed on billboards and subway posters, as if AIDS was something that could be defeated by a catchy slogan. The mere notion that the best shock troops society could muster against AIDS were public relations specialists only made Maggie furious.

No one knew how to deal with it. Even genuine public sympathy had come to be expressed in ways that were intolerably artificial and unbearably sentimental. Maggie gagged on one particular public television story of a young man, a thirty-five-year-old public schoolteacher, who was abruptly afflicted with AIDS. It was intended to be a touching, heartbreaking, and moving account of the man's ordeal. It turned out to be a mushy collection of clichéd lies about how getting AIDS was really a good thing since it made this poor sap suddenly smell the flowers.

Gazing ardently into the camera, the teacher said that after he found out that he had AIDS, his life actually took an upbeat turn. AIDS—and he used these very words—had been his "wake-up call."

"This is just the beginning," he said with the same kind of smile Maggie had seen displayed by undertakers. From an aesthetic point of view, he was an appealing young man; he didn't look sick. Except when the camera caught something in the eyes—a burst of dumb fear.

Such tinny, false positivism could be excused from the dumb bastard with low T-cell counts, Maggie thought, but it was unforgivable for the station to broadcast such goo. No one recovered from AIDS. No one got better. There was no hope. Life didn't begin when your HIV test came back positive. The presence of HIV signaled the end. This was too serious a business to be coated with thick, starry-eyed, new-age, touchy-feely mega-bullshit.

Staring at the straight lines of the large letters in her dead friend's diary, Maggie was on the edge of tears. Cissy would have run through all the known bolstering sentiments, given herself a pep talk; then she would have peered blindly at the notepad (Cissy always took notes on the phone). It would have said *HIV Positive.*

Like almost everyone else, Maggie believed that apart from the victims of bad transfusions and innocent infections from a spouse, there was some behavioral, moral transgression attached to people who got AIDS. She could not absolve people who stuck contaminated needles in their arms. She could not bring herself to exonerate reckless gays who took wild sexual risks. In spite of all of her up-to-date, enlightened, and broad-minded opinions about *alternative* lifestyles, blame was attached to AIDS.

Maggie was, alas, still a prisoner of her blue-collar, bluestocking upbringing. Promiscuity still violated those ancient codes of morality with which she had been raised. And drug abuse was not within her range of social norms. No, she could not hide the fact that she held the victims of AIDS accountable. Cissy was not excluded. And Cissy would have known that, too.

This was hard for Maggie to swallow. To be doomed with AIDS and silenced by shame—it was a ghastly modern curse! In the end, was Cissy all alone, without a soul on earth left to confide in?

"It's Scott," said Sam.

She looked up, nodded, then heaved the diary into the drawer and locked her desk. "Okay," she said gravely.

The chief of detectives came through the door, his face flushed with excitement. He was trailed by an aide. Outside the office Bannion and Queen leaned against a wall and sipped coffee, watching every move through the window like vultures.

"Okay, what've we got?" asked Chief Scott, placing himself on the lip of the chair across the desk from Maggie.

"We got a maybe," Maggie said. "A thin maybe."

Chief Scott, still in a tuxedo, dragged away from a preholiday campaign party, looked stunned. He glanced at his aide. The sergeant shrugged. "What are you talking about? This was supposed to be a likely. I thought this was a likely?"

He turned and looked at the aide full in the face, demanding an answer. The aide shrugged.

"No," said Maggie. "We got a maybe."

The chief's face tensed and he was silent for a long moment. "I told the mayor," he said. "Sergeant Rosen said you had a suspect."

"I told you we were questioning someone," said Sad Sam to Sergeant Gil Player, Scott's aide. He avoided speaking directly to Chief Barnes. "I don't believe that I put any stronger emphasis on it than that."

"You told me you were questioning someone," began Sergeant Player. "Naturally, I took that to mean—"

Chief Scott cut him off, waving a hand at his aide and

at Sam. "Everybody out," he said. "I have to talk to the lieutenant alone."

The chief was quiet for a moment after the door closed. Maggie slumped down in her chair. Finally he spanked the desk. "You shouldn't have let me tell the mayor we had a suspect."

"I didn't," replied Maggie evenly, keeping her temper. "I was told to keep you informed, I was keeping you informed."

She was right. He knew that she was right. He was just frustrated and angry. He pulled at the tight collar. His face was a patchwork of blushes and pale blotches.

"He told me a suspect," said the chief, motioning over his shoulder. He smiled sheepishly. He meant his aide. He rolled his eyes. "So I told the mayor." He ran a hand carefully across the safe parts of his scalp, where the remaining hair wouldn't be disturbed.

"You know, we could have one," replied Maggie. "Maybe."

He squinted at her. "I never know when you're being insubordinate," he said.

"I have that trouble, myself," she said almost apologetically.

He got up, turned, walked to the inside window that looked out on the Manhattan North command bay, chasing Bannion and Queen and Sam and his aide to a corner. "Trouble is, I told the mayor we have a suspect," he said sorrowfully.

"Sorry, Chief," said Maggie, trying to be consoling.

"We need a break in this case," said Chief Scott, turning away from the window, staring at his hands.

"I am doing my best," said Maggie. "But, really, we only have a four-day-old case. It's not like we hit a brick wall."

He shook his head; she didn't understand. He was

under pressure. "Well, lemme ask you, what're the chances of this hardening into cement?" he asked.

"That's a definite maybe, Chief."

He weighed whether she annoyed him enough to break her out of this job against the clear fact of her competence. Finally, he decided that he was in midstream and not about to change this irritating horse. "Gimme a fill," he said.

Nodding, she picked up the notes and told him about Associate Editor Carol Sinclair and Sinclair's complicated relationship to the murdered woman. The chief sat up straight in his chair.

"You mean she was a dyke?"

She shook her head.

"Well, what about this editor? She could have killed."

Maggie shook her head.

"Well, she's a fucking lesbian, isn't she? She's married, right? She could have killed her to protect her marriage."

Maggie took a breath. "I don't think so, Chief. We got her coming home at the time of the murder."

"Who makes her?"

"Doorman. Pizza guy."

"What about the husband?"

She shook her head. "He's our thin maybe. Nobody makes him," she said. "Not even the wife. Doorman has him comin' in late."

"Opportunity. Motive. So he sounds promising."

She nodded. Then shook her head in her infuriatingly ambiguous fashion. "There's the matter of the blood...."

"What about the blood?"

"Not enough." she said.

"What the hell does that mean?"

"It means that she didn't emit enough blood from that wound to convince me that she was killed by having her throat slashed."

"What does the medical examiner say?"

She shrugged. "Could go either way. Says she could have died from the knife wound, it's possible. Sometimes the heart quits pumping. But he agrees that there are indications of something else. Anyway, he wants more tests."

Scott waved away the reservation. "Well," he said, clapping his hands together and brightening, "I think that's more than a thin maybe, Lieutenant. I'll go with my instinct on that."

"It's early, Chief. We haven't applied any real pressure yet."

Chief Scott sat back. He clasped his hands together and put his two index fingers over his mouth. "You don't realize how important it is that we catch a break. This is a holiday weekend," he said.

"Groundhog Day," she said.

He ignored her. "July Fourth is a very big campaign event," he continued. "The mayor is going to be hitting all the beach clubs and cabanas. Some of those clubs have people who are going to say that the city is a rat hole and nobody's safe from crime. They're going to be thinking of that girl killed in her bedroom. It would be nice if the headlines on the *Post* and the *Daily News* said that he just caught the killer."

She sighed and got up. "Why don't you watch from the goldfish bowl while we put matchsticks under his fingernails?"

Not a care in the world, thought Maggie, taking in the relaxed manner of James Sinclair, who was sitting sideways on the chair in the interview room. The man had a bad attitude, she thought; his expression was a mixture of contempt and bravado.

Actually, she thought that he looked much younger than his thirty-nine years. He had a smooth, clear, handsome face with a thin mustache, and he was one of those naturally graceful men who wear clothes well. The suit jacket fell faithfully along the contours of his body and his shirt was unwilted after hours in the sweaty station house. He looked elegant. The only thing missing was an adoring woman hanging from his arm.

Had to be six two or six three, judging by the size of the coil he had wrapped himself into. Broad shoulders. Came on to her like she was a lady in a bar—flashing rings and bullshit. Big, fearful men were volcanos, she knew. Couldn't picture him with Carol, a woman of some polish, but then she had been educated by Sam to know that Black women of accomplishment had a smaller talent pool than White women. They often married down.

"I am Lieutenant Van Zandt," announced Maggie, taking the command chair behind the desk. Bannion and Queen flanked Sinclair and Sam stood behind Maggie. Sinclair smoked and the ashes fell into the palm of his cupped hand. He studied her with sulfuric intensity. She turned away.

The file in front of her showed that Sinclair had a decent army record, a good credit history, and that one arrest ten years earlier when someone had tried to rob him. The charges had been dropped because Sinclair was so clearly in the right, and the only one injured—and not very seriously, with only a minor wound to the hand (a hand that held a weapon of its own)—was the would-be thief. After some rocky financial episodes Sinclair's computer consulting service was flourishing, attested to by the man's expensive linen and imported shoes and gold watch.

Flipping through the detective reports, Maggie saw that Sinclair was not at home on the evening of the murder, that he had had a loud argument with his wife the evening before, and that there was a long history, according to neighbors and friends, of a very stormy relationship. He often stayed away for days at a time.

She looked up and smiled and Sinclair smiled back. No one else in the room smiled. Maggie didn't think that Chief Scott or Sergeant Player, hidden behind the one-way mirror, were smiling either.

"You've had your rights read to you?" she asked.

He nodded and blew a smoke ring at the ceiling. "Didn't do it," he said disarmingly.

"Didn't accuse you," replied Maggie.

"So what are we talking about, you see what I'm sayin'?"

"Well, let's see where this takes us. Okay?"

"Takes us around the block," he chimed back musically.

The glide was all surface, she thought. Maybe nerves, maybe attitude. She couldn't tell yet.

"So, where were you Monday night?" she asked.

He lit another cigarette off the burning tip of the last. "Working," he said, exhaling a small cloud of smoke.

"You were working?"

"That's right, I was working. I run a computer consulting service. Takes a lot of hard work. Black man has to work harder. Be available. Somebody can't figure out a program, I gotta be there, boot it up, if you see what I'm sayin'."

"Uh-huh."

"You know what it's like."

"What makes you say that?"

"Well," he said, drawing it out, spreading his hands, "a lady cop." He smiled. "Got to be a lot of folks want you to look bad. Lot of brother officers, so to speak, who don't like the idea of a lady cop giving them orders."

She didn't like him putting her on, trying to dazzle her with all that phony street shit. Then she decided that he was afraid. That was what was behind the show. Maybe he was afraid of getting busted. At first she had missed it. He was a big man, and the automatic tendency was to ascribe boldness and courage to a big man. But not Sinclair. He had the peculiar, covered-up fear of a big man.

"Was there someone who saw you at your office?"

He shook his head.

She looked up from her notes. He turned and leaned closer. "In my business, I hafta be out picking up work. Convincing Black businessmen to use me—another Black man," he said. "That's not easy. Requires some capital. Gotta have an office and cards and a fox secretary. We don't always have a lot of capital. So I hustle. Hang out. You know."

He turned away again.

"Where were you?" she asked with a brittle firmness. She didn't want to leave him too much wiggle room. She wanted to lay down the rules.

He couldn't remember. He had had too many drinks. He had talked to too many potential clients, putting out his line of shit. Black man in business is always drowning, he said.

"Where do you usually go on a Monday night?"

"Fat Jack's," he said. "Place up on One thirty-eighth Street, see what I'm sayin'? That's probably where I was."

"Did you know that your wife was friendly with another woman?"

He laughed. "I know that she is friendly like I am friendly with a lot of folks who don't give a shit about her one way or another, you see what I'm sayin'?"

"You had a fight with her." It was not a question.

"I always had a fight with her. We fight like cats and dogs."

She believed him.

eighteen

A lightbulb went on over his head. Eric Miller had a bright idea. There were four oversized translucent 150-watt lightbulbs over the bathroom mirror in the blood clinic. Gazing at them from his perch on the tub, he knew they would do the trick. A lightbulb would deliver Harry to him.

Now that he was under emotional control, he coolly refined his homicidal plan. Scheming, he found, was a satisfying way to dodge disagreeable thoughts. And for Eric Miller there was no more unpleasant thought than the future.

He could envision the next hour, he could even picture the next day. But the next week or the next month lay far beyond some harrowing horizon. He had no future.

With a sigh, he pushed off of the tub and stood, then reached over the sink and grabbed one of the two middle bulbs. It burned his fingers and he pulled away, stifling a little cry.

"Ooohhh!"

Shaking his head at his own stupidity for not anticipating the heat, he deliberately reached out again and put his hand around the blistering bulb, ignoring the pain, and unscrewed the bulb from its base. Now the sting was welcome. It was life, he told himself. It was the price of doing business.

Pain was a new factor in his life. He couldn't let it stop him. He had to accept it, forge ahead. He had his plan. Samurai detachment was what he demanded of himself.

He took the blistering bulb, held it for a moment, longer than he had to, allowing the hurt to take root, to sink in and become part of his injured sensibility, savoring the slowly diminishing commotion of pain. Then he turned and, with deliberation and aim, flung it down, smashing the lightbulb in the porcelain bathtub. Its exploding sound made him jump.

Outside in the clinic area, he heard Harry react, rushing to the door and calling, "Are you okay? . . . What's going on? Eric, are you all right?"

Eric smiled. It was working. "No, I'm not," he shouted in a stifled and breaking voice. "I hurt myself. I need help."

Eric was fully prepared. He made certain that he had taken his disposable scalpel out of its plastic sheath, and kept it hidden by a towel in his right hand. Harry would guess that was where Eric had injured himself. Then Eric reached over and turned the knob, unlocking the bathroom door to let Harry in. Crouched over, he held the unsheathed scalpel concealed against his chest, cradling the right arm.

Into the bathroom, toward his own doom, rushed Harry. Vulnerable, he opened the door uttering solicitous murmurs and reaching down to comfort his injured colleague, who had turned away, showing only his back.

"What is it, Eric? How bad is it?"

This is what Eric had counted upon—Harry's innate goodness. He knew that Harry would come running, letting down his guard.

"Ooohhh!" cried Eric.

Harry reached over and around the doubled-up figure of Eric Miller, who seemed to be in excruciating pain. Harry strained to locate the injury, intending to lead his colleague to the examining room, where he could do something: stop the bleeding, stabilize a broken bone, assess the damage. He stretched over Eric's back, his neck exposed, his arms spread out in a gesture to contain and assist a casualty—presenting a perfect target. That was when Eric wheeled like a cobra and struck.

It was blindingly quick. The blade of the surgical scalpel moved cleanly and briskly from left to right across Harry's neck, severing in one devastating motion blood vessels, muscles, cartilage, and tendons. The blade cut clean through the larynx and bounced off the spinal column, almost disconnecting Harry's head from his trunk. The blood from the main carotid artery pumped straight up in a perfect stream of red; seeing it gave Eric a strangely tranquil aesthetic satisfaction, as if he had just opened a lovely new fountain.

In a tiny fraction of time, Eric saw, too, the startled pop in Harry's eyes. They bulged with surprise and horror. In that same first, flickering second, Harry took in everything; he understood it all: the fact that he had been duped into a trap, the fact that Eric was a ruthless murderer, and the clear, indisputable fact that he was a dead man. He saw it all, recognized the extent of it, yet had in his eyes an unremitting question: Why?

For an instant, they both hovered there in a moment of frozen horror, like two men suspended in space before the last plunge. Harry's mouth opened and closed, but the only sound that emerged was the gurgle from the flow of blood and mucus that dribbled between his lips; his hands moved up and down, as if he couldn't decide where to try to stem the hemorrhage.

And then he collapsed in a bloody, lifeless heap.

* * *

Harry Graham was late. In her nervous state, as she waited for him, Laurie Drake had nothing better to do than inspect her environment.

There were only a few last customers in the diner on the southwest corner of Eighty-sixth Street. There was an old man eating a late dinner, bent over his plate, giving it all of his attention. He made wet, slurping sounds that seemed to echo throughout the diner. Although there were a lot of empty tables, the old man sat at the counter. He wore a heavy coat—too heavy for summer. He carried his wardrobe on his back. A bedouin of the streets, she thought.

There was a couple who kept checking the clock, trying, no doubt, to time a movie. The sandwiches were only partly eaten—they were still so besotted with each other that they had trouble swallowing. It was that early in the romance.

There was a gray doorman from one of the tall buildings along Eighty-sixth Street in his gray tunic with gold braid. He was waiting for a take-out order of coffee and smoking a cigarette deeply. No doubt he worked in one of those glittering high-rises where tenants didn't approve of smoking in the lobby. He wasn't old, but he had the sad, sagging face of an ex-cop forced to bolster his pension with mean work. They all got that look—proud men who were now bitter and flattened by circumstances.

Laurie Drake could see all this from her booth in the rear of the diner. She held up her hand and asked for some more coffee. The waiter, who had a sinister-looking five-o'clock shadow, gave her one of those unhappy sideways servings, demonstrating with body language that refilling a coffee cup for an hour was not his idea of good business.

"You want to eat?" he said.

It was more of a push than a request.

She didn't want to fight. "Toast," she said. "Whole-wheat toast."

"No toast," he replied. She looked up. He had a toothpick dangling out of his mouth. "Pretty soon we close," he added.

"Okay," she said. "A turkey sandwich." She hadn't eaten dinner. She wasn't hungry, but maybe the sight of the sandwich would revive her lost appetite. She hoped that it wouldn't make her sick. "No mayonnaise."

"No turkey," he said belligerently.

"Really? Well, then, how about tuna salad?" she said. "Whole-wheat toast." She smiled up at him, trying to force a truce. He had no smile.

"We don't have no whole-wheat toast," he said.

"Rye," she said, starting to feel a birth of temper along her back.

"No tuna," he said.

He had his hairy arm on the back of the booth. It seemed presumptuous. She said evenly, "Fine. Okay, let me put it your way: what do you recommend?"

He shrugged, raised his eyes. "Brisket," he said.

"Good. I'll have the brisket."

"What vegetables?"

"Sandwich."

"What on?"

"Toast."

"No toast."

She forgot. "Rye," she said.

"No rye."

"What bread do you have?"

"Roll."

"I'll have it on a roll."

"You want gravy?"

He was trying to provoke her. She didn't know why. It

didn't matter why. Not in New York City, where moods were volatile and sudden. They shifted in mysterious, baffling, and unpredictable ways. Anyone could turn on you. The tailor, the bus driver, the waiter. When you lived in New York, she understood, you were always feeling the lash of someone else's bad day. The problems came when two bad days collided. Most of the citizens were resigned and backed away. You either accepted that brute truth about the city or moved to some less socially inclement stadium.

"No," she said mildly. "No gravy. I'll just have the brisket. On a plain roll."

Laurie checked her watch again, although she sat facing the clock behind the counter. Nine-fifteen. Harry hadn't stood her up—she was certain of that. When she had met him, he didn't strike her as the type who was late or canceled or didn't show up. When she had spoken to him on the phone, the feeling was reinforced; he didn't sound careless. But he was an hour overdue, and she had to face a plateful of brisket.

She walked over to the phone and punched the number of the clinic. There was no answer. She came back to the booth and the man with the hairy arm was dropping the plate with the brisket sandwich from a distance high enough to announce his irritation.

"Some more coffee," she said.

He scribbled on his pad and dropped the check and walked away. "No more coffee," he said over his shoulder.

She ate the dry brisket, finished the water, then demanded another glass. The waiter saw the glint of something already resolved in her eyes and refilled the glass without giving her any more trouble. She decided that she would wait another half an hour for Harry. Then she would get help.

* * *

The blood was everywhere. How did it get on the walls? wondered Eric. The ceiling he understood. The fountain. But the door? That was behind him. It had sprayed everywhere. A broken pipe. He didn't try to scrub it off, just made certain that he blotted up the larger puddles. Eric did not expect to leave a perfectly clean crime scene. All he wanted was a decent head start. Just the weekend.

He had to put Harry in the tub, seal the office, and get some distance between himself and the clinic. They would be looking for him. There was no way he could avoid that. The thought of answering questions, being pushed around by cops, was unbearable. He was not up to that, sticking around and letting them arrest him, drag him down to the precinct, fight off the firefly cameras. He didn't want all that trouble and humiliation on top of everything else.

When Eric first tried to lift Harry's dead body, he was amazed at the sloppy weight. He was prepared for some difficulty; after all, Harry was stout. But he thought that he could handle it. What they said about dead weight was true. It was heavier and harder to lift. He'd never appreciated how heavy and slippery that could be. Harry was a big fish who kept sliding out of his hands. He grabbed an arm and tried to pull, but nothing moved. He tried for the waist, but quickly realized that was hopeless, too.

He sat on the closed toilet seat sweating and trying to devise a plan. Maybe he should just leave Harry on the floor. What difference would it make if they found him on the floor or in the tub? Somehow, it made a difference. He thought that Harry should be in a tub if for no other reason than to catch the fluids still oozing out of him.

Better get it done, he told himself. The longer he stayed, the greater his risk of getting caught and the shorter his head start. With a heavy heart, he got up, stretched, then bent over and reached under Harry's arms. Harry had been sweating and the feel and smell of the perspiration and the blood made Eric slightly sick. He could only push and shove Harry's body close to the tub. Inch by inch, he got him flat against the side of the tub.

The phone kept ringing. Eric was afraid that someone had heard all of the moving and noise and called the police, thinking that it was a burglary. He kept listening for the crash of police rams against the door, the shouts and threats. If they came, he decided, he would charge the police brandishing his scalpel. Let them kill him. Better to go out that way than face the ordeal of the criminal justice system.

Already it was after ten, long past closing. There were residents who might notice that fact, who might dial 911 as good citizens. If they came now, he would be caught, he thought, glancing at the ocean of blood, red-handed.

In the end, it really didn't matter. He was already gone, already living in that other world south of hell. Hadn't he been executed first? It was like *Alice in Wonderland*, punishment first, crime second. He was already gone and living in that grim netherworld of eternal woe. He was numb with his own cold, unfeeling death. And he was very angry with his thoughtless, safe, smug executioners. As he imagined a wrongfully dead man would do, he despised the living.

It was not altogether unreasonable. The only odd thing was the reversal of the order of things. The sequence of crime and punishment had been twisted, that was the only truly unusual part. Now, in the light of events, Eric thought that his own death carried a semblance of justice. First he had been condemned, then executed. Now he had to commit the crimes so that the sentence was a reasonable one. He was in the middle of his great crime spree. He had no choice—he had to kill. To restore a moral balance in the universe. To vindicate the punishment.

The scope of the injustice made him strong. With renewed energy, grunting like a pig, he managed to get Harry's head and shoulders over the side of the tub. He flinched as he banged Harry's head against the hard tub. It didn't matter that Harry couldn't feel anything anymore. The hollow clunk of flesh and bone on solid porcelain was disgusting, made him want to retch.

There were other factors, things that made Eric wince as he wrestled with the body. Buckets of blood sloshed over the floor, onto his shoes, into his socks, between his toes. He could feel the sucking, gummy mass attaching itself to his own flesh, as if Harry were reaching back from the grave to place an accusing hand on his murderer. But in the end, he got it done. Harry was buried in the bathtub.

Deliberately, carefully, fighting off the queasy feeling in his belly, Eric took off his shoes and his socks and washed the socks in the sink. He took off his pants and his shirt and his lab coat and he stood naked. He studied himself in the mirror. He didn't look sick. But he shook that off, knowing that the disease was not in the obvious, overt stage.

Then, with another burst of effort, he pushed Harry's body over to a corner of the tub with the shards of broken glass from the lightbulb and stood under the shower.

The water felt nice. It was cold and he needed the refreshing feel of cold water. Harry's body kept slipping back toward him—a hand touching his feet, the head slithering at his ankle. But he ignored the creepy feeling and scrubbed himself thoroughly.

Always conscious of the time, he remained in the shower for ten minutes. Reluctantly, he got out and dried himself with a roll of paper towels. Then he walked naked through the clinic. Someone peering in might have seen him from the backlight of the examination and treatment rooms, but he had gone too far and was too exhausted to care about that.

He dressed in a fresh outfit from his locker. He placed the bloodied garments in a plastic bag along with the towels, which were already growing stiff. Then he gathered all his personal items, including his own file from the personnel cabinet, and put them in his backpack along with the scrubbed scalpel. Looking everything over once more, satisfied that he had forgotten nothing, he closed and locked the clinic door behind him. As he turned the key, he heard the phone again.

nineteen

Sam knew the routine, understood the way it worked, but it still made him cringe as he watched James Sinclair turn and twist and lose his way beneath the relentless braid of Maggie's taut cross-examination.

"Why do they call you Coffee?"

"Why do you think?" James "Coffee" Sinclair looked around, as if for support. He laughed nervously. "See what I'm sayin'?"

He addressed that last aside to Sergeant Sam Rosen, who stood there, adding little except his own fraternal presence to the interrogation. The ethnic factor had an effect, thought Sam. It always had an effect. Poor Sinclair kept looking at him for help after each bumpy answer, as if Sam would fix it, reinterpret him to his White lieutenant, get him off the hook. Or maybe sink him deeper in whatever hole he was going down.

"So let's say you tell me," pressed Maggie. "Why do they call you Coffee?"

She was good at it. Just repetition. The slow, relentless drip of water on a rock. It never failed to wear down the stone, unless the suspect was psychotic, and James "Coffee" Sinclair didn't seem crazy.

Maggie worked by instinct and the book: ask a simple, guileless question, as if it was the first layer in an artichoke of meanings. Ask it again and again, making the poor guy in the bull's-eye search for other possibilities, question his own answer. What's she getting at? What am I missing? And Sam knew that James "Coffee" Sinclair could feel the subtle tightening of Maggie's rope.

"I do most all my business over a cup of coffee," he said again. Then, as if he realized that each little detail was a trap, as if his nickname was somehow incriminating, he held out his hands. "Man, I *am* coffee-colored."

Sam felt a small ember of pity and shame. There was no more banter in the interrogation room, only the blunt, entangling pressure of official impatience. Even Sam recognized the shrewd push to offer some better explanation, to further clarify, and thus force a critical stumble or a ruinous slip of the tongue. Sinclair was close to the edge of hysteria. The big men, the ones you didn't expect to shatter under questioning, often enough turned to mush when things got rough, Sam knew.

"Just a name, man, that's what they call me on the street, you see what I'm sayin'? What the hell!"

James "Coffee" Sinclair was moving out of the "Maybe" category and headed down that long, one-way perp walk. Sam could tell that Maggie was leaning; she was definitely on the brink of making her move.

Sam was not convinced that Sinclair was their villain. He sensed something essentially soft about him. Something not quite lethal. He was, concluded Sam, one of those street-corner braggarts whose worst sin was exaggeration. In the hood, a certain amount of self-ornamentation passed for charm.

They had spent an hour and a half going over Sinclair's version of his behavior on the night of the murder, and by now Maggie had the glazed look of an accountant. She was no longer making artistic distinctions about the plausibility of Sinclair's story (given the poetic license of the street); she wasn't even listening for the likely kernels of truth in what was clearly a self-serving narrative. Sam could tell that she was just adding up debits and credits, looking for the bottom line.

She had peeled away the shaky alibis and puffed-up boasts and had come down to the raw facts. No, he could not strictly account for his time on the night of the murder. No, he could not name a reliable witness. Yes, he had once used a knife, in self-defense. Carried one now. Everyone carried something. A knife wasn't so bad. Yes, he fought with his wife—fought the way a man fights who is trying to keep his dignity when the whole world schemes to whittle it away, and even his wife has high ambitions that rob him of a peaceful household sanctuary.

But he was no killer. That was his bottom line.

Maggie kept at him, like a sniper.

"So you admit that you carry a knife?"

"Man . . . !"

"So where's your knife?"

His eyes were rolling around the room. He looked from Sam to Maggie and back again. He didn't have a good answer.

"You didn't have a knife when we picked you up."

He shook his head emphatically. "Lost it."

She nodded with doubt. There were fresh sheafs of detective reports on her desk. Bannion and Queen took turns coming into the room, dropping papers and reports meaningfully on her desk. The detectives were quiet, padding back and forth, their faces closed for business, delivering contradictions like hand grenades. She was looking down, reading one report intently.

"You knew Edith Severan," she said. It was not a question.

He shook his head. No, but he was uncertain. Lies kept bouncing back in his own face. "Yeah, yeah," he said, retracting. "Yeah. She worked with Carol."

"You knew her."

He didn't answer. Just sat there, sullen.

Maggie put down the paper. Looked at him squarely in the face. "You were seen."

His voice rose to a high tenor of denial. "Listen, I did not kill nobody," he almost sang. "I swear on Jesus Christ!"

She nodded. "But you went to her apartment." She looked down at the report. "The night of the killing. You were seen."

He shook his head. "You are not listening to me. I didn't kill her. Didn't even go upstairs. No way!"

"You knew about her and Carol."

He was caught, and when he spoke his voice had the frenzied velocity of a man's with a hand in the cookie jar. "Okay, yeah, I went there. Not to catch my old lady. I didn't give a shit about that." He shook his head.

He leaned closer. "I got a business," he said. "An office on Ninety-first Street! I employ people. Two full-time technicians."

"What's your point?"

He was sweating. His hands ran back and forth over his forehead and across his mouth. He looked around wildly—maybe for a way out, maybe for a friend. "It's hard," he said. "You see what I'm sayin'? Bank gives me a loan and I gotta make the payments. But who do I do business with? Black folks. Money is tight." He slapped the desk. "You don't know." He laughed and it rattled around the room. "Black folks I do business with, they're gonna pay their bank loans first, before they pay me. I'm the last on the list. But I gotta pay the damn bank. They just look at me and see a deadbeat nigger.''

Sam nodded in sympathy. Maggie Van Zandt was tight-lipped.

''Where's this going?'' she asked.

He lowered his head. His voice was a whisper. ''I gotta make some money,'' he said. ''Bank loan due. Payroll late. The old lady, she can't help. We don't get along, but she knows what a Black man has to do and if she could help me out she would. But she can only help but so much. In the end, I gotta make some money.''

''So how did you make some money?'' asked Sam gently.

''I sell a little blow. Not much. Just a little. Carol's friend. That's all. Just to make the mortgage and the payroll. You understand what I'm sayin'?''

The lieutenant's lips were tight. Sam didn't say anything.

''Oh, Lord, this sounds bad,'' said Sinclair. ''I didn't kill nobody. I got a call to go to the apartment with something, but nobody answered the door. I swear to God Almighty. Oh, I should have a damn lawyer!''

Maggie nodded. ''You should have a lawyer.''

He leaned closer, causing everyone in the room at the time—Sam, Bannion, and Queen—to follow his movement and press around him protectively, to defend Maggie. ''Do I need a lawyer?''

Maggie stopped, straightened the papers. ''Get him a lawyer,'' she said to Sam. Her voice had the steel clamor of a cell door slamming shut.

''No, no,'' he said, reaching out, putting a restraining hand on her arm. He quickly pulled away; it was just in time to prevent Bannion from cracking his wrist. ''I didn't kill nobody.''

Maggie sat there for a while, waiting. There were some

who would crack in that lull, who would find the hush unbearable. Her voice softened. "What time were you there?"

He looked up, startled. Then his face unclouded. "Nine," he said. "Ten. Can't exactly remember. Rang the bell. Hit the door. Nothin'."

"What'dja do then?"

"I left."

"You didn't go home."

"No." He shook his head. "I didn't go home. Went out. With friends. I was pissed off. Needed the money. I guess . . . I don't know. I was pissed off."

"Maybe when you were high you went back?"

He shook his head, almost sadly, almost as if he regretted it. "I ain't like that," he said. It was, to him, a shameful admission.

In the technical part of an outer office there were cameras and recorders working overtime. Sam was aware that every expression and every word were being recorded and inscribed. The lies and denials, the backtracking and pleas, they were all going around together on the hissing spools of tape. Maggie took notes, but she didn't need them, not for the record. She had the cameras and the tapes for that. The note-taking was for Sinclair's benefit. To show him that this was official. It was, thought Sam, one more form of intimidation, one more reminder to Sinclair that this was serious police business.

"I ain't like that," he said again.

If he sounded believable to Sam, Sinclair didn't convince Maggie. Sam knew the signs from watching her at work. He could tell when Maggie developed a soft spot for a suspect. When she bent in that conspiratorial direction, Maggie would joke, and her face adopted a forgiving, understanding crinkle. But not now. Now she was brittle, now she was ice. Sam sensed that Maggie was about to come down hard on James "Coffee" Sinclair with all of the thunder and weight of the law.

She broke off the questioning suddenly and went outside to brief Chief Scott and to keep Sinclair off balance. The pause was another textbook tactic. Let them stew, that was the approved method of breaking a suspect's spirit. Dazzle them with motion and the show of brisk efficiency. The coming and going gave the impression of new battlefield bulletins, fresh troops arriving—an unbeatable, machinelike enemy. The ones who could not take the show would snap.

Sam nodded when Maggie got up and told him to stay with Sinclair. He felt the man's panic as Sinclair realized what he was up against. This was no small beef with negotiable lesser counts of misdemeanors. This was a front-page felony. Sam tried to break the tension with the offer of a soft drink. Sinclair shook his head. Probably couldn't swallow, thought Sam. "You were in the Gulf War?" said Sam, sitting casually on the desk, trying to make human contact with the sweating, suffering suspect.

Sinclair nodded, looked around. They were alone. One more trick, he no doubt suspected. He took a handkerchief from his pants pocket and wiped his forehead.

"Where'd you serve?"

"What? Oh, in a reserve unit," replied Sinclair. He wasn't paying much attention. Looking for the next trap to spring. Looking for a way out. "You think she believes me?"

Sam shrugged. Then, brightening, "You in Kuwait or in Saudi Arabia?"

Sinclair's eyes were wide with shock. He looked like a man who'd been hit by a truck. Then he turned his attention to Sam and shook his head. "No, no," he said. "Not there." Trying to regain his balance, he straightened out his slacks. Brushed away some phantom lint, and laughed.

"Fact is, I never got outta New Jersey," he said, amused with himself. "I was in logistics, you see what I'm sayin'? Supply. Working in my specialty—computers. Sending out guns and catchin' body bags comin' the other way. I never left McGuire."

Sam understood. "Didn't see no action, then?"

He laughed a deeper, throatier laugh. "Oh, I didn't say nothin' like that, bro. I seen some action. Plenty of action. Over in the town. Nothin' that would look good on my record, you see what I'm sayin'?"

Sam saw what he was getting at.

"Excuse me," he said, and went out to find Maggie.

Chief Scott was waiting for Maggie when she came out of the interrogation room. He pulled her into a small conference room and shut the door. "Good work," he said.

"We'll see," she said. "I don't like the feel of it."

"I called for an *ADA*," continued Scott, ignoring Maggie's clear signal for caution.

She shrugged. "That's okay; I don't mind you having one handy, but aren't we racing a little fast here, Chief?"

"What the hell are you talking about?"

"I'm not through with my interrogation," she said. "I haven't even gotten around to checking alibis and matching stories. I have to talk some more to the wife. I have to talk to him again. I'm not even working up a good sweat yet."

"This is going fine. Fine."

"Chief, I gotta tell you, I can feel you in the fishbowl and I know you have pressure on your end that I do not have to deal with—thank God—but I gotta tell you, I'm not comfortable moving at this rate of speed."

He was planted at the head of the table, under a portrait of Teddy Roosevelt, the patron saint of the New York City Police Department. Maggie was leaning against a wall, fingering her clipboard.

"I don't know what you're talking about. This guy is way beyond prima facie. He did it. I know it."

"How do you know that, Chief?"

"You saying that you think he's wrong?"

She shook her head wearily. "All I'm saying is that we are in the third or fourth inning," she added. "Let's not go home yet. I want some corroboration, something solid. We're really gonna look stupid if we parade this guy around and he's clean."

Chief Scott stood up. He was trying to control himself. "Listen to me, Lieutenant, this is a first-class suspect who had motive and opportunity. A man with a record of violence, who admits being there at the dead girl's apartment, who . . ." He sputtered, looking down at his own notes. "I already called the ADA."

"Hope you didn't call a press conference," said Maggie.

"What the hell do you need for an arrest?"

"Well, I'd like to feel better about it, for one thing," replied Maggie. "I'd like to finish my interrogation."

He started to pace, fuming. Then he stopped in front of her.

"What, exactly?" he asked.

"I want some more time," said Maggie, who pushed herself off of the wall and was standing toe-to-toe against her boss.

"You're not gonna get much. You better wrap this quick."

Sam caught up with Maggie in the small rec room where the snack machines were lined up side by side, offering everything from coffee to hot meals. They sat in a corner.

"So?" she asked.

He shrugged. So Jewish, she thought, how did Sam ever get to be a cop? All that doubt and Talmudic reevaluation. All that Black sympathy for the underdog.

"Tell me," she said.

He sighed and stood up and brought back chemical coffee and Maggie got ready for a story. "Last year I drove to Florida to visit an aunt," he began. "Great-Aunt Alicia."

"She the one with the turnip pie?"

He nodded. "Well, I got to South Carolina and I was pulled over by a trooper. Now, you know when I go south, I drive nice and slow, well within the speed limit. And I always wear a necktie and a suit jacket. Matter of fact, I always make a point of dressing well when I go shopping."

She smiled sadly.

"Saves aggravation. Otherwise, they pull you over or watch you like a hawk. Black men always have to think and act defensively. Saves wear and tear, but it does leave a scar."

He looked up and she nodded to show that she got his point. "Well," he continued, "I got pulled over and this cracker takes my police ID and he says, 'Sam Rosen?' And I knew that I was in all kinds of trouble. He drags me outta the car and he says, 'Boy, you stole this from some Jew cop, didn't you?'

"So I point out my picture and he says, well, anybody can fake a picture and I try to get him to call and run a make and he doesn't want to. He wants to bring me into the county sheriff and show him this New York Jew nigger. Because, the truth is, he believes me, this cracker cop. He suspects that I may be a fellow cop. But I am also a mighty fine trophy if I'm not. In any case, he just wants me to suffer. And—here's the tricky part—there's no downside in South Carolina. Nobody would blame him for pulling in a Black guy with cop credentials in the name of Sam Rosen. You couldn't even call him malicious. Unless you were me and knew that he was enjoying it so much."

She took it in. It was, in its way, shocking. Maybe more shocking because White people never know the full price of being Black. The small, incremental insults. The ones you can't even prove. "You never told me," she said.

"That's my point. We don't always tell. We don't always list and enumerate the million little affronts because, well, it is embarrassing. It cuts away at your manhood and leaves a scar."

"And you think that explains Sinclair?"

He shrugged and smiled and drew her own shrug and smile. "I think the man's okay. He has some cash-flow problems and he moves a little cocaine. That doesn't make him a killer."

"Why?" she asked.

"It is partly hunch."

She nodded. "I don't think I can hold back Scott. Not for long. I can slow him down a little. And I don't know if I agree with you. But," she sighed, getting up, "go find some witnesses if you can, and I'll see if I can part the Red Sea."

twenty

"Hello." He was groggy with sleep.

"Hi." In spite of herself, she chirped. Maggie was angry with herself for calling, yet glad to hear his voice. "You know who this is?"

"It's probably some magazine subscription thing, right?"

"It's Maggie."

"I know."

Even on the phone, they were still at the fresh, daffy stage of their relationship; the moment they made any kind of contact, they were blushing and bright-eyed and enthusiastically awkward. Everything tasted better, everything was funnier, everything was more cheerful, sparkled, contained an astonishing amount of inferred wit and important meaning. Even just before seven o'clock in the morning.

"Sorry about last night," she said finally.

"You mean about sticking me with the check?"

"No. That was deliberate. I'm pretty old-fashioned about sticking guys with the check."

"Right. You're about as old-fashioned as Roller-blades."

"Okay. So what do I owe you?"

"A lot. You ran out pretty fast."

"It was business."

"I know, but the thing is, you cost me a restaurant."

"That's expensive. How did I do that?"

"Robert. You remember Robert?"

"I call him Row-berrre," she said with a rolling French accent.

"So I was sitting there after you fled into the night, just sitting on the banquette sipping some wine, trying to appear calm after this woman bolted out of the restaurant as if I did something bad under the table, when good old Row-berrre came over. He looked a little concerned. No, let me amend that. Actually, he seemed flat-out distressed. As if the wine had turned. So I smiled and said, Yes, Row-berre? And he asked in his most Gaelic, food-attentive manner, was everything all right?

"I thought he meant the meal. Well, you know the French. Too much garlic in the salad and you have to hide all the sharp instruments.

"So I reassured him. I said the meal was perfect. I held up the glass of wine to prove it, and I smiled."

"That was nice," she said approvingly. "Didn't that put his mind at ease?"

"No, as a matter of fact, it didn't. Row-berrre leaned over and whispered—very discreetly—that the lady with whom I had shared the meal, the one who left in a sprint, had dropped something in her haste. Oh, I thought, a comb, perhaps, or possibly a glove."

"Yeah? So what did I drop?"

"It was a bullet," said Jerry.

She laughed.

"Not funny. Poor Row-berre, he opened his hand—

first looking around to make certain that no one was watching—and there in the immaculate white-gloved palm of his hand was, indeed, a bullet. He couldn't have been more horrified if he was showing me an insect plucked from the dessert tray. I took it from his trembling hand. His face was very pale.''

"Oh, c'mon, it's no big deal. I happen to keep some loose bullets in my purse,'' Maggie explained. "For emergencies. Don't go ballistic.''

"You know, Maggie, most people keep some loose tokens for emergencies. You'd be surprised how few people consider live bullets no big deal. Loose bullets are frightening all by themselves. They suggest a certain laxity when it comes to, say, danger. This conjures up loose morals, which is usually followed by loose women!

"Robert is a restaurateur. He is not accustomed to ladies who carry live ammo in their purse. He thinks it violates the spirit of the meal. Or, possibly, it can put too much pressure on the chef. Personally, I don't mind, but if you're going to leave behind a bullet—you know, as a kind of souvenir or calling card—it should be made of silver and you should definitely wear a mask.''

"Good thing I didn't drop the gun.''

"I may not be able to go back to that restaurant again.''

"Sure you will.''

"Maybe I will, but you won't.''

She laughed. She sat at her desk holding the phone, quietly. There was something on her mind, but she was uncertain about naming it. Why had she called? That was an ominous portent. The first sign of a craving. She had called to talk to him, to hear his voice, to sniff around. And she was upset to find that she was happy to hear him, with his complaint. Even the silences were crowded with excitement. That, too, was unsettling.

"What are you wearing?'' she asked.

He paused. "I gotta look."

"I'll wait."

"Yeah, wait a sec. Here. Oh, yeah. It's that Delta Force camouflage outfit. Accessorized. I've already got one bullet."

"Sounds exciting."

"Listen, is this . . ." He didn't know how to put it. "I wanted to tell you something, but I feel dumb."

"What?"

"Well, you know, Maggie, I like you." In some ways, he found it easier to talk to her on the phone. In person, she was a little too impressive for intimacy. On the telephone, however, there was that built-in curtain of distance. It had been the same thing when he was a reporter: putting something (distance, professional drapes) between you and the subject so that you could ask impertinent questions that would never dare ask on your own.

"Did you hear me?"

"Yeah, that's okay," she replied, clearly embarrassed.

"I'm not sure."

She knew what he was getting at. She had the same sprouting emotions. She just didn't know if she wanted to hear it. She wasn't ready to get too explicit with this man. It was a phantom thing. In some portion of her mind, he was still Cissy's man. Consciously, she understood that Jerry never met Cissy and Cissy never met Jerry (except in a figment of her imagination). Nevertheless, it still felt like cheating.

"Do you get what I'm trying to say?" he asked.

"Don't worry about it," she said.

"Okay."

That was enough. She was surprised. He seemed relieved. It was a good sign. He knew when to back off. "We could have breakfast," she said.

"I don't know. I got hit with dinner. Gonna hafta be a pretty hearty breakfast."

"Today's a good day for breakfast. And it's still early enough."

He looked at the clock. It was 6:50. "It's too early. I could use a little more sleep."

"Yeah. That's good for me, too. I still got a few things to do."

"How's the tooth?"

"Coming through my scalp."

"You're not gonna make it through the weekend."

"I'll make it."

"We'll have soft-boiled eggs."

"I'll call you in an hour."

Outside of Maggie's office, in the bay of the command, Professor Lauren Drake was pulling herself together, trying not to explode. She made the statement slowly, carefully, and in complete earnest. "I am trying to explain to you that the man was going to meet me and he didn't show up."

The big-bellied detective taking the statement was being infuriatingly, patronizingly patient. "Which man is this? The one who has AIDS?"

"No," she said through clenched teeth. "The man from the clinic. The *Gotham Medical Laboratory*. He was trying to help me find the man with AIDS. The man with AIDS worked at the clinic, I think."

"So did this second man," said the detective.

"I think they both did."

Because of the concentration of forces on the Edie Severan murder case, this was almost the only place in Midtown Manhattan to find a real gold-shield detective. After going back to the clinic and finding it shut for the weekend, Professor Laurie Drake lay awake all night before deciding to yell cop. Now she found herself sitting at the desk of a sarcastic detective.

Detective Third-Grade Leonard Gilson, who had only been given a gold shield because he was on the verge of retirement, gazed at her intently as she sat on the flank of his gray metal desk. His manner was correct, but insulting. He was clearly humoring her as Laurie tried to present coherent testimony. He leaned in her direction, his brow heavily furrowed, nodding, breathing hard, for he was a man who carried an extra fifty pounds on his thick frame and was in a perpetual state of panting at the effort. He was not writing a report, he was gathering a locker-room story for the boys, she was convinced. Laurie had to fight herself to stay put, to spell out the humiliating details.

"Okay," sighed the fifty-one-year-old detective third-grade, who had spent the last twenty-nine years sitting in a radio car in Queens eating free pizza and french fries when he wasn't ducking mostly unfounded calls for help from people he regarded universally as crackpot civilians. "Let me see if I got this straight: you meet a guy at a party. Correct?"

She nodded.

"He infects you with AIDS. . . ."

"No. That's not the way it happened." She was shaking her head.

Len Gilson was regarded as a good guy among his peers. He was a little lazy and a little slow on the uptake, which made him a safe candidate for pranks, of which he endured more than his share. But he was generous and didn't blame anyone for his low achievement—anyone, that is, who was a street cop. He had the cop's grudge against civilians, especially brilliant college teachers who got knocked up with AIDS on the first date. When he grasped the gist of Professor Drake's story, old Catholic codes of childhood training kicked in and he lost all sympathy for her plight.

"So tell me again. Try to make it simple, Professor."

She knew that there was no point in being angry at him. He was just a small functionary, an apparatchik in a world devoid of serious compassion for the victims of AIDS. Cold Catholic eyes stared back at her.

"The man I met at a party called me and told me that he had tested positive for the AIDS virus."

"You slept with this man?"

He seemed to want her shame on record. Repeated. A catechism of guilt.

"Yes." She understood the intended humiliation and suffered through it, partly out of a shared sense of mortification.

"On that first and only date?"

"Yes."

"Uh-huh." There was harsh judgment in that acknowledgment. "Then what?"

"So, he called me and informed me that he had tested positive."

He sighed. "You know, it's not a crime to have AIDS, lady. And, he didn't know he had it when you dated. Is that right? In fact, in some eyes, it sounds like he was just being considerate calling you."

"That's not my point," she said, exasperated. "He was not being considerate. He was being malicious. He hung up on me. I wanted to see him, to confirm it. I went up to the *Gotham Medical Laboratory* on the East Side and one of the technicians there called me back after thinking it over. I'm certain that he knew this man. We made an appointment to meet, but he never showed up. I went back to the lab, but it was closed for the weekend."

"I gotta tell you, Professor, this is a little thin. I don't know what kind of crime you're reporting."

Maggie was out in the bay, making certain that she was getting all the use of her manpower, when she spotted Detective Leonard Gilson taking a statement from Professor Drake. She motioned to him and he excused himself.

"What've you got?" she asked, nodding at the professor.

The detective shook his head. "Some woman sleeps with a guy who's got AIDS and now she's all shook up. Thinks she's got it, too."

"What's she want here?" asked Maggie.

Gilson held out his hands and shrugged. "Beats me, Lieutenant. Says that this bum called her up to rub it in. I told her it wasn't a crime, but she's a college professor. Literally."

Maggie frowned, annoyed at his dismissal of so large an event in the poor woman's life. He was right, of course, there was no crime. But it disturbed her all the same. Then, walking past him, she whispered, "Listen, let me talk to her." She smiled caustically. "This is a girl thing."

Detective Gilson hung back as Maggie introduced herself to Lauren Drake. "I'm afraid there's no crime here," she said mildly, leaning close. "I'm sure the guy is a son of a bitch, but that's not against the law. Too bad."

"I wish I could find him," said Professor Drake, shaking her head.

"We really can't help you there. I'm sorry."

"I think I know the name of the laboratory."

"That'll help, if you want to find him."

"I *have* to find him."

"You know the name of the lab?"

"I overheard it when he called. Someone picked up the extension. It was the *Gotham Medical Lab*. I'm pretty certain."

Maggie felt the voltage of an important discovery. *Gotham Medical Lab*. That was where Cissy took her blood test. It was more than coincidence. Slowly, she made Professor Drake run through the whole story again, including the broken appointment with Harry Graham.

"This Mr. Graham, he seemed a little hesitant. I thought that he knew exactly who I was talking about. From my description. Then when he called me back and arranged to meet me, I was certain of it."

"And he never showed?"

"He didn't seem like the type to stand me up."

"Did you check your answering machine?"

She nodded. "Nothing."

Maggie leaned back to think.

"I went back there at nine-forty-five," continued Professor Drake. "I rang the bell. There was a light on. I could see it. And I'm sure that I heard someone. But they didn't answer the bell."

"Coulda been the janitor. They don't answer bells."

"I don't think so. It was someone."

"How do you know?"

"The noise inside stopped when I rang the bell."

The name of the clinic had set off Maggie's alarm. But something else rang even louder: Maggie believed in coincidence. Not that she didn't rely on the potency of deduction. But in her years in the department, she had found that the highest order of police work depended on significant leaps of luck and intuition and coincidence.

It was always part mystical. Details accumulated, facts attended, but there was some other force that determined the outcome of distinctive cases. After all, crime itself was peculiar and could not be understood by plain logic. More often than not, Maggie had been helped along by some component of luck or coincidence. And a good detective kept his or her eyes and ears open for that possibility. As a good detective, she was receptive to the signs.

Maggie asked, "You know the name of the technician? The one you were supposed to meet?"

"Harry Graham."

Maggie nodded, then turned to Gilson. "Excuse us," she said to Professor Drake.

Gilson lifted himself heavily and walked with his boss to a part of the bay out of earshot.

"I think we have something here," she said. "I smell it."

He shook his head. He was an old-timer, unable to translate past cop chauvinist lingo into modern tactics. "Aw, just some dame gets laid and finds out that the guy has AIDS. Now she wants to find the guy and he don't want to be found."

"Maybe. Maybe not."

"Well, it happens. All the time. Tell you the truth, Loo, I do not see a crime here."

She was firm. "Call the lab people," she said. "Ask about this guy Graham. Talk to him. Find out why he stood her up."

"Hey, Loo, it's Saturday morning," protested Gilson.

Maggie got tough. She'd been up all night fighting Scott. This jumped-up beat cop giving her a hard time was fresh. "That's a pity," she said. "Wake them up. Track down Graham. I'll get you some help."

Maggie wasn't the only one who had been up all night. Jack Fox had been sitting in a leather chair in his library sipping scotch, watching a blank television screen.

Betsy was upstairs sleeping. He listened to the deep silence of the apartment, as if the serenity itself were a living, breathing enemy. What would she do, he wondered, when they took him away in handcuffs? How would she react? Would she appear before the cameras and proclaim her steadfast support for her husband?

No. She would calculate. Leave herself an escape route. She would, in the public arena of the pampered luncheon crowds at Lespinasse and Demarchelier and La

Côte Basque, adopt a pose of heroic, undaunted pluck in the face of adversity. She would wave off questions about guilt and innocence—if anyone dared raise such questions—as trespassing on the sacred ground of legal privilege. All she would safely say was that she had complete faith in her husband's eventual vindication. She would avoid the ensnaring declaration of complete faith in her husband's innocence, an omission that would be silently accepted without further question.

It would go without saying that she could not discuss the details of a case now before the courts—especially not one in which she, in all innocence and ignorance, was cast as the surviving victim. A slight hint of blame would remain unspoken. Naturally, no matter what, everyone would agree that the whole mess was all his fault. They would find clues and signals in past behavior to explain his sudden breakdown.

And Betsy would become a tragic martyr in that gilded circle of languid shoppers and restless travelers and fasting guests at life's great feast. She would accept with a kind of melancholy grandeur the unspoken sympathy of her peers.

Perhaps she would write a book. Of course! There was an occupation requiring no talent whatsoever. They would hire a writer and she would disclose one or two juicy tidbits around which a professional would weave a blockbuster best-seller. Out of such foam she could command a seven-figure advance. At least. There would be, he was certain, a lot of eager editors who would leap at such a project. Too bad Jack could not negotiate the deal—they could both clean up.

Each time he took a sip from the glass of liquor, he gazed up at the ceiling, imagining her sleeping peacefully in her plush, perfumed bedroom. Until this moment, he had not realized how much he resented her detached dependence. She lived in a cushioned world without risk of repercussions.

Well, one thing: if it came to that, this would be the end of their marriage. She would keep the trainers and health-club memberships and put a lien on the solid assets. He might have enough to defend himself in court, but she would take the bulk of the investments, the apartment, the summer house, the friends, and the sympathy.

He had lost all track of time when the telephone rang. It was Tom McCord.

"Did I wake you?"

"No," said Fox bleakly.

"Listen, you can't quote me, and don't go out celebrating, but I have it on some reasonably good authority that they have caught a guy in that murder case."

Jack Fox did not speak. He lifted his glass, stood up, and took a long, last swallow of the whiskey.

"Did you hear me?" asked the lawyer.

"I heard," replied Fox. "It's not a joke? Please don't joke with me now. It's on good authority?"

"I am not supposed to say, but, yes, I think you can relax."

"Oh, God!" said Fox. "Oh, dear God!"

"Well, you weren't really worried, were you?" asked McCord.

"No. Of course not."

When he hung up the telephone, he studied himself in the mirror and saw a face that looked like butcher's meat. The eyes were bloodshot and popping out of his head. His hair—arranged and neat even in his sleep—was flying every which way, as if trying to escape his head.

"Not very fucking worried!" he said to his own image.

Then he heard something stir upstairs. Betsy. His awakened spirit had a momentary relapse. The reprieve meant that he was stuck with her.

twenty-one

The sun blinded him awake. Eric Miller jumped off the bed as if he had been touched by fire.

How had he gotten back to his apartment last night? How had he gotten to sleep? What had been wrong with him, that he fell asleep in his clothing when he should have been running all-out to get away, putting as much distance as possible between himself and . . . what? The world was still spinning, an early morning blur. He felt danger, but it was something vague, unfocused, and unconcentrated. He couldn't shake off the fuzzy feeling.

And then he remembered. He looked down and saw the blood that had caked into the cuticles and under his fingernails, felt it stiff in his hair, and the hard clots and flakes in the shafts and tunnels of his ears. In spite of the shower, the blood clung. No wonder he had fallen asleep. No wonder he was exhausted beyond all caring.

It had taken a lot of energy to kill that way. All that blood! All that work!

At some point, and he couldn't remember exactly when, but it was during the battle with the sweat and blubber when he was trying to get Harry's corpse into the tub, he had realized that the attempt at a decent cleanup was hopeless. The place would never be made spotless. Not even reasonably tidy.

He'd decided then that he could only hope to get it under a semblance of control. He'd known that he couldn't get himself clean, but he'd spent an hour washing and scrubbing anyway, just to make it possible to walk in the street without causing instant panic.

In the middle of the struggle, when he'd been all out of breath and pushing the body up the slope of the tub—cursing and praying and muttering oaths—he'd heard the front doorbell chime. Not once. Persistently. His heart had frozen and he'd realized that the bell might have been ringing for a while. He'd been unable to tell. Maybe someone had heard the commotion. Maybe someone had seen the light. The bell had chimed and chimed and he'd sat quietly, holding his breath, in the thick of the gore, until it had stopped.

Then, when the bell had ceased, he had been so grateful that he had wept. And contained within the soft little sobs had been a touch of self-pity. Hadn't he suffered enough by innocently contracting AIDS for something he had not ever done? Did the penance have to be doubled now that he was only committing acts that he had already paid for? Where was the justice in that?

The emotions had come and gone with lightning speed. He had been filled with self-pity one moment, crying the next, giddy with his own antics after that. He had slipped in and out of moods so quickly that they had blended together and he had been crying and laughing at the same time.

He had finished his chores quickly, carelessly, because his knees were wobbly. He was past fatigue. Afterward, he had stood out on the street, bewildered. He didn't know where to go—he'd run out of plans. He had thought of going to a hotel, but that was too exposed, too risky. Someone would notice the commotion in his eyes and the bedlam of his appearance. He had thought of trying to get out to his aunt's apartment in Queens, but he would have had to ride on a public subway, and then he would have been seen in bright lighting, and certainly reported. It was a chance he couldn't take.

The only place left was his own apartment. There, he could pick up a few things—checkbooks, automated teller machine card, passport—then safely vanish. Get that good head start that he badly needed. But when he had gotten back to the apartment, he had sat on the bed and fallen asleep. He didn't even remember lying down. All he had felt was the tug of lassitude and finally his willpower giving out.

But when he awoke, in the unrestful aftermath of a very bright morning, he heard the high-pitched sound of riot and hysteria in his ears. It was a bad feeling, a cry from inside that he had to get going. And he didn't know: was it the sun or a knock on the door that woke him up?

Time to get going, he told himself. Time to move! Maybe some hot coffee would start his engine.

But first, he felt that same longing for respite again; just one more second of sleep. Just a taste of real sleep. A moment of escape before the last burst of . . . whatever lay in store. And he fell gently back against the pillow.

For June 25, the diary entry said *Gotham Lab, 9*.

Maggie confirmed it. Looked at it in black and white. Then turned the page and saw again *AIDS ?* She sat there looking at it, turning away, looking back again. It kept shifting; one moment she was certain, but as soon as she turned away, the doubt returned. And she had to look again.

"I just spoke to Birnbaum," said Detective Leonard Gilson, leaning into her office.

She looked up, her wide eyes rattled. "Who's Birnbaum?" she asked belligerently. She really didn't like this big-bellied old cop with bad, labored breath and a worse attitude. He didn't like female cops, that was clear, and he especially resented them when they were in charge. He came at her blowing the foul stench of archaic precinct-car wisdom, as if she should accept his views as hard-earned street insight. She was sorry he had caught the case, but there was nothing she could do about that now. There would be time later to push him aside, if it came to that. So far, there was no case. She was operating on nothing more than a wisp of a hunch.

"Dr. Samuel Birnbaum, he runs the *Gotham Medical Laboratory,*" said Gilson, taking her question as an invitation to step into the office. He plopped down on the chair, his gut quivering like jelly.

"Oh," said Maggie. "That Birnbaum. You spoke to him? And?"

Gilson shrugged. "Said this is the second time in twelve hours that the police have bothered him at home about something at the clinic."

"Really?"

"Yeah. The precinct got a call of a possible break-in last night and had a sector car take a run past it. It was a blank. There was no sign of forced entry and all the lights were out, so they called the doctor, just to check it out, make sure someone wasn't inside working. He didn't seem concerned. Said that there's nothing there to steal. Just some office machinery and stuff."

"What time was that run by the sector car?"

"About ten."

"Not sooner?"

He looked at his notes. "Matter of fact, they were on

their meal until ten. I checked with the dispatcher. They got the run at ten-o-two."

"And Professor Drake was there at nine-forty-five."

He glanced at the notes again. "That's what she says."

"The mystery of the dog in the night."

"What's that?"

"Sherlock Holmes. The mystery of the dog in the night is that it didn't bark."

"So? What's strange?"

"The sector car didn't see the light. Fifteen minutes earlier, Professor Drake said that she saw a light."

Gilson looked down at his notes. "She say that?"

"She said that she saw a light through the front window. It was a small light in a back room, but she was positive." Maggie felt the heightened thrill of making solid connections. "Who called in the complaint?" she asked.

"It was a 911 call. Anonymous."

Maggie nodded. "Where's our professor?"

"I sent her out for breakfast."

"Good. Keep her around. Now, get hold of the guys in the sector car. Ask them if they looked into the window and saw that light. Make sure."

"The light?"

She tried not to show her irritation. "The light that Professor Drake told us that she saw when she looked through the front window."

"Oh, that light. Check."

"And start a file; gimme Birnbaum's number."

"He's not too happy about being bothered today," offered Gilson. "Said he gave everything to the cops last night and he was late for an appointment. Asked if I could call back later."

"Well, that's too bad," said Maggie. Doctors were always pulling rank, claiming that they were answering higher calls. Mostly, they were abusing their privileges.

She took the number, waved Gilson off. It felt good. She had a mug of coffee on her desk and she was hot on somebody's tail, although she didn't know who she was chasing or for what. But she felt the wind at her back.

The area code for the doctor was out on Long Island. "Garden City," he said after she identified herself and asked for him. He could not keep the irritation out of his voice, claiming that he was just out of the door.

"Doctor, can you tell me, what time did the clinic close last night?" she asked.

"I gave this information to the police last night," he said.

She was calm. Maggie had a purpose. Her friend's diary. Not even the unwilling doctor's grudging collaboration could dent her determination. "Tell me again," she said. "Make believe I'm brand new. Humor me."

He sighed with exasperation. "The clinic was supposed to close at eight, depending upon the traffic. Actually, it's always supposed to close at eight. Sometimes, when tests get a little backed up, or when it's a holiday weekend—such as this weekend—the technicians run a little late. It's not unusual."

"You were there when they closed up?"

"No. No. I told this to the officer who called, what's his name? There were two technicians on duty. Harry Graham. He was the senior technician. I gave his number to your man."

"Who was the second technician?"

"What difference does it make?"

"I would think that you would be concerned," she said, faking innocence. "I mean, supposing that burglars have cleaned you out. I would think you would be worried."

"I'm late for an appointment. The police checked the doors and windows. There was no sign of a break-in. Besides, I believe that this is a matter for the insurance company. I believe that this is their business."

Her voice grew a little more firm. "What time did you leave the clinic, yourself, Doctor?"

He had run out of patience. "Listen, Lieutenant, the truth is, I am already late for a golf date. That may not seem very urgent to you, but I work very hard during the week and I look forward to my Saturday morning golf game. Now, I just told you that I gave a full and complete statement to the officer who called last night and I repeated the very same statement to the officer who called this morning. Why don't you people check with each other? Compare notes. Christ, all this fuss over nothing. We don't even know if it was a burglary or a false alarm. Can't it wait until Monday?"

"I'm sorry, Doctor, I appreciate your irritation." She was brisk now, but polite. "But this is an official police investigation. Tell me where you are playing golf today?"

"Why?" His voice rose in suspicion.

Maggie became almost soft in her answer. "Well, maybe it'll snow."

"What?"

The rough edge returned. "Tell me what golf course you will be on. You don't have to, but I'll find out."

"Why?"

"Because I intend to send a squad car to your golf club. My officers will then place you under arrest. Then they are going to handcuff you and march you back to the squad car. You will make a very uncomfortable trip back to the city, where I will personally charge you with obstruction."

She was bluffing, but he couldn't know that.

"What do you want?"

"Who was the second technician?"

"Eric Miller."

He fumbled for a moment, retrieving his address book,

then gave her Harry and Eric's telephone numbers and addresses.

"Now," she said, finally. "I want you to cancel that golf date and drive into the city and open your clinic. I want to know what went on there last night. I will have a few detectives waiting there to meet you."

"Yes, Lieutenant."

She felt good. She was moving along nicely.

Jerry Munk couldn't get back to sleep. He lay in his bed, his eyes wide open, thinking of Maggie Van Zandt. Trouble, nothing but trouble. A woman of mulish opinions and iron will. Still, appealing, in a strange, unfathomable fashion. She was an unbroken female and he knew that he would suffer bumps and bruises from the alliance. Not that he wanted to stop the tipsy spin of their unspoken, unwritten, unchartered understanding.

When he thought about her, he knew that she would bring a great disruption into his life. She would have demands and preferences and loud inclinations. And yet, there was that other truth when he mused on Maggie: she made him happy. The mere thought of her made him laugh out loud.

There was no point staying in bed, so he got up and showered. The water felt good, broke his sluggish mood. He got dressed quickly. He was eager to hear her voice.

She sent Detective Gilson for two search warrants. It took half an hour after she explained the facts to the sleepy judge. The uniformed cops who examined Harry's Brooklyn apartment reported it clean. The superintendent of Eric Miller's building kept addressing himself to Gilson, as if he was in charge. Maggie let it slide.

The rooms were bare of Eric Miller's scent. There were no pictures, no personal items, no clues to the personality or identity of the person who sublet the apartment. It might have had no tenant. Maggie checked the clothes, neatly hung or folded. He was a medium-sized man with bad taste and a tight budget. He shopped at the Gap and mistook color for style.

Maggie stood near the window and listened to the growl of the traffic coming out of the Midtown Tunnel. It would have been a dispiriting sound to hear in the morning. There were some containers of juice in the refrigerator, a few dried-out bananas, and a loaf of stale bread.

There were piles of books and pamphlets on treating AIDS, fighting the virus, coping with the mental anguish—indeed, an entire library for the infected. In the front drawer of an old secretary in the dining room she found the medical report that showed that one Edward Barnes tested positive for the HIV viral antibody. Edward Barnes was the name of the man for whom Professor Lauren Drake was searching.

But the freezer held the decisive, chilling proof that Eric Miller was not a peaceful citizen. The evidence was wrapped in a plastic bag and jammed in the back to blend in with the ice: it was a scalpel.

Wearing her latex gloves, Maggie removed it carefully and sealed it in an evidence bag. She wrote her initials on the front to keep intact the chain of evidence, then sent Gilson back to the precinct to keep Professor Drake occupied and ship the scalpel to Forensics for tests. There was nothing to do now but await the lab report and find Harry Graham.

From the phone on the kitchen wall, she called Jerry Munk.

Munk didn't want to grab the receiver on the first ring—didn't want to seem too eager—but he did. It was 8:50 when he picked up the receiver. He was sitting in the living room, his hand poised over the phone.

"Yes?" he said.

"There's a diner on Thirty-sixth and Second," she said in her singular, abrupt manner.

"Uh-huh."

"See you there at nine-thirty."

When he hung up, he was amused. For all she knew, it could have been the wrong number. There was no way for her to know, not from the quick "Yes?" and "Uh-huh."

She was standing at the cash register showing her shield to the owner when he got there. Nodding to Jerry, she continued to question the man.

"He's a young guy, about thirty," she said. "Very nondescript. Sort of guy you'd pass in the street."

"This is the guy you want to know if I remember?" asked the owner sarcastically.

"Well, we have a name."

"Names! Who knows names. I got nicknames for everybody. There's the sugar man who puts four spoons of sugar in his coffee. There's the tea lady. But I don't know anybody's names. You got a picture? I know faces."

"No," admitted Maggie. "Just the name. Eric Miller."

The owner gave her one of those long New York looks, as if to say, Gimme a break! Don't I have enough trouble?

"He lives around the corner," she said. "He must have come in here. Not a lot of stuff in his refrigerator. This guy doesn't cook."

"I got two, three hundred people come in here every day," said the owner, a middle-aged man with hairy arms. "What did he do, this guy?"

She shrugged. "We just wanna talk to him. He works in a clinic; he's a medical technician. Maybe he talked about it?"

"We don't have time for talking. People come in here to eat."

The line at the cash register was backed up. Customers at the tables, booths, and counter were glancing over sideways—not wanting to display too much interest (this was, after all, New York City, where all manner of the fantastic was common)—but no one showed any more than ricocheting interest.

"If you hear anything . . ."

"What am I gonna hear?"

"Okay." She was defeated.

She and Jerry slumped into the booth near the window. There were two booths facing the street. In the other a pale, youthful man bent over his third cup of black coffee.

Maggie ordered eggs, bacon, sausage, toast, coffee, and juice. Jerry just wanted fruit.

"I called the dentist," she said.

"Yeah?"

"You were right." She held her jaw.

"The tooth won't wait?" he asked.

"No. It's about to launch something through my scalp. The dentist said he'd see me at one."

"Who is this guy? You know him?"

She plucked the card out of her handbag, slipped on a pair of glasses, and read. "Dr. Fred Raphael. Fifth Avenue. Convenient."

"Today?"

"Yeah. I told him it was an emergency. He's coming in at one. Special."

She wasn't able to bite on the eggs or the bacon or the sausage or even the toast.

Meanwhile, the young man in the next booth left a dollar tip and paid his check. Outside, when he was out of range of the window, Eric Miller took out a pad and a ballpoint pen and wrote down the name of Fred Raphael, a dentist on Fifth Avenue.

twenty-two

It would come down to a fight. Without a doubt. Maggie parked Jerry Munk outside and marched into the Seventeenth Precinct to head off Chief Scott before he embarrassed the department by naming the wrong suspect. Over the phone, Scott was adamant. He intended to hold a two-o'clock press conference to announce the arrest of James Sinclair.

She looked at her watch. It was just after ten as she ran up the stairs to the detective command. The exertion made the tooth throb. Could she hold out until one? Did she have a choice?

Waiting at the top of the stairs was Detective Thomas Neeley. She had almost forgotten about Manny and Lydia Stern. The reports should be coming in by now. Probably the medical examiner's papers were in her office, along with some results on Severan.

"Got a minute?" asked Detective Neeley, whom she had recently renamed the art lover. Now that she knew of his aesthetic inclinations, the colorful sports jacket and bright silk handkerchief flowing out of his breast pocket seemed appropriate expressions of his artistic bent.

Standing behind him, looking uncomfortable, like a small boy, was the rough Detective John Bukowski.

"No," she said. "I got maybe ten seconds."

Neeley and Bukowski followed as she led them into her office. Maggie plowed through reports from the medical examiner and detectives while listening to Neeley, who read from a small leather notepad about the deaths of the lawyer, Manny Stern, and his wife Lydia, the couple found shot in their plush Fifty-fifth Street apartment. The first assumption—an open-and-shut case of a devoted husband who killed his dying wife because he couldn't watch her suffer, then turned the gun on himself—was wrong, Neeley said.

"They were both murdered," he said flatly.

Maggie shoved her glasses back on top of her head and gave Neeley her attention.

"Definitely a double murder," said Neeley.

She nodded. It was no surprise to Maggie. After all, she had been the first to spot the flaw in the picture, or rather, the shadows in the photographs of the apartment walls. A cheap little Utrillo print floated in a space where she knew that a large Picasso painting had once hung. The Utrillo print could not cover up the false note.

"Tell me," Maggie demanded.

"Manny Stern was shot up close in the head. There were powder burns." He nodded emphatically.

"So?"

"That was okay, but that wasn't all. We found another hole in Manny Stern. In his back. Hard to spot, but it was there. Maybe wouldn't even have found it if you hadn't pushed. That second shot makes it a homicide. The ME says suicides don't shoot themselves in the back. The head wound was intended to throw us off."

Neeley smiled. He looked quite young when he smiled, she thought. The serious planes of his face softened, breaking the severe bearing he tried to affect to offset all of the colors and contrasts in his attire. It was very appealing, the smile.

Maggie couldn't help smiling back. "Well, it looks as if we have a double homicide on our hands," she said brightly; she was glad that she could clear her old friend Manny Stern. "Good work. Let's get on it."

"Well, actually, Loo, we got a pretty good head start. I mean the paintings. At least we have a motive. Theft. 'Lot of missing pictures," said Neeley. "According to the insurance people, at least a couple of million."

She nodded. "This case stunk from the go," she said. "Let's put a blanket on it, quick. I don't want people matching stories, having second thoughts, worrying it to death."

It happened in cases that lent themselves to scandal and gossip. Witnesses compared notes, adopted versions that seemed ultrasensitive, or cast themselves in a better light. Maggie found that it was better to grab the witnesses swiftly, before the revisionism set in.

"Let's make this like Watergate. Follow the money. Find out about the paintings. They'll turn up, won't they?"

Neeley shrugged. "Maybe. Who knows? Art theft is typically a professional thing. But maybe this wasn't professional. As a rule, pros don't kill. A violation of aesthetics. Good art thieves are meticulous and fussy. They like to admire their work. Talk about it afterwards. Like a painting. But it could be professional. If this was pros—something that went bad—they will probably get cute and hide the stuff away for a long time." He shrugged. "Who knows? They can be out of the country already."

"Okay," said Maggie. "Let's assume we don't know who killed them. We can keep the friends and relatives on ice. Put a tag on them. If it's something else, if it's some band of sloppy art criminals, we have to heat up informers, contact art experts. Go to the museums, call in some specialists. You know, I hear drug people are into stealing art."

"That's true."

"Maybe that's a lead. Meanwhile, and I know it may be too late, but cover the airports and the borders. Notify Interpol. Canadian Mounties, Mexican cops. The whole deal. I'll give you some manpower."

"Right."

"Now I have to deal with this Severan thing." She rolled her eyes. "Soon as I straighten out that I'll be back with the cavalry," she said. "At the moment, I have to try to remove a big foot from Scott's mouth."

Sam Rosen came into Maggie's office, his face twisted and worried. God, she thought, I'll never make it in time to stop Scott!

"Gotta go," she said.

"A second," Sam demanded.

"You know, this is really a hard job," she said.

A plainclothes officer stuck his head in the doorway. "Sorry, Lieutenant, but your dentist called and said you should move up the appointment, make it by noon. And you can't be late—he's gotta be outta there by one."

"Good," she said. "The sooner the better."

The plainclothesman held up his hand, continued. "And the chief, he's in the small conference room and he's having kittens."

"No he's not," she muttered as the plainclothesman retreated. "He's having more worms."

She turned to Sam and asked, "You got something or what?"

Rising from the chair, he stretched his large frame and yawned. "Been up all night," he said. "Talking to Mr. Sinclair's clients."

"Computer people?"

"You could say that. Alibi types." He shook his head. "You would not put one of them on the stand. I could break them all with a little feather."

"Never mind that. Does the man have a real computer business?"

Sam's brow furrowed. Then he nodded, shook his head. "He does. If you call living on the knife-edge of bankruptcy a business. Owes everybody a fortune. Getting by by the skin of his teeth, day to day."

Maggie nodded. "I think that makes him look pretty good."

Sam smacked his forehead, leaned across the desk. "I think it makes him look pretty desperate to me."

She shook her head. "It's gotta be hell keeping a small business afloat for a Black man. You wouldn't understand. Sinclair is worried about money and staying open; he isn't going around snuffing his wife's girlfriend. He doesn't give a shit."

He sensed something. "You're holding back. What've you got?"

She held out the medical examiner's report, pushed down her eyeglasses. "Edie Severan was suffocated," she said triumphantly. Looking at the report, she read, " 'Anoxia to the brain. Dilated pupils. Body cold and clammy and gray.' " She pushed back the glasses. "Not consistent with a big bleeder."

"What about the knife wound?" asked Sam.

"She was already dead," said Maggie. "Look, there was very little blood on that bed."

"Meaning?"

"Meaning she was already dead. She was cold and clammy and her mouth was open, like she was struggling for air. Muscles clench from a knife wound. Wouldn't have an open mouth."

"How the hell would you know that?"

"I saw a snuff film once. And I asked the ME."

Sam raised his eyebrows.

She shrugged. "Some people like to get close to the edge with sex. Have someone hold a pillow over them. Only sometimes it goes too far."

"Maybe Sinclair . . ."

"No," she said emphatically. "Not Sinclair and not the wife. Women do not do that to other women. It's a man-woman thing. And poor old James." She shook her head.

"Why not?"

"Because he didn't come there for sex. He came to deal some dope to save his business. And he wouldn't use a kitchen knife to slash her throat. He carries a knife. A sharp knife. Something you use to stick, not slash."

"Where did you get the business about the kitchen knife?"

"There's one missing. I had that inventory include the silverware, remember? She bought a set of knives from Williams-Sonoma two weeks ago. There were six in the set. Now there are five."

Sam was silenced. Then, "You know, Scott is about to charge your friend."

"I know. I gotta stop him."

She leaped out of her chair, turned back, and grabbed the reports, then smiled at Sam. "Let's talk to Mr. Fox again," she said. "And I'd like the telephone records."

"Whose?"

"Everyone. Fox. Sinclair's beeper. His wife. Edie Severan. Get on it."

On her way to the conference room she spotted Detective Leonard Gilson. "Aren't you supposed to be meeting Dr. Birnbaum at the blood clinic?" she asked, pulling him along in her undertow.

He looked a little startled, spilling some melted butter from his toasted bialy on his tie as he trailed after her.

"He's got some problem with the car. Gonna meet me there at eleven-thirty."

"What about that other guy, Graham?"

Gilson shook his head. "Nothing."

She was openly annoyed. "Have someone from the eight-six make a run past his apartment again. He lives in the Heights, right?"

"Right."

She stopped in her tracks. "Listen, Gilson, get some enthusiasm, okay?"

Indignant, he replied, "I'm enthusiastic."

"What did you do with the professor?"

"Had to send her home. She was tired."

"You put her in a cruiser?"

"Well, I didn't give her cab fare."

Chief Scott wanted to stage the press conference at the Manhattan North command center where the combat look of an active precinct would serve as a gritty backdrop for the cameras.

Sergeant Gil Player was on the phone in a remote corner of the conference room, summoning friendly members of the media to a two-o'clock press conference. First, there was Dan Force, the crime reporter for *Newsday,* a dull drone who could be counted on to give all the credit to Scott for cracking the case. It was payback for a lot of early tips that kept him on the newspaper payroll.

"You didn't hear it from me," Player told Force.

"I appreciate it, Sarge," Force said conspiratorially.

The picked reporters thought that they were being given the inside scoop; they didn't seem to notice that when they arrived at the press conference, everyone else from every other newspaper and television station was there, too. They preferred to think that they were chosen members of some charmed, favored circle.

It worked. Force would now whisper to his editor that

he had inside information that the Severan murder was about to break; the editor would call the publisher, and the publisher would tell his friends. A complicated transaction was taking place. Everyone would think that they had an edge, and everyone had a stake in not breaking the spell. The media business depended upon cultivating that mythical advantage. Every public servant and press agent knew how it worked, learned to strip like Gypsy Rose Lee, dropping tantalizing hints and tips to the naive dupes of the working media.

When Maggie banged open the door of the conference room, Player made one last call to the Associated Press. He always saved that call for last. The AP would put the two-o'clock press conference on their daily schedule, which went to every studio and newsroom in the metropolitan area. It was a last guarantee that no one in the tristate area would miss the press conference.

The thing that amazed Maggie about the process was that in spite of the clear evidence to the contrary, those few moments of exclusivity gave the reporters called by Player and the editors plugged in by the reporters and the upper-management types who traded in the ephemeral gossip an illusory sense of privilege. The fact that they had been called, not brushed off as the pests, elevated them all, gave them status.

After he completed his media calls, Police Sergeant Player called Police Commissioner Charlie Quinn, who remained on the open line while Player called Mayor Roger Wolf. All three high municipal officials were placed on the conference line as Chief Scott broke the good news about Sinclair's impending arrest.

"Thank God!" said the mayor when he heard that there had been a solution to the Edie Severan murder case.

Police Commissioner Charlie Quinn had a brittle and

well-grounded suspicion of convenient and timely breaks in important cases. It was not superior intelligence, but a lifetime of cunning that made him suspicious. Quinn was an old cop who had risen from street patrol to head the department. Along the way, he had learned to trust no one, not even his chief of detectives, especially when it came to good news. His moods were saturated by a deep and sulfuric pessimism.

"There's no mistake here?" he asked with a high arch of seasoned, professional doubt.

"I was present at the interrogation," replied Chief Scott, as if that resolved all doubts.

"Thank God!" the mayor said.

"Who is this suspect?" pressed the commissioner, who was never satisfied with the answers of the officers serving underneath him. He operated on the principle that all cops were essentially lazy and therefore liars. He was convinced that they would do anything to deflect the unwanted attention of superiors. That was his own nature and he assumed it was universal. He had learned, as he rose in grade, to challenge each and every statement until he was satisfied that he had pulled out the truth.

"It's a jealousy thing," replied Chief Scott. "He was a jealous husband."

There was a pause on the three-way connection as each of the men tried to digest the implications of that opinion.

"She wasn't married," declared the commissioner.

"Yes. I know. But her lover was," said Chief Scott, who couldn't contain a note of glee at that particular complication.

"Wait a minute. You mean, she was . . ." began the mayor.

"A lesbian," interjected the commissioner, who grasped immediately Scott's little surprise.

"That's right," said the chief of detectives.

"What's our case?" asked the commissioner.

"The suspect—he's a Black male who runs a business of dubious legitimacy—was seen going into the deceased's apartment on the night of the murder. He had already had a fight with his wife over her affair with the deceased that same evening. . . ."

"Was the wife Black?" asked the mayor, fearful of any ethnic ingredient in the tinderbox city.

"Yes," replied Scott.

"What about forensics?" asked the commissioner.

"Well, we're still pulling stuff together. We have no prints and no weapon yet. But our guy has a record. With a knife."

"I have doubts," said Maggie, who had been waiting for a strategic moment. "I don't think we should run with this suspect yet."

"Who the hell is that?" growled the commissioner.

"Lieutenant Van Zandt," said an unhappy Scott.

"Who?" asked the mayor.

"She's head of the homicide squad," said Quinn. "Let's hear it, Lieutenant."

Maggie cleared her throat. "The ME has a cause of death that doesn't fit the story. Asphyxiation. The suspect is a businessman. He does deal a small amount of drugs, but it's just to keep his business going. I think he's innocent."

"What about the motive?" asked Commissioner Quinn. "His wife cheating on him."

"I don't think he gave a shit about her," Maggie replied. "Sorry. My read is that he was passionate about his business."

There was a long, painful pause on the conference line. Maggie thought that she detected a tilt in her favor.

"What about that, Scott?" asked Quinn.

"I do not agree," insisted Scott, glaring at Maggie.

"What does the suspect say?" asked the mayor.

"Naturally, he denies it. But he's shaky. Very shaky. Has no alibi, claims that he was out partying . . ."

"Sounds like we got the shaky end of this stick," said the commissioner. "Where's Van Zandt?"

"Here, Commissioner."

Scott was shooting her fierce, restraining looks.

"I think you have a point," said Commissioner Quinn.

"There's still a possibility that he's our guy," she said cautiously. The tone carried her attitude. "But I think that there are some open questions."

"It would be good to reach closure," said the mayor, who wanted to bring the gift of a solution to the weekend cabanas, but who recognized the danger of a bad arrest.

"I think that this suspect will hold up," insisted Scott.

"Maybe," said the commissioner, settling it with that one equivocating word that landed like a hammer. "But we are under no particular pressure. Let's not jump too quickly. Let's get some more case so we don't look like fools."

The hate in Scott's eyes was only matched by the satisfaction in the eyes of Maggie Van Zandt.

"You gotta get your fucking priorities straight," Scott hissed at her as he pulled her aside out of earshot.

"Oh?"

"You got half your manpower chasing some burglary in a blood clinic," he said. "Don't think I don't know what's going on. Your friend committed suicide. Period. Let it alone! That's an order."

"I got a few cops chasing down a few leads on some open investigations."

"What are you talking about? You got shit. It's a fucking burglary, for Christ's sake! Those people should be out chasing down proof against Sinclair."

She pulled away and started gathering her things. "Where the fuck are you going?" he asked.

"Dentist," she said, pointing to her swollen jaw. "I'll give you a fill when I get back."

"You better get on top of this Sinclair shit!" he called after her.

Sergeant Player was frantically punching buttons on the phone, trying to get the Associated Press to remove the press conference from their schedule.

Trailed downstairs by Bukowski, Neeley wanted to chew over some more speculation about the case. Maggie sensed the excitement and fed her detective.

"What do you think?" she asked. "The sister-in-law?"

Neeley shook his head. "Little, birdlike thing. She couldn't break an egg."

She leaned against the wall at the top of the stairs, thinking. Then, "Okay, lemme hear."

"We need help now," said Neeley.

He was a good cop, she thought. She nodded. "Okay. I'll give you four more people as of right now. You grab them. Tell them it's from me."

She was in a fierce, sour mood as she rushed off to the dentist.

twenty-three

Outside, on Fifth Avenue, the street was stifling hot and empty of traffic. As usual on a Fourth of July weekend, the city was freakishly silent; the stylish New Yorkers had all fled far out on Long Island, launching the annual summerfest of barbecues and softball tournaments. Only a few bewildered tourists emerged from their dark hotels, to blink in the Midtown sunlight.

The tourists had come to see St. Patrick's Cathedral and Rockefeller Center and to drink in the spectacle and bedlam of midsummer in Mid-Manhattan. If drained of natives, the boulevard was still redolent with cooking meat as vendors peddled everything from Middle Eastern lamb sandwiches to homegrown hot dogs. A man in a high red, white, and blue hat and green beard hawked seats on a psychedelic bus for a tour of the city. Mute, stick-thin West African pitchmen wearing ill-fitting suits opened instant sidewalk stands selling fake Rolexes and copies of designer silk scarves. And the absence of quick New York pedestrians made everything seem slower and less urgent.

Inside the lobby of one particular office building on

Fifth Avenue the air was both humid and cold. The gray fifty-story building was closed for the weekend, although in such a skyscraper there were always a few tenants working overtime. In the deep interior hush there was also the ghostly, lonely echo of janitors pulling rolling buckets like prison chains through the empty hallways.

A security guard, hearing the click of Eric Miller's heels against the polished marble floors, looked up from a mangled copy of the *Daily News*. He was a bored, embittered sentinel who slouched in a kind of officious, low-level ambush at the security lectern. For a moment, he held what everyone in New York City wanted: genuine power. He could bar the door.

A sign-in book was chained to the wooden counter, and the guard said not a word as Eric nodded a passive greeting and took the pen and filled in the empty blocks of space in the book.

"ID," demanded the guard, and the voice matched the cold malevolence of the eyes.

Eric looked up from the book and smiled and reached back for his wallet.

He was not an old man, the guard; somewhere between fifty and sixty, Eric guessed. The face was broken and crisscrossed with the lifelong log of his scowling temperament. His uniform was frayed and shiny in spots. There were stains of spilled food and liquid encrusted into the front. Just another worn-out victim of too much pressure, passing along his misery like a baton in the brutal urban relay race, Eric thought.

"Sure," Eric said in his most winning fashion. This was no time to start a fight. The guard wanted to provoke something, Eric could easily see that. He had that plain, open, defiant belligerence of a nasty, pushy drunk.

But there were more important matters on Eric's agenda. He had to deal with Lieutenant Maggie Van

Zandt. He had to stop this meddling cop now. He had a goal. He intended to set the world on fire. He needed havoc. Sooner or later he knew that they—someone—would stop him. But not now. Not yet. Once he had overheard a doctor telling a patient that he was not going to let the patient die. "Not this day," the doctor had said. "Not this day and not this way." In his moment of supreme rage, this became Eric's thunderous battle cry. He was not going to be stopped before he exacted a full-throated, wild, bring-down-all-the-pillars-of-the-house revenge on the world. Not yet. Not this day. Not this way.

It was not simple revenge. He had thought about it. He was convinced that his was a virtuous sin. Because of some stupid social qualms about guarding the privacy of plague-bearing fools, Eric Miller was doomed. He was going to die because everyone was too priggish to pay attention to common sense. Well, he was not going to go quietly, softly, without some supreme solace.

He insisted upon peace of mind.

How would he achieve it? In a feverish inspiration it had come to him. Eric Miller would not die alone. He could not attach an exact number to the people he had to destroy to ease his mind, but he felt certain that he would recognize the state of serenity when he reached it. He trusted his instincts to tell him when he was done. And as he stood in the lobby absorbing the benign abuse of the sadistic security guard, he knew that he was not even close.

For tactical reasons, Eric grew meek in the face of the guard's cruel aggression.

"I'm here to assist Dr. Raphael," he said mildly, showing the guard his medical license. It only attested to the fact that he was a bachelor of science in Medical Technology and entitled to work in that field. There was no reference to dentistry, but that didn't matter, not to an ignorant security guard. The laminated certificate was official looking.

"I'm from Medical Temps," said Eric. "Didn't Dr. Raphael notify you?"

The guard frowned and then looked at a scribbled list of instructions on a clipboard hanging from the side of the night desk. He held up the clipboard so that Eric could read the stained piece of notepaper.

"Says here dental emergency."

"On a Saturday," said Eric, shaking his head sadly. "Ain't that a bitch?"

"I'm here," the guard pointed out.

Eric shrugged, but kept that harmless smile on his face. "Yeah, well, I guess some of us have to keep the machine running even on the July Fourth weekend."

There was a digital clock over the entrance to the building. It said 11:24. "You're pretty early," said the guard. "Thought this was for one."

"No, the appointment was for noon," said Eric Miller, twisting his face into an expression that reflected the never-ending complications that came from widespread incompetence. "Somebody screwed it up. Probably got the message wrong. But my office said it was definitely noon."

The guard hesitated—his mind turning over the implications of pushing this a little farther—then he grunted, and decided to skip a showdown. He locked the front door, placed a sign over the knob that was visible through the glass. It said: GUARD WILL RETURN SHORTLY. Then he escorted Eric to the elevator and they rode in ringing silence to the twelfth floor.

The bare, sterile hallway smelled of ammonia, Eric noted. Not a medical brand, the liquid cleaner type. The dentist's office was at the end of the corridor. It had an opaque window. The guard fumbled until he found the master key and then he opened the office door and stood there for a moment, deciding something, finding another impediment.

"How will you know where things are?" he asked with malice.

Waving a hand, Eric pushed past him and said that all dental offices were alike. He'd find his way around. By now, he was ready to break. This son of a bitch was itching for a fight and he had bent over backwards to pacify him. But Eric decided that he had gone as far as he was willing to go. He had a grip on the handle of another throwaway scalpel inside his jacket pocket. He felt the start of the red blur—the dizzying, uncontrollable fury. One more word, one more obstruction, one more irritating sound, and he was prepared to end this security guard's bad mood forever.

"Okay," said the guard. "But stay out of the doctor's private office." He couldn't help throwing in that last jab.

"Check," said Eric loosening the grasp on the handle of the scalpel. "And, by the way, if the patient shows up, just send her right up." He looked down at a notepad, as if he didn't have it memorized. "Her name's Van Zandt."

"Okay," said the guard. "Key to the bathroom is in the top drawer of the reception desk."

Eric listened to his footsteps fade, then found the supply closet. There was a key nicely labeled in the same drawer as the bathroom key. There was a small can of liquid spray to lessen the pain of an injection. Eric found a white lab jacket, a sanitary mask, a pair of latex gloves, and, finally, a pile of various-sized syringes. He took a large one.

He was sweating a great deal; he found a thermostat and turned the air conditioning up high.

In his pocket he carried a capped bottle. The liquid was milky white and thick. After getting himself dressed in the white jacket, he arranged the bottle on the instrument tray. His hand was steady, although he was still perspiring as he plunged the needle through the cork bottle top and filled it. It was too bad, he thought. He preferred the idea of using the needles contaminated with the AIDS virus. He took some pleasure thinking about the incubation. But there was no more time for that. He needed something quick, something that would knock out the immune system, and every other life-support system. This would do. Then he placed the loaded needle under a towel on the preparation counter, put the mask on his forehead, and familiarized himself with the switches for the high-intensity lights, the drill, and turned on the water spout. Then he waited.

It was 11:39 when Plainclothesman Felix Ramon pulled ahead of the hydrant on Manhattan's Upper East Side and parked. From the passenger side, Detective Leonard Gilson got out of the unmarked cruiser heavily, and adjusted his belt, which kept slipping below his belly. He motioned for young Officer Ramon to trail closely as he made his way to the front door of the lab.

Across Ninetieth Street, Dr. Samuel Birnbaum, a short, stocky, impatient man wearing a bright yellow golfing outfit, shot them both a harsh, disapproving look.

"Phew!" whispered Detective Gilson to his partner, catching a whiff from a pile of fresh dog droppings cooking in the sun, "I would say that our pooper-scooper laws are being openly flouted."

"You're late," said the doctor, looking at his watch.

"Yeah, we had a jumper on the Brooklyn Bridge," replied Detective Gilson sleepily.

Gilson thought that there would be relief when they entered the office. He expected a blast of cool, scented air. But that's not what struck all three men when they walked into the blood clinic.

"My God!" cried Dr. Birnbaum.

"Holy shit!" said Officer Ramon.

It was hot and close and dark and foul inside the office. It took Dr. Birnbaum a moment to shut off the alarms and to turn on the lights and to switch on the air conditioning. That was when Detective Gilson abruptly came awake.

"Don't touch anything," he said quickly. His hand reached down to his side and he touched the handle of his pistol.

"What the hell is that stink?" Officer Ramon asked, putting a handkerchief over his mouth.

The sluggish Detective Gilson was now taut, alert, scanning the waiting room with fresh eyes. His body, so slack a moment before, was now folded slightly into a semicombat crouch, as if he expected something to leap out at him from the other rooms.

"What the hell is that?" Officer Ramon repeated, also driven to a higher state of alert by a combination of the odd smell and his partner's reaction.

"Something dead," Detective Gilson replied. He recognized the odor. In almost three decades of answering radio runs, he had come across his share of decaying bodies.

He ordered Dr. Birnbaum to wait outside.

Recognizing the sudden shift in tone, the doctor obeyed without objection.

Gilson held out a hand, a signal, putting his partner on his flank so that they could provide covering fire for each other. Then they inched toward the closed door of the bathroom. It was from behind that door that the stench seemed to emanate.

Gilson took the left side and Ramon took the right. Slowly, the old detective twisted and reached his left hand around and turned the knob. In his right hand he held his service revolver pointed at the ceiling. His breathing was shallow. Swiftly, he flung open the door. Both policemen automatically dropped into firing position as the wooden door flew back.

They were not prepared for what hit them. The second shock of odor sent Plainclothesman Ramon reeling. He fell back against the wall of the corridor, muttering, "Oh, Christ! Oh, sweet Jesus! Oh, Mary, Mother of God!"

This stench was far worse. Even Detective Gilson was staggered by it. It was as if they had broken open an oven in hell. Harry Graham—jammed like a roast into the tub—had been cooked in the closed, windowless bathroom. There was no ventilation and the temperature in the room was high.

Detective Gilson advanced slowly into the room, making mental notes as he went. The rug and tile and walls and sink were covered with gore. A bulb was missing from over the mirror. Then he gazed down into the bathtub where Harry's face stared up blind at the ceiling. The expression in the dead man's eyes was one of horror and shock and disbelief.

Always disbelief, Gilson thought. No one ever accepts the possibility that someone will do the worst. It is beyond comprehension. That's why they always look surprised, he thought grimly.

Plainclothesman Ramon forgot all his training, all fear of danger, all other considerations, and vomited his breakfast in the corridor.

Gilson was pleased that he had passed that queasy stage and could control himself. "Call in," he said while Ramon was still heaving. "Get Forensics and get some uniforms down here to seal off the scene."

Gasping, then nodding, Ramon wiped his mouth with his handkerchief and started for the phone at the reception desk. "Not there, you asshole!" Gilson hissed. "Let's keep the scene virgin."

Ramon looked confused. "Use the radio," Gilson said, nodding at the car. "And notify the lieutenant."

Dr. Birnbaum was standing outside, chewing on a fingernail. He saw Plainclothesman Ramon run from the office toward the unmarked cruiser. When he looked back at the lab, Detective Gilson was standing in the doorway, motioning for him to approach.

"Hope you didn't have a big breakfast," Gilson said.

He led the doctor to the bathroom, warning him not to touch anything—they were in the midst of a crime scene—then pointed at the body in the tub. "You know him?"

The doctor's face was pale, and he took a step away in horror. But he still had a little control. "It's Harry Graham," he said. "He's my senior technician."

"He the guy that closed up last night?"

The doctor nodded. "Along with Miller."

Outside, the doctor took a few deep breaths. Detective Gilson walked over to the cruiser where Ramon was also sucking air while radioing in.

"The lieutenant's out; they have to beep her," he explained to Detective Gilson.

Before she went across town to the dentist, Maggie read her mail. There was an envelope with a familiar large, generous script. Cissy. It was dated June 28, the night she died.

Dear, dear Maggie. Dear: By now you know why I did what I did. I am too cowardly to face it. All the sickness, all the pity, all the horror and fake sympathy! No thanks. The amazing part about this, now that I have come to a definite decision, is that I do not feel too bad about it.

Suicide is painless. They promised. Even if it's not . . . Listen, Maggie, there's one thing that I want to say—I have no idea how I got this damned virus. Really. (At this point I have absolutely no reason to lie.) It's a real mystery. I have not been with a man for more than a year and I was tested negative before and after. I have not had a blood transfusion. The only needle that entered my body was when I took the blood test for the job. Dear, dear Maggie. Don't feel bad.

Love,
Cissy

"ID," demanded the guard, not even giving Maggie time to fill in the blanks on the sign-in sheet.

Oh, this one was undoubtedly a real asshole, she thought. A genuine hero when it came to bullying bicycle messengers.

"Here," she said, showing him her badge and police-department photo identification. Her voice had a gravelly rasp. It was from all that commotion in her mouth—her tongue tickling the sore tooth and little swallows of saliva catching in her throat. The pain had changed from an aching pilot light to a roaring fire.

A police ID left the guard flustered and Maggie couldn't even take any satisfaction in his trouble. The aroused tooth saw to that. They rode up together on the elevator and the guard remembered when they were half-way there that he'd forgotten to lock the front door. "Just down the hall," he said pointing, then pushing the "Down" button to get back to the lobby. "Far end."

She growled and cupped her hand protectively over her jaw and moved down the corridor. What was it that made the tooth throb as if it was going to split the flesh and erupt out of her mouth? Did the tooth know that it was about to be assaulted?

The man waiting at the door looked young for a dentist. The mask riding up on his forehead gave him some authority, and Maggie fell into the submissive role of a suffering patient. She took no notice of his features, no notice of the surroundings. She only wanted the tempest ended.

"I cannot tell you how grateful I am for your coming in and taking care of this," she said.

"It's okay," he said soothingly. The voice had a gagged, uncertain sound. Even in her state of distress Maggie recognized the wavering quality. It was an incriminating hesitation, how most people sounded when they first spoke to a detective. He smiled. "Let's get you into the chair."

She tried to smile back, but any movement of her face now felt like cracking cement. The office was cold, so she kept her suit jacket on. Discreetly, she took her gun from her shoulder holster and tucked it into her purse, which she left in the outer waiting room. Then she followed the young dentist into the treatment room. He pointed to the high, reclining chair, and she climbed, sighing with pain and dread, into the squeaky leather seat. He stood behind her and gently slipped a bib around her neck.

Maggie tried to recapture her usual state of unruffled and detached acceptance. But the pain made her mood and head unsteady.

"I'm going to need Novocain," she said emphatically.

He fiddled, searching for the water spout, standing close alongside her, then nodded and lowered the mask, covering his nose and mouth. "Don't worry," he said. "The right rear top, right?"

He held the dental mirror in his right hand and she opened her mouth and muttered something. In the other hand he held a probe. He moved the mirror gently to the top of her mouth and she groaned. "Oh, God!"

"Uh-huh," he said, peering in. Her eyes were clenched shut.

"Turn to me," he said. The voice was firmer, more assured, and she obeyed meekly. There were no heroes in a dental chair, she thought. Then he touched the throbbing tooth with the probe and she screamed.

"Sorry," he said. "But we've found our culprit."

"Oh, Christ," she said, "this is really going to hurt."

"Don't worry," he said, "I'll deaden it."

He picked up a pencil-thin cylinder and sprayed her upper gum to numb the area where he would apply the primary anesthetic. The liquid felt cold. Then the dentist turned to the counter and reached under the towel for another instrument. When he swiveled back, he held a large, loaded syringe.

Maggie shut her eyes against the thought of that needle driving into her sore gum.

"It will take a second for the spray to work," he said, watching her twist in the chair; her face was mottled by the bright light and the blood rushing to her head. He looked away. He didn't want her to notice his eyes. Later, when it was too late, when she was writhing in her final agony, he would watch her die.

Her life would end almost mercifully, he thought. The poison that he held in his hand was quick. She would have a few bad moments. But nothing compared to the long, lingering torment of waiting for the AIDS virus to become active. Nevertheless, strychnine was painful. In a technical sense, he knew exactly what would happen. The alkaloid would instantly shut down the central nervous system. That would set off a chain of catastrophic physical events. For a start, she would go into violent convulsions as her muscles twitched and burned off the last spasm of energy. Then her back would arc like a bow as she strained for one last elusive breath. It was then that he would look into her dying eyes. The eyes would plead and cry out in mute panic (she would not be able to speak) as she strangled to death on the hard tile floor. And as her face reddened, then turned blue, as she slipped into final unconsciousness, he would stand back, content, knowing that in that last terrible moment she was completely aware of her destruction.

Maggie began to calm down when she felt the numbing effects of the spray. The dentist had a tranquil look in his eyes as he placed the mirror back in her mouth and probed gently. It was an awkward position and he had to reach high to see inside her mouth. "Let me lower the chair," he said, hitting a foot pedal. She heard a motor kick in, but it wasn't the chair. It was the drill. Blushing, the dentist hit the pedal again and it shut off the drill motor. Then he hit a second pedal and it tilted the chair back, giving him an even more unmanageable angle. Finally, on the third try, he got the chair down. He was nervous, Maggie thought. It was both comforting and unsettling. "You are Dr. Raphael?" she said jokingly.

He stiffened. Nodded. Maggie dismissed her disquiet. She was afraid of dentistry, not dentists. She watched him take the syringe, hold it in a firm grip, and move toward her, gazing intently at her mouth, searching for the right spot to insert the point.

"Open wider," he said.

"What is that?" she asked, stalling, nodding at the barrel of the syringe with the milky liquid inside.

"Novocain," he replied brightly.

"It looks funny," Maggie said; she no longer felt much pain, although her blood was pumping.

"It's a new combination," he replied. "There's a mild sedative mixed in."

"I never heard of that," she said.

He was poised over the chair. "It's okay; just open up and stay still," he said firmly. She obeyed. This was stupid. This was paranoia and plain cowardice.

"Wider."

She opened her mouth wider. He reached over to plunge the needle into her gums, but she shook him off. She still wasn't ready. She took a few gulps of air, nodded, then shut her eyes and opened her mouth in imitation of a silent scream as he hunched over to administer the contents of the syringe.

It was at that instant that Maggie's telephone beeper went off. Quickly, she pulled away and held up her hand. "My office," she said, smiling. "An emergency. Where's the phone?"

Witlessly, he looked at the syringe, then nodded toward the private office. Maggie leaped out of the chair and dashed into the adjoining room. She exhaled and wiped away a patch of sweat, then called her office. She made herself comfortable behind the desk, enjoying her reprieve, waiting to be connected.

"Maggie?"

It was Sam on the phone. He was still at the precinct.

"They found Graham," he said.

She was still rattled. Her reactions were off. "Oh, good. They found Graham. Who's Graham?"

"The technician. From the clinic."

"Oh, *Graham.*" She forced herself to remember why Graham was important. He was the lab technician who had stood up Professor Drake. "Did Gilson ask him how come he didn't meet the professor? What did he say?"

"Nothing. He couldn't. His throat was slit. They found him in the blood clinic, in the bathtub."

Her mind was starting to clear. She lowered her voice. "What about the other one? What's his name?"

"Miller. I think he's the one we're looking for."

She paused for a moment. Took a breath. Everything was crowding in too fast. She had to get back to the precinct house. But first she had to put a patch on her tooth. "I'll be done here in ten minutes," she said. "Send a car for me." She gave the address and hung up.

She got up quickly. "Let's go," she said, marching past the dentist, who was waiting in the treatment room. With alacrity, she got into the chair and opened her mouth wide. The prospect of urgent business deadened her fear.

The dentist reached for the can of spray, but she shook him off.

"Just stick that needle in," she said, leaning back in the chair, her eyes open and fixed on his diploma on the wall. *Frederick Raphael, D.D.S.,* it said, and then there were the Latin inscriptions. His shadow fell over her face as he took the syringe in his hand and loaded her jaw with cotton packing. She turned to look away and Maggie's gaze fell upon something else next to the diploma on the wall to her left. It was a family portrait.

It could have slipped past her, but she was a cop and paid attention to discrepancies, contradictions, incongruities. The family portrait was nice: a middle-aged man, his wife, and three children. Very ordinary. Very happy. The only thing that seemed strange was that the family was obviously African-American. And the man hovering over her with the large needle about to penetrate her gums was obviously Caucasian.

She held up her hand, blocking the needle. "Tell me, Dr. Raphael," she asked, finding it hard to speak through the cotton packing, "did you drive in today?"

"What?"

She did not understand it yet, but she felt a palpable danger. The accumulation of abnormalities: the dentist's unfamiliarity with his own equipment; his jolting, guarded manner; and the family portrait. It was then that she became aware of a distinct Afro-centric pattern in the decor: scenes of tribal life; green, black, and red flags; a knit map of Africa hung in a frame. Maggie felt the naked absence of her gun. She remembered that she had left it in her purse in the other room. She leaned away, making certain that the point of the needle was out of range. She lifted the arm of the dental chair, making it a barrier between her and the dentist, who was on her right.

"We should get this started," he said briskly. "I don't have time."

"Look, I'm feeling a lot better," she said, spitting up the cotton in her mouth and starting to get out of the chair from the left side.

"This won't take long," he said, pushing her back in the seat. His hand was on her shoulder and she knew that she was in danger. He held her tight in his grip.

"Get your fucking hand off me," she said in a low voice.

She rolled off the chair to her left and as she went she swung the arm of the overhead high-intensity light into the dentist's face. He grunted, but she was still trapped. She had to go around the chair and past the dentist to reach the door. He was muttering something under the mask, and unexpectedly he lunged at her. She was not prepared. The needle jabbed into her arm and she looked down in horror as it protruded from her suit jacket. She could feel a thin trickle of blood from where it had entered her muscle.

The dentist had attained the limit of his reach in getting the needle into her arm. But he was straining and cursing, trying to reach the plunger. He couldn't inject the contents of the barrel into Maggie's arm. Her reflexes had slowed, but she finally understood what he was trying to do and she backed away. Maggie was unable to pull the needle out of her arm, afraid that she might jar some of the contents through the syringe and into her arm.

"What the fuck do you want?" she yelled, then faked a move to the left and ran to the right. He wasn't fooled and got between her and the door. Instantly, she pulled up her skirt and rammed her knee into his groin. He was too intent on hitting the plunger of the needle to see it coming, and he straightened up and cried out.

Maggie bolted past him into the outer room, but he recovered and tackled her. As she fell, she thought, If the plunger hits the floor it will drive the contents into my arm. She twisted and rolled to her left to avoid that possibility.

On the floor, Maggie kicked his head, then at last grabbed the large needle and pulled it from her arm. Meanwhile, the dentist reached into an inside shirt pocket, pulled out one of his throwaway scalpels, and yanked off the protective plastic sheaf.

"You're fucking dead!" he screamed.

He flung himself across the dental tray to get within range, catching her arm with the blade. A stitch of blood ran down her arm. She pitched the needle like a dart at his face. He screamed. The needle hit him sideways, striking harmlessly.

She was wounded and vulnerable and reached inside her jacket. Damn! The gun was in her purse in the other room. She forgot. However, all he saw was the leather holster and the optimistic motion and assumed that there was a gun.

When she looked up, he was racing out of the front door of the office. He ripped off his white coat, mask, and gloves, leaving a trail behind.

He didn't wait for the elevator, but ran down the fire stairs. She stopped to call for backup, then tried to follow him down. The guard at the door looked stunned when she reached the lobby.

"What's going on?" he asked as sirens ripped through the traffic and uniformed officers began racing for the door.

"You saw him? You saw which way he ran?"

"Out there," he said, indicating the holiday throng. "What the hell's going on?"

Then she realized that she still didn't know what he looked like, couldn't describe him. The blood was dripping down her arm, and the guard pointed dumbly at the little puddle forming at her feet.

twenty-four

Eric Miller vanished into the throng.

Jerry Munk, who had been waiting for Maggie outside the office building, watched him bolt from the building and head east and then north, and it stirred in Jerry nothing more than the usual curiosity at the high-wire antics of New York's colorfully unbalanced population.

Jerry had been sitting on one of the low marble walls surrounding the building where, on sweltering summer days, people lined up like pigeons, eating their lunch from the rolling food carts, drinking in the sunshine, and enjoying the perfumed, seductive atmosphere of the passing parade.

While he was waiting, Jerry thought of Maggie and the great change she had brought into his life. Out of nothing, really, he mused. Just a great-hearted presence. She had burst into his life like a clap of emotional thunder. There was nothing gentle or coy about her. But she had reliable sentiments and a generous nature. And she made him glow. Before her, he had always felt a dull sadness about life.

And so, because his mind was wandering in two or three directions, he was not concentrating on the man running away from the building. He stood as the *Radio Motor Patrol* cars came screaming at him from every point of the compass. At least eight of them. Squads of grim-faced cops came flying out of both sides of the cars, guns drawn and tensed for action. They left the cars there in the middle of the street, parked at odd angles, doors open.

Instantly, as if they were acting out of a prepared script, the pedestrians backed away, forming a barricade, sealing off the scene. Other police units arrived now, taking blocking positions around the building.

Then Jerry noticed Maggie. She walked toward him slowly, deliberately, holding her right arm. The sleeve of her light blue jacket was soaked with blood. She looked very annoyed.

She shook off a helping hand from another cop and came straight to Jerry Munk. "Where did he go?" she asked.

It took a second to make the connection, but then Jerry nodded north, toward the park. A uniformed sergeant took Maggie gently under her uninjured arm, and she shook her head. "Get some pursuit after that guy," she ordered. "Put out some word on the radio. About five eight or nine, hundred and forty pounds, light hair, Caucasian. Attempted homicide. Of a police officer." A uniformed officer asked specific questions for a report. She took charge. "Get a lab report on the contents of the needle in the dentist's office. Check the security guard and the sign-in sheet."

"You're bleeding, Lieutenant!" said the sergeant.

"I know I'm bleeding." Then she turned to Jerry Munk. "Did you happen to see what he looked like?"

He shook his head. "I didn't know anything was happening. It was too fast," he said.

She nodded and let the sergeant usher her into a sector car. "Go home," she told Munk through the open window. "Go to the store. I'll give you a call." She smiled weakly.

The sudden transformations left Jerry rattled. He nodded dumbly and wandered away, uncertain whether he should head home or to the bookstore or go back to Manhattan North headquarters.

Meanwhile, the RMP sped Maggie to Cornell Medical Center, where an emergency-room doctor sewed up her arm with six large stitches. He gave her a tetanus shot and a sermon.

"You could have torn up a lot of tissue," said the young doctor with disapproval. "There could have been some nerve damage."

The sergeant was smiling.

"I did not do this on purpose," Maggie said with controlled ferocity.

Sam arrived in the middle of the procedure, and she shook off his concern. "I'm all right," she said. Then she turned to the doctor and told him to hurry up. She had work to do.

With the fresh bandage and a couple of aspirins, she and Sam headed back to the detective command. "Bring in the security guard and the sign-in book," Maggie said. "They have a sign-in book for that building. And I want Jack Fox brought into the house."

"What's he got to do with this?" asked Sam, pulling out into traffic, squealing around a bus.

She stared straight ahead, still seeing in her memory the deadly needle coming at her; she still couldn't make out the face of the man who had pretended to be a dentist. "It was his dentist."

He had one more bottle of strychnine, but no needle. Eric Miller got off of the subway train at Seventy-second Street and made his way north. Along the way, clusters of alcoholics and drug addicts nodded off on benches or swayed in the fabricated wind of liquor and chemicals. They bunched together on the median strip, where the grass had been trampled to mud and the benches converted to shanties. Carefully, Eric Miller zeroed in on a small group and peeled off one of the addicts, a young man wearing a winter coat on a summer day.

"I need a set of works," Eric said when they were out of earshot of the rest.

The youth with red, needy eyes grew sharp, looking for a trap. He waved Eric away and started to stagger back to the group, who were watching every move over their shoulders.

Eric grabbed the addict's coat. "I'll give you twenty bucks."

"Man, leave me alone," whined the youth, pulling away. "I'm in a fucking program!"

"Thirty bucks," Eric said. "Last chance." He held three ten-dollar bills like bait.

It was too much temptation. The youth looked around, then led Eric to an empty storefront on the east side of the street. It was deep and dark and they were not visible from the street. Eric reached for the needle, but the youth pulled his hand back. "The money!" he demanded.

Eric smiled and handed him the cash and took the bent, filthy needle. He stopped in an army and navy store and bought a light bush jacket, a cap, a hunting knife, then headed north, toward City College.

It was after one o'clock and Maggie was reading the files and reports when they brought Jack Fox into her office. He was flanked by detectives Matty Bannion and Joey Queen. Sergeant Rosen stood behind Maggie, his arms folded across his chest.

"You want your lawyer?" she asked without looking up from the spread of reports.

"I already called him," he replied. "But that's okay. We can talk."

She detected a slight unsteady note in his voice. "I saw your dentist," she said.

"Oh?"

"Nice guy." She looked up, smiled. "Thanks."

"Glad to be of help."

"Not many Black dentists," she said.

He shrugged. "I hadn't thought of him as a Black dentist."

"Really? What, then?"

"Just a good dentist. Who happens to be Black."

"He have an assistant?"

He looked puzzled. "Not that I know of."

She nodded. The other detectives in the room had a puffy, chesty confidence, as if they knew the secret of where this line of questioning was going. "Boy, you really don't like me poking around about this Edie Severan killing," she laughed.

His eyebrows rose. He stammered. "I thought that you had a suspect."

She shook her head. "Thought we did, too," she said. She shook her head sorrowfully. "James Sinclair. You know him."

He nodded.

"Nice guy. Soft, you know? I don't buy him as a killer."

His smile was strained. Bannion and Queen looked at each other.

"He deals a little cocaine," she said, pulling one of the reports from the pile. "But he's not a serious dealer. He moves a little dust to keep his shop alive. He runs a computer consulting service. Ambitious. His wife works for you. So, tell me, how come you took Edie Severan to The Four Seasons?"

It was a shocking switch of topics, and he looked around, as if someone could explain it. "She worked for me," he said weakly, conceding the dinner.

Maggie nodded understandingly. "And after dinner, you took her home."

He didn't reply, just sat there.

"Well, you wouldn't let her go home unescorted, would you? I mean, you're not that sort of man; it was on the way and you had just treated her to a two-hundred-dollar dinner." She looked down at another report, pushed down her glasses on her nose, then looked up at him. "Actually, two hundred and forty-seven dollars, with the tip," she said, pleased with the wealth of her data.

"Listen, Lieutenant, I had dinner with her, okay. I took her home. But I left her there and she was fine."

He was squirming in his seat, looking back and forth, trying to convince everyone with his intensity.

"You were having an affair. No big deal."

He lowered his head. Another concession.

"So what time was that, that you left her?"

"Nine-thirty."

"That tallies," said Maggie brightly. "Time of death is after that. About ten. So you couldn't have killed her if the time is right."

"No."

"Sinclair was there after that."

"That's interesting."

"It is. It really is. Because we have some reports that Coffee Sinclair was in a bar with some friends at . . ."—she pulled down the glasses and read the reports—"ten-fifteen. His beeper went off. He told his friends—all of whom gave us statements"—she held up sheafs of paper—"that he had to do some business. Funny the doorman didn't remember seeing you leave."

"What? He might've been away from his station."

"Or, you might have waited until he was away." She

was smiling, but there was the menace of a cobra in her expression.

"Why would I do that?"

"Let's see." She bent into the reports again. "Sinclair showed up about eleven. Had some stuff for Edie, but he never got an answer to the bell. The doorman remembers him going up and coming down." She held up a report. "Said that he looked mad as hell."

"Really?" Fox said brightly.

Maggie shook her head. "Sinclair wouldn't look angry if he killed her," she said as if explaining the rudiments of crime detection. "He'd be frightened. Trying to leave unobtrusively. Besides, he didn't have time. No, he didn't kill her."

She got up, leaned one hand on the desk, and with the other slammed down a batch of reports. She said in a hissed stage whisper, "You did."

He stammered, "I want my lawyer."

She nodded and shook her head and spoke mildly. "I'm not saying that you meant to kill her. I know that she liked that kind of sex. You know, slightly dangerous. Testing the envelope. You hold a pillow over her head and it heightens the kick." She held up a batch of reports. "Faking orgasm with fake strangulation. She liked that." She leaned back in her chair. "Kids used to use poppers for the same effect. But this is tricky." She held out both hands, as if holding something. "You hold a pillow over her face for twenty, thirty seconds. She's thrashing around in ecstasy. Only she's not. She's dying. Then, all of a sudden, she's quiet. You figure it's the aftermath of the big thrill." She pulled her hands back. "But when you take the pillow off of her face, she doesn't move."

He was silent. Then, weakly, he protested, "You are violating my rights."

She rifled through the reports. "That's what killed her, according to the medical examiner. Asphyxiation."

Sergeant Rosen stepped out, summoned by a detective waving from the window.

"Besides, I thought she was killed with a knife," Fox said.

She shook her head and walked back to the window. "That was to implicate poor Coffee. Like the phone call. We checked his beeper. 'Ready Beeper.' It's got a memory. A good feature. For him. The call from Edie's apartment came in at ten-fifteen." Maggie came back and rested a hand on the desk. "At ten-fifteen she was already dead." She waited, letting her evidence sink in. "You made that call."

"No."

"Yeah, sure you did. You wanted to make it look as if Coffee Sinclair killed her. Because he was jealous. You'd bought some coke from him before, and you knew about his history from his wife, who also works for you. So he was a perfect fall guy. He had a police record. All you had to do was to slice Edie's throat with a kitchen knife. That must've been tough, her already dead."

"No . . ." he began. "It was an accident."

Maggie sat down at her desk, wound her fingers together in front of her chin. "I can understand that. I can understand everything. What I can't understand is why you tried to have me killed."

For the first time he looked truly bewildered. She saw his hand tremble and continued. "That will boost this to Murder One." She held up the sleeve of her suit, ruined with dried blood.

"What the hell are you talking about?"

"The so-called dentist. Who tried to stick me with a knife!"

Sam came back into the office. His expression was grave. He leaned over and whispered into Maggie's ear. "The dentist is in my office. The real dentist. And the security guard with the sign-in book."

"I didn't," Fox said.

Maggie blinked, looked at Fox, looked at the detectives around the room. Bannion and Queen and Sam quietly and subtly closed in around Fox now that he was an admitted killer. They would pounce if he made any attempt to move.

"So who else knew that I was going to . . .," began Maggie, then stopped. She had a cold premonition. "Wait a minute."

Maggie got up and motioned for Sam to follow. Turning to Bannion, she said, "See if he'll make a statement. Check with the lawyer." Then to Fox, "It doesn't matter, you know. We have enough without a statement. But it might reduce the manslaughter charge. You little weasel."

She pulled Sam along in her wake and when they were outside in the hall, she asked, "Where's the security guard?"

"My office."

She went straight for Sam's office. The guard was puffing and complaining to the uniformed man guarding him. "Where's the book?" she asked. It was right in front of her on Sam's desk. Everyone in the room became quiet as she opened the ledger, fumbled with the pages, and found the current entries. Her finger ran down the page and then she looked up. "Why would he use his real name?"

She was speaking to Sam, who came around and looked at the next-to-last entry. It said, *Eric Miller.*

"Holy shit," Sam said.

"Why would he use his real name?" Maggie asked again.

"Well, he had to show some ID."

It was the security guard, a busted old shield who held everyone's feet to his fire. Maggie wanted to kiss him.

* * *

Meanwhile, Chief of Detectives Larry Scott still wanted to stage a press conference. He calculated that the sand in Maggie's hourglass had run out. He poked his head into Sam's office. "We're going to charge Sinclair," he said.

"Bad idea, Chief," said Maggie.

"It's out of your hands," Scott said. "I'm pulling you off this case."

"Yeah, okay, but Mr. Sinclair has a great defense."

"Oh, really?"

"Jack Fox did it."

Scott's mouth moved up and down. "Bullshit!" he finally uttered.

"He made a statement. Bannion and Queen will give you a fill."

On the way back to her own office she ran into Tom McCord, Fox's attorney. "You can't question my client," he said.

"Okay. But I think you're too late, Counselor. He made voluntary admissions in front of four detectives. After he had his rights. How's the wife?"

Laurie Drake was not at home and Eric guessed correctly that she would be at the campus, working. Convent Avenue was empty as he approached the entrance to the Great Hall. He waited until the guard at the entrance went to the men's room and then slipped the lock on the front door with the hunting knife.

The staircase smelled of apple juice and disinfectant and he climbed to the second floor without making a sound. He was still mulling over the brush with the detective, Maggie Van Zandt. She should have been dead.

He would have liked to kill her—she was tough and quick and erupting with life—but he knew that at best he only had one or two more killings left before they shut him down. Maybe he could escape to another city, but he was too exhausted. He was worn out in some deep, irrevocable way.

Just one or two more lives, that was all that he wanted. It was a prayer. He watched through the glass window of the door while Laurie Drake worked on her computer. She had an intensely concentrated expression. Her desk faced the door, but she was turned to the side, facing a blank wall, working on a computer console, and he inspected her profile. She was frowning at the screen, focused hard, but he knew that if he stood there at the door, sooner or later she would look up.

He backed away so that he wouldn't be spotted. He saw a supply closet down the corridor. His footsteps were muffled in the empty hall. The door of the supply closet was open—nothing much inside except mops and pails and a sink. He stepped into the dark, pulled a chain, and a light came on. Carefully, he loaded the last vial of strychnine into the filthy needle he had bought from the street addict. His hand was steady and his resolution unbending. Then he capped the tip of the needle with a cork, reached down and filled a rolling pail with water, propped a mop inside, and went forth, moving slowly down to Laurie's office. The sound of the pail was like an alibi. He pulled the cap low on his head and ducked his head away from the light. No one would challenge a man pushing a pail on a holiday weekend. No one noticed a janitor.

Maggie drove. Laurie Drake had left the address of the two places where she could be found: her home and her office. Dr. Birnbaum had a picture of Eric Miller in the personnel files and Laurie Drake would be able to identify him. Maggie's sense of urgency was dulled by her ordeal and her wound. But when she didn't find Professor Drake at home, she began to feel a slight uneasiness, along with the continuing throb in her tooth. The professor must be at the college, she thought, getting back into the car. She swung the cruiser around, and when she hit Convent Avenue she was struck by a grave possibility. She slapped the spinning red light on the roof of the cruiser, hit the siren, and mashed her foot down on the accelerator.

"What's up?" asked Sam.

"He's not done killing," she said over the wail of the siren and the rush of the engine.

"How do you know?"

She shrugged. But she knew. She remembered sitting in the dental chair with the needle coming at her. She thought that she might be racing Eric Miller to the City College campus.

Professor Drake grunted something when Eric knocked at the door; he entered carefully, hiding his face in a shadow. She didn't look up from the glowing computer console, assuming that he was a member of the janitorial staff. Eric bent over, keeping his face hidden, and pushed the pail, all the while getting closer. There was a window behind Laurie Drake and he intended to block it, put himself behind the desk so that she would be trapped.

"Would you mind doing that a little later?" she said without taking her eyes off the screen.

By now he was within striking range. Only the desk stood between them. He could lunge across the desk and grab her throat, he thought. He was safely within killing range. She had to be killed. Lauren Drake exposed him, stopped his rampage. She might or might not be infected, but she had to die. It would be his last act. Closure.

"You know," he said, grinning, "the funny thing is that I had a really nice time with you."

Lauren Drake opened her mouth but nothing came out. Eric moved around the right side of the desk. The left was already blocked since the desk was only a few inches from the wall. She was trapped. It took her a moment to grasp it all. Then she saw the hunting knife in his hand. "I had a nice time, too," she said through her dry throat. It was a high, hollow sound.

"But you know," he said, inching closer, every inch a closing-off of any chance of escape, "you really are a bitch."

She saw that she could wedge herself out of his way. There were about six inches between the desk and the wall. But it would be tricky and he would surely grab her before she had a chance to get away. Her voice came back a little. "I don't mean to be," she said passively.

"Why did you call the cops?"

"I didn't."

He laughed. "Now you're a lying bitch!"

She couldn't sit there paralyzed, waiting to die. She started to get up, but he was there already and he pushed her against the wall. In the hand he used so roughly, he held a syringe. She looked around, but she was panicked into numbness. He placed the hunting knife that he clutched in his right hand against her throat. There was an unsteady rage in his eyes. Lauren Drake started to plead and babble and cry. Her knees began to buckle, but he jammed the blade against her flesh and she rose to prevent being cut.

"Shut up!" he demanded.

"Please, Ed, please! I didn't do anything to you. I'm sorry if I did something wrong. Please, I don't want to die!"

He found it curiously satisfying, this single moment, feeling the strain of the knife leaving a thin necklace of blood around her neck. The strain was half pressure to restrain her and half holding himself back from murder. Like when he saved a last bite of candy; he didn't want to kill her yet. He had so much power! This golden college professor with a bright future and keen mind was reduced to a whimpering, slobbering mess. It made it easier, now that his life was over, knowing that he would take her with him. He would not be the only victim of immense injustice. It was a soothing thing to cut short someone else's promise.

"This won't hurt," he said. "Much." He shook the cap off the needle and stood poised. Savoring. "It is just a neuromuscular inhibitor. You'll feel a tightening sensation. That's all." He was almost singing. "By the time you can say Socrates, you will be dead."

Her eyes were wide and pleading. She wanted to fall, but she was pinned to the wall by the knife.

"Put it down!"

It was Maggie standing in the doorway, her service revolver out and leveled in a combat crouch. Moving to her right was Sam Rosen, his gun also pointing at Eric. They had come in undetected. Sam was maneuvering for a clean angle for a shot, but Eric still had the advantage, with the knife at Lauren Drake's throat.

"There's no place to go," Maggie said evenly. "The building is locked up tight."

Eric took in the situation quickly. He heard the approaching sirens, glanced over his right shoulder, out of the window, and saw the blue-and-whites forming a circle around the entrances.

He smiled. "Don't," he said to Sam, who stopped in his tracks. Then he bent over, shielding, for an instant, his motions, and drove the dirty syringe through the skin and into the swollen vein on the back of his clenched left hand. Then he dropped the knife, his eyes rolled back in his head, and he fell to the floor. He twitched for a moment, but he couldn't speak.

Professor Drake collapsed. Maggie and Sam closed in,

suspecting a trick. Eric's back arched and a white froth came out of his lips. By the time Professor Drake was out of his range and behind the protective ring of Maggie and Sam, Eric Miller was dead.

epilogue

There were, in all, an even dozen victims of Eric Miller's revenge. All agreed to remain silent in exchange for large settlements from the clinic's insurance company and free medical treatment. After all, as Dr. Birnbaum argued, what was the point in alarming the entire world over one lunatic?

Who will pay for Cissy? Maggie asked.

Meanwhile, Chief of Detectives Larry Scott took full credit for cracking the Edie Severan killing. An unfortunate accident, he told reporters. A modern parable against greed and excess.

Betsy Fox cleaned out all of her husband's accounts so that he had to defend himself with a legal aid attorney. None of her friends blamed her.

On the twelfth of July, Detective Thomas Neeley said that he thought that he had a break in the Sterns' murders. A woman arrived in Paris bearing large parcels thought to be paintings. Her name was Dolly Grove—the sister-in-law of the slain attorney. Unfortunately, the French police had lost track of her.

"How's about a vacation in Paris?" Maggie asked Jerry Munk.

"Great. I can go see *Shakespeare & Co.*"

"I had paintings in mind."